The Destination
for Art and Culture

KW-361-752

Aesthetica

THE ART & CULTURE MAGAZINE
www.aestheticamagazine.com

Issue 124
April / May 2025

MIRRORED IMAGERY
Sarah Meyohas presents new
interactive pieces at Desert X

ANCIENT ECOSYSTEM
Documenting old-growth trees
that form a vast network of life

ALTERED LANDSCAPE
Photographers are responding
to life in the Anthropocene age

BENEATH THE WAVES
Sculptures constructed out of
plastic collected on the beach

24

UK £6.95 Europe €14.99 USA $16.49

Since 2003, Aesthetica has published in-
depth features and visual narratives with
today's most innovative practitioners.
Be Inspired! Save 70%. £12 for 12 months.

CONTENTS

From publishing insider **GERALD HOWARD** comes the incredible story of an under-known man with an astonishing impact

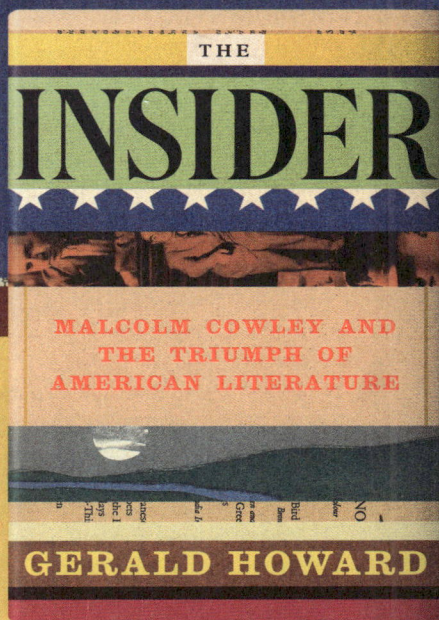

THE

INSIDER

MALCOLM COWLEY AND THE TRIUMPH OF AMERICAN LITERATURE

GERALD HOWARD

Witness the life and legacy of **MALCOLM COWLEY**, the editor extraordinaire responsible for transforming **Kerouac, Cheever, and Faulkner** into household names and inspiring the American literary canon as we know it today.

"*The Insider* brings to life—through the key figure of Cowley and with a remarkable amount of warmth and tenderness— a thrilling piece of social history." —VIVIAN GORNICK

P PenguinPress | PRH.COM/THEINSIDER

GRANTA

12 Addison Avenue, London W11 4QR | email: editorial@granta.com
To subscribe visit subscribe.granta.com, or call +44 (0)1371 851873

ISSUE 173: AUTUMN 2025

EDITOR	Thomas Meaney
MD & DEPUTY EDITOR	Luke Neima
SENIOR EDITOR	Josie Mitchell
MANAGING EDITOR	Tom Bolger
ASSOCIATE DESIGN DIRECTOR	Daniela Silva
ASSOCIATE EDITOR	Brodie Crellin
EDITORIAL ASSISTANT	Aea Varfis-van Warmelo
PHOTOGRAPHY EDITOR	Max Ferguson
SPECIAL PROJECTS	Janique Vigier
CONSULTING EDITOR	Karan Mahajan
PHOTOGRAPHY CONSULTANT	Veeranganakumari Solanki
COMMERCIAL DIRECTOR	Noel Murphy
OPERATIONS & SUBSCRIPTIONS	Sam Lachter
MARKETING	Simon Heafield
PUBLICITY	Pru Rowlandson, publicity@granta.com
CONTRACTS	Margaux Vialleron
ADVERTISING	Renata Molina-Lopes, Renata.Molina-Lopes@granta.com
FINANCE	Thomas Smith
SALES	Rosie Morgan
IT SUPPORT	Ravi Dhir
PRODUCTION & DESIGN DIRECTOR	Sarah Wasley
PROOFS	Katherine Fry, Gesche Ipsen, Jessica Kelly, Jess Porter, Will Rees, Francisco Vilhena
CONTRIBUTING EDITORS	Anne Carson, Rana Dasgupta, Michael Hofmann, A.M. Homes, Rahmane Idrissa, George Prochnik, Leo Robson
PUBLISHER	Sigrid Rausing

p.21–39 'A Measure of Martyrdom' is excerpted from *Ooru Bhanga* © Vivek Shanbhag 2015, translation © Srinath Perur 2025; p.167–173 is excerpted from the forthcoming *A Public Circumcision* by Saharu Nusaiba Kannanari; p.247–251 is excerpted from the novel *All at Once (Sah-sa)* by Geetanjali Shree; p.255–268 is excerpted from a work-in-progress by Devika Rege. Special thanks to South Asian Literature in Translation (SALT) for a research and translation grant for the issue.

This selection copyright © 2025 Granta Trust.

Granta (ISSN 173231 USPS 508) is published four times a year by Granta Trust, 12 Addison Avenue, London W11 4QR, United Kingdom.

Airfreight and mailing in the USA by agent named World Container Inc., 150–15, 183rd Street, Jamaica, NY 11413, USA.

Periodicals postage paid at Brooklyn, NY 11256.

Postmaster: Send address changes to *Granta*, ESco, Trinity House, Sculpins Lane, Wethersfield, Braintree, CM7 4AY, UK.

Subscription records are maintained at *Granta*, c/o ESco Business Services Ltd, Wethersfield, Essex, CM7 4AY.

Air Business Ltd is acting as our mailing agent.

The manufacturer's authorised representative in the EU for product safety is Authorised Rep Compliance Ltd, 71 Lower Baggot Street, Dublin D02 P593, Ireland (arccompliance.com)

Granta is printed and bound in Italy by L.E.G.O. S.p.A. This magazine is printed on paper that fulfils the criteria for 'Paper for permanent document' according to ISO 9706 and the American Library Standard ANSI/NIZO Z39.48-1992 and has been certified by the Forest Stewardship Council®(FSC®). *Granta* is indexed in the American Humanities Index.

ISBN 978-1-909-889-76-7

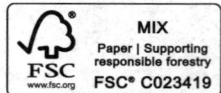

MIX
Paper | Supporting responsible forestry
FSC® C023419

To worship my country as a god is to bring a curse upon it

– Rabindranath Tagore, *The Home and the World*

Modi-Land

I arrived in Delhi this year to find the city in the midst of a minor literary dust-up. Arvind Kejriwal, the former chief minister for Delhi from the center-right Aam Aadmi Party, had made a passing reference at a campaign rally to how the evil king Ravana from the *Ramayana* had transformed into a golden deer to lure the princess Sita away from the hero Ram. For the next twenty-four hours on national television, ministers from the ruling far-right Bharatiya Janata Party (BJP) lashed out at Kejriwal, saying he had disgraced the nation by getting a crucial detail of the epic wrong: of course it was the evil demon Maricha, Ravana's uncle, who had transformed into the deer at Ravana's instructions, not Ravana himself! Kejriwal was denounced as a 'Chunavi Hindu' – 'Election Hindu', with pundits speculating about how many prayers to Hanuman it would take to expiate his sin. Kejriwal said his critics were worse than Ravana, and was called Ravana in return.

It would have been little more than an extreme form of literary criticism were it not for the fact that for the BJP, the *Ramayana* is worth killing for. The party cemented its place in Indian national life with the destruction of the Babri mosque in 1992, claiming it as the birthplace of Ram. When I met Kejriwal the next day at a meet-and-greet with voters, he was glum and appeared to be on a verbal fast. A Congress constituent had just lambasted him for doing nothing about the air of Delhi, which was 'like a Nazi gas chamber', while a man in an ascot berated him for distributing 'freebies' among the poor. But Kejriwal was more concerned about his electoral fortunes than the state of his soul. There is only so far you can get these days in Indian politics with a program that is BJP-lite. In India under Narendra Modi, the ancient epics are ammunition, and the archaeological sites are political dynamite. If you want to win people over, you better have Ram on your side.

Twenty-five years ago, I came to Banaras to teach English at a small school funded by the Ford Foundation. Thinking they might cause trouble, I carried books by Salman Rushdie and Arundhati Roy with their covers wrapped in brown paper so as not to draw attention to their contents. For half a year I lived in a *barsati* – a small concrete block on top of a building on the outskirts of the Banaras Hindu University. The India of the early 2000s was already well into its economic liberalization, and the country's intellectuals were breathless about how far it had come. India, the political scientist Sunil Khilnani claimed, represented 'the third moment in the great democratic experiment launched at the end of the eighteenth century by the American and French Revolutions'. 'We have flourished,' the liberal guru Pratap Bhanu Mehta declared, 'because we are "diverse in our unities."' Finally, the clientelist cushions of the early decades after Independence were being stripped away. The inaugural flight of Sahara India Airlines served caviar in economy. India was on the up and up. There would be no stopping it.

What no one predicted at the time was that this ascent would not be presided over by the Congress, which had ruled India almost uninterruptedly since 1947, but by a highly disciplined outside organization that could master the wounded sentiments of the nation and put them to work. Today, the BJP – the largest political party in the world – rules over nearly half of India's twenty-eight states and commands the national government without any challenges to its dominance. Like Recep Tayyip Erdoğan's AKP and Benjamin Netanyahu's Likud, Modi's BJP can credibly claim that it channels the religious passion of the majority of the population, a passion that was temporarily blocked during the nationalist struggle. The story of the BJP's ascent is remarkable. Backed by its social base, the Rashtriya Swayamsevak Sangh (RSS), the BJP started as a party of upper-caste Hindus. But it faced a growth problem. In India's electoral system, no political party could afford to ignore the Other Backward Classes (OBCs), who constitute more than half the population. How was the BJP able to gain the votes of OBCs while continuing to serve its upper-caste constituency? By including more OBCs in its political ranks – 63 percent of the BJP's representation in the Lok Sabha now consists of OBCs, scheduled castes, and tribes – while backing policies that further increased the wealth of its upper-caste supporters. One of the first initiatives of the Modi government was to abolish the 1957 wealth tax and install the world's most regressive tax regime. Why, even with the sop of more representation, would the poorer OBCs go along with this? Because they were simultaneously galvanized by the BJP's anti-Muslim campaign, which raised their social status above the Muslims, who became enemies of the state. Muslim hatred became the BJP's trusted solution to dilute intra-caste resentments. The Congress had always relied on the Muslim vote in elections – to the point of upholding Islamic legal exemptions and favoring to some of the most hidebound Muslim leaders. The BJP discovered it could do without these votes if it doubled down hard enough on Hindutva – the idea of India as a country for, by, and of the Hindus.

To bring about this new dawn, the BJP turned to one of the great political showmen of our age. I remember seeing Modi for the first time in 2014 at Madison Square Garden in New York. He had recently become prime minister, and his travel ban to the United States for presiding over the massacre of Muslims in Gujarat a dozen years before, had been duly rescinded. The crowd – IT programmers, Sikh businessmen, cowboy-booted Indians from Houston – chanted 'Modi, Modi, Modi' and pumped their chests, where the leader's face was emblazoned on their T-shirts. In his element on a revolving dais, with a projection of the Ganges pulsating behind him, Modi could barely restrain himself from treating the American senators and congressmen who had come to pay him court like parasites. Then he began speaking in conversational Hindi, using his fireside voice: 'Our country has undergone a lot of devaluation,' he said. 'Our ancestors would play with snakes . . . Now our youth are able to shake the world with a click of their mouse!' The Garden shook with pleasure at this slender offering of wit. One sensed the Hindu nationalists had their man, a martial grandfather in a saffron vest, determined to make the Indus Valley Civilization great again.

Narendra Modi claims he is immune to poison and that as a child he tried to domesticate a baby crocodile. He changes his clothes several times a day, uses holographic avatars of himself to appear in multiple locations at once, and sees fit to self-publish some of the most guileless poetry *Granta* has ever encountered:

> We are buddies for life
> We are seekers of joy
>
> No one dare stop us
> No one dare daunt us
> We are law unto ourselves

This bard is the most popular Indian leader since Gandhi, with whom he has much in common. Both fashioned themselves as soft-spoken, supremely indigenous spirits of the soil, when their guiding intellectual orientation was in fact Western. In Gandhi's case, the Victorian esoterica and theosophy he picked up while a law student in London; in Modi's, the highly Protestantized hymnal of Hinduism arranged by the British colonizers who vaulted action-orientated books like the *Bhagavad Gita* over other sacred texts. (The *Gita* was also a favorite of Gandhi's.) Like Gandhi, Modi has a gift for mismanaging pandemics; his decision to send Covid-stricken urban Indians back to their villages mirrored the Mahatma's refusal to recognize the risk of his ashramites spreading smallpox to the villages of Gujarat ('Shall my heart quail before that catastrophe, or will I persevere in my faith?'). Like Gandhi with his Salt March, Modi is a man of the road, who first made his name in 1991 with a procession for Hindu unity from Kanyakumari on the southern tip of India to Srinagar in the north. Like Gandhi, Modi adamantly defends the interests of the upper castes, despite being an OBC himself, and the wealthiest strata of Hindu society. Where Gandhi had the textile tycoon G.D. Birla in his corner, Modi counts on the industrialist magnate Gautam Adani. (The Adani Group's opaque accounting practices and fraud may have made it a nemesis of Wall Street and the US Treasury, but its capacity to build infrastructure to rival China's Belt and Road cannot have been lost on the US State Department.) The differences between Modi and Gandhi are also significant.

In contrast to Gandhi's anti-modern reverie of India as a land of wheel-spinning villagers, Modi dreams of a utopia where Indian entrepreneurs perform yoga behind their computers. As a political organizer, Modi may even have an edge on Gandhi. Behind the BJP is the intricately coordinated RSS, the paramilitary organization that assassinated Gandhi in 1948 for straying too far from the cause of Hindu nationalism. For decades, Modi, who joined the RSS at the age of eight, journeyed across India, sleeping in monastic quarters, while helping to build the organization's cadre base, today estimated at some four million members. The tentacles of the RSS now reach into nearly every village, as well as Indian communities as far away as Kenya and Texas, and enforce a form of shadow rule that is often more formidable than the national government. If there is any threat to Modi's hold on power, it comes not from the Congress or the parties of the center-right, but from the hard right, if the leadership of the RSS ever loses patience with its son in the limelight.

M odi has been a full decade in power since *Granta* last devoted an issue to Indian writing. We have found extraordinary work across all genres, but almost all of it runs against the grain of the broader culture. While reality has dramatically shifted in neighboring Bangladesh and Sri Lanka, where regimes have imploded, and in Pakistan, which has been wracked with a series of political oustings, India under Modi has been comparably stable. The effect of this political atmosphere on Indian literature has been stultifying. Indian non-fiction today is full of case studies of Modi's 'fascism', as if a political concept drawn from interwar Europe were adequate for the scale of the Indian present. For many young fiction writers, Modi's India is the only one they have ever known. In several of the stories *Granta* considered for this issue but did not publish, characters from lower castes are either murdered or punished, as if these acts in themselves constitute social commentary; or caste position is revealed as a thudding epiphany, serving only as a plot point. The situation has not been helped by the prize juries of the United States and Britain which, in their desire to be seen as champions of the oppressed, increasingly honor the didactic strain of Indian fiction, mistaking their good intentions for courage.

The diasporic Indian novel written in English suffered a stroke in 2008. As Sanjay Subrahmanyam pinpointed at the time, Aravind Adiga's Booker-Prize-winning novel, *The White Tiger*, which was set in the business parks outside Delhi, exhibited the exhaustion of literary fiction that catered to two audiences but satisfied neither. The novel is about Balram Halwai, a village boy and the son of a rickshaw-wallah, who ascends into the booming entrepreneurial class and leaves his caste behind. It was not simply the overly stuffed storyline that made *The White Tiger* unpersuasive – the book is told as a series of letters from Halwai to the former Chinese premier Wen Jiabao – but the dialogue: characters in it speak in a kind of baffling simulacrum that sound neither like Indian English nor a plausible rendering of any Indian vernacular. Something had gone wrong since the days of Salman Rushdie's highly original, chutnified English, and the high-octane volleys of Arundhati Roy.

Meanwhile, thanks to better translations, another major strand in writing was on the rise in India. The unfortunately named category of 'Indian Regional Literature', which comprises works in India's many languages outside English, is often rooted in distinct cultural histories and animated by questions of social justice and local experience. This year, sixteen years after Adiga won the Booker, the jury for a sister prize – the International Booker Prize – selected *Heart Lamp*, a collection of short stories by the Kannada writer Banu Mushtaq. I was in Bengaluru when the award was announced, among a group of writers who were both delighted by the recognition of a Kannada-language writer and bemused by the choice. Banu Mushtaq is a lawyer who is revered for her work championing the rights of Muslim women. In the 1970s, she was a young member of Karnataka's Bandaya Sahitya movement, which sought a prominent place for a specific type of self-reflective Dalit consciousness in poetry and fiction, and declared subjects, like the state's development projects, ripe for literary treatment. The trouble with Mushtaq's fiction is that her stories can read like the undigested testimony of her clients in the post-*Shah-Bano* era. *Heart Lamp* could have been titled *The Bad Deeds of Muslim Men*. We are treated to one tale after another of callousness and cruelty at the hands of evil husbands who make the lives of their wives a living hell, whether by insulting their bodies, running off with nurses, or beating them when they cannot cook their favorite meal. Despair reliably takes the same shape to the point that one wonders whether it would not be more efficient simply to read the court transcripts of the victims themselves rather than these mildly varnished ventriloquisms. Mushtaq's is the same kind of moralizing fiction of village life that was produced in heaps by Russian Narodniks in the late nineteenth century, which Chekhov reduced to dust.

In India, the divide between modernist literature and more explicitly political fiction has always been hazy. In the lead-up to Independence, the country's best-known writer in English was R.K. Narayan, who treated the Independence movement with gently affectionate irony. But in 1935, another much more critical strain of Indian fiction sprouted in London. The Indian Progressive Writers' Movement closely studied European modernist forms but demanded they be mobilized to address the horrors of misogyny, colonialism, and especially caste. In writers like Ismat Chughtai and the communist Rashid Jahan – whose story 'Woh' (That One) about a decomposing untouchable woman may be the most powerfully affecting Indian fiction about caste – the movement found searing artists for its cause. Their most valuable asset was Saadat Hasan Manto, the Punjab-born short-story master who moved his fiction with ease through the bordellos of Bombay to the atrocities of Partition. Manto was an enemy of everything and everyone, not least himself, but the result was a wry, fleet-footed, merciless prose that showed up the hypocrisies of the world around him. By the 1940s, Manto was quick to turn his fiction on his fellow Progressives when he felt they had become self-satisfied swamis, coddled in their own pieties. (Find the story 'Progressives' by Manto, newly translated by

Matt Reeck, in the online edition of this issue.) In the end, Manto sat astride multiple traditions in the best cosmopolitan style of his beloved Bombay.

In the wake of Manto, the two most formidable Indian writers of the postwar decades occupied different ends of the political spectrum. In 1965, U.R. Ananthamurthy published his Kannada-language masterpiece *Samskara: A Rite for a Dead Man*. Ananthamurthy studied English literature in Birmingham, where he wrote his dissertation on the communist novelist Edward Upward, and was steeped in English modernism. The novel, though, was a deeply local tale about Praneshacharya, a learned Brahmin man, who has to decide what to do with the corpse of an apostate neighbor who kept an untouchable mistress and supported the Congress party. The comedy of manners is heightened by the fact that the Brahmins of the colony shape their entire lifeworld around taboos and restrictions. Substantively, *Samskara* presents a terrific picture of what the early Congress was up against in traditional India. Stylistically, Ananthamurthy makes every use of modernist techniques as he dances through the minds of his characters on a canvas saturated with the *Ramayana* and a brush borrowed from Virginia Woolf. Much has been made lately of deliberately awkward translations from Indian languages that reveal the 'seams' or 'scars' of the original, holding back from imposing a smoothness associated with colonialism, but there is little doubt that Ananthamurthy's work benefited from the skilled translation of the great poet A.K. Ramanujan, who brought the prose into incisive English. Whatever the merits of deliberately awkward translations, foreign works have the best chance of expanding English literature if the *first* translation reads well.

In his later years, Ananthamurthy receded into a posture every bit as stoical as Narayan's: India would go on, it would go on forever; the BJP were time-serving charlatans, but there was no point in participating in politics; the country was too set in its ways, and besides, when it came to organizing things like the harvest or your dinner table, the caste system could be rather convenient. The second great writer after Ananthamurthy was Mahasweta Devi, a radical communist whose greatest fictions appeared during and after Indira Gandhi's Emergency. Though known today as the darling of Subaltern Studies, Devi, like Ananthamurthy, applied a thoroughly modernist technique to the most local of subjects. In her case, these were not the Brahmins of Karnataka, but the Naxalites of Jharkhand. No one can read *Mother of 1084* or 'Draupadi' without feeling the jarring juxtapositions of a novelist who expects familiarity with Shakespeare and Antonioni as she plumbs the consciousness of Maoist guerillas. Her interest in how not only the guerillas, but also the Indian officials fighting them were thinking and feeling, allows her to deliver a panorama unlike any other in Indian postwar fiction, a kind of long-running *The Battle of Algiers*. If Ananthamurthy showed how hard it was for the Congress to make inroads into the stubborn villages, Devi showed what the savage excesses of the Congress looked like up close – a litany of horror that stretched from Nehru's crushing of hill tribes in the 1940s to his daughter and grandson's sterilization programs against the rural and urban poor. The fact that writers like Devi and her epigones had become so fixated on resistance to the Indian state was enough of a reason for the old devil V.S. Naipaul to drag himself out of retirement for one last rodeo. In *Magic Seeds*, by far his weakest novel, he tried to produce an Evelyn-Waugh-like satire of the follies of empty-headed Naxalites who waste their lives on half-felt ideals.

'English is not merely a language in India, it's a kind of power,' the novelist Vivek Shanbhag told me over coffee in Bengaluru. Even Modi reverts to English when he needs a word to accentuate his rhetoric: 'operation', 'nuclear', 'devaluation'. But no language in India, not even English, commands literary hegemony anymore. The state's Hinduization efforts have, if anything, raised hackles in states outside the cowbelt. Across the Karnataka state earlier this year, customers protested post offices where officials only spoke Hindi. India, with its close historical ties with British and American houses like Penguin (where no less a figure than Krishna Menon, minister of defense under Nehru, was once an editor), publishes a large amount of writing read in the West. At *Granta*, we developed several methods for working through fiction in Hindi, Gujarati, Bangla, Assamese, Telugu, and other languages. Although we sometimes used AI translation tools to get a sense of the shape and content of some stories, our work primarily relied on an extraordinary network of translators, many of whom feature in our symposium on translation. This set of essays each centered on a single word from thirteen of India's twenty-two scheduled languages, from the Malayalam of Kerala's southern coast to the Punjabi spoken across the northern plains. Our main aim with the fiction in this issue was to avoid both the exhausted elite Anglo-Indian writing of the New York–London–South Delhi corridor and the overhyped 'authentic' fiction of the regions, in order to concentrate on what is most alive in contemporary Indian fiction.

We are pleased to feature an excerpt from a recently translated novel by Vivek Shanbhag, the most Russian of Indian writers. With his tight concentration on the manners and slips of the Indian middle class, Shanbhag has become one of the most sure-handed fictional chroniclers of contemporary India. In this story, a corporate man who writes fiction on the side goes to a party, and a *Pnin*-like comedy ensues. In 'Transformations' by the Gujarati writer Umesh Solanki, a man is transported back to his childhood, and the friendship he formed with a boy from the Valmiki community. Wary of the imagined differences the narrator perceives between them, and of how the alliance will warp the social hierarchy at school, an intimacy develops tentatively, their lives eventually interlocking with animation and care.

In Geetanjali Shree's 'All at Once', a retired judge's heart skips a beat when he glimpses his grown-up daughter secretly devouring a motichoor laddu, a sweet she loved in her youth but has since shunned. He recalls a time in which pleasure was found in fairy tales, in rote and formula, when the roles of father and daughter were simple to perform. In Saharu Nusaiba Kannanari's story, a young Muslim boy succeeds in escaping his scheduled circumcision. Time and again he evades the procedure, ultimately managing to persuade his mother to adopt the fiction that his foreskin has been removed by a surgeon in a neighboring village. The great Tamil writer Jeyamohan banishes all of the clichés of writing about caste in his story 'Kazhumaadan'. In the exacting tradition of Ivo Andrić and Marguerite Yourcenar, it is a tale of an ancient Tamil court in which a young man finds an extraordinary exit from his caste – deification through impalement. Finally, we present a new story from Devika Rege, whose 2023 novel *Quarterlife* is the most accomplished political novel of the Modi years. In 'Homa', Rege examines the life and fate of an ambitious woman who comes into the orbit of a religious-political movement that seems to offer a solution to her isolation.

In the photography for this issue, Dayanita Singh returns to *Granta*'s pages with a striking series on Calcutta's Durga Puja festival twenty-eight years after her debut in *Granta 57*. Her work is introduced by long-time *Granta* writer Amit Chaudhuri, who remembers how the transient palaces of the festival's pandals contribute to the 'delicate fiction of the Pujas'. In the Mumbai monsoon photographs of Yash Sheth, the novelist Ruchir Joshi, another experienced *Granta* hand, explores how they defamiliarize the city. Looking at the images, Ruchir writes, 'it feels as though Bombay has invented rain for itself, that it has the first full use of it before it ruthlessly licenses it to other places for a price.' This summer Keerthana Kunnath traveled across the south to the new sites of India's space technology. In her sharp series, she captures the labs and clean rooms where the country's second space age is being assembled.

Non-fiction writing about India has often concentrated on stories of poverty and pain or uplift and gain. The last *Granta* India issue featured an essay by one of the most well-regarded non-fiction writers of the decade: Katherine Boo, author of *Behind the Beautiful Forevers* (2012). The book is a novelistic look at the slum-dwellers of Mumbai and a tale of 'resilience' amid some of the worst living conditions on earth. Boo's way of freely entering into the consciousness of her subjects was starting to be questioned at the time, but her reflexivity about her own methods has made the book a classic of literary reportage. The greatest non-fiction book about India since Boo's has been Sujatha Gidla's *Ants Among Elephants* (2017), a memoir about a Dalit family, one member of which takes up arms against the Indian state. Gidla's prose is a strikingly effective instrument. For Western readers, for whom 'caste' is still often a metaphor, Gidla brings home the reality of life as a Dalit:

> The caste whose occupation is the most degrading, the most indecent, the most inhuman of all, is known in coastal Andhra as *pakis*. In print, they are called manual scavengers or, more euphemistically still, porters of night soil. In plain language, they carry away human shit. They empty the 'dry' latrines still widely used throughout India, and they do it by hand. Their tools are nothing but a small broom and a tin plate. With these, they fill their palm-leaf baskets with excrement and carry it off on their heads five, six miles to some place on the outskirts of town where they're allowed to dispose of it. Some modernized areas have replaced these baskets with pushcarts (this being thought of as progress in India), but even today the traditional 'head-loading' method prevails across the country.
>
> Nearly all of these workers are women. They don't know what gloves are, let alone have them. As their brooms wear down, they have to bend their backs lower and lower to sweep. When their baskets start to leak, the shit drips down their faces. In the rainy season, the filth runs all over these people, onto their hair, into their eyes, their noses, their mouths. Tuberculosis and other infectious diseases are endemic among them.

Gidla appears in this issue with a memoir of caring for her mother, whose determination to be independent is in reverse proportion to her ability to care for herself. Snigdha Poonam last reported for these pages on female wrestling in India and its tussle with politics. For this issue, she returns to her hometown of Ranchi to dip into the history of the Naxalite insurgency that formed part of the background of her childhood. In the forest of Jharkhand, Poonam meets a legendary Adivasi Maoist who shows her how the state has co-opted the local Maoists with methods different from what one reads about in most of the Indian press, which celebrates the military's counterinsurgencies and ambushes. In his reportage from the tunnels of Barnawa, Raghu Karnad enters the vexed terrain of Indian archaeology. Karnad takes a skeptical view of the BJP's uses of the past for national mythologization, but with a concern, too, that just because the Indian epics are myth does not mean they cannot be of use to scientific archaeology, as the *Iliad* and the *Odyssey* once were for Heinrich Schliemann.

Every country imposes its national myths on the heavens. In the 1930s, masses of Indian peasants in southern India claimed to see Gandhi's profile on the moon. In his essay, Srinath Perur examines the history and present of the Indian space program, for which his mother worked as a scientist. What was once a national effort determined to fight poverty appears these days to have more glamorous ambitions. The novelist Karan Mahajan happened to be in British Columbia a month after the Sikh activist Hardeep Singh Nijjar was assassinated there in 2023. This year, Mahajan returned to Canada, where he unspooled the logic of the Indian campaign in North America and what it means for India to join the extrajudicial murder club, where Israel, Russia, Saudi Arabia, and the United States are long-time members. If there is a running thread through the non-fiction of this issue, it may be that Modi-Land is becoming more like everywhere else. Until that day comes, there will still be *Granta* special issues on India, home to many of our most loyal readers. ■

TM

SOHRAB HURA
Bangalore, 2018
Magnum Photos

A MEASURE OF MARTYRDOM

Vivek Shanbhag

TRANSLATED FROM THE KANNADA BY SRINATH PERUR

My colleague Samir Sahu called in the afternoon to remind me that my wife and I were invited to his housewarming party that evening.

'She may not be able to make it, but I will certainly be there,' I said, deciding not to go.

Sahu, who grew up in Calcutta, had moved to Bangalore for work. He's a few years older, but my subordinate. I suspect he slights me behind my back. We may have something in common when it comes to how we try to transcend our corporate lives. I write. He is interested in painting and likes to associate with artistic types outside the office. He apparently used to be a member of the Communist Party, something he brings up every now and then. I have a way of startling him in conversation by adopting a leftist position fiercer than his: 'Just wait,' I might say, 'there will come a day when we break the chains of corporate oppression.' He looks at me warily, as if it might be a ploy on my part.

I was hesitant to enter his bastion, but I felt it might not be a bad thing to show some magnanimity to one's juniors. Besides, Sahu had called despite being on leave. I decided to go.

It was dark when I arrived. The new house was not hard to find in its sparsely built neighbourhood on the city's outskirts. Cars and scooters were lined up outside. A van pulled out, and I parked my car there. The house had a picket fence, which was rare in this city. The exterior was done with a spareness that gave the impression that some construction work still remained. From outside I could hear the clamour of voices and an occasional flare of laughter.

On entering the house I ran into Sahu immediately. He beamed at me. 'Please come, please come.' He shook my hand and drew me in.

His wife, a short woman struggling in a grand sari and a sweat-soaked blouse, produced a tired smile of welcome. Her lipstick was wearing off. As if her display of deference was somehow inadequate, Sahu said: 'You know who this is, right? None other than Mr Manmohan.'

Despite her exhaustion Mrs Sahu tried to remind me of our having met at an exhibition four years ago. 'We met once. You were wearing a blue shirt. It was evening. You remember?' she said, in strangely accented English.

As she went on about blue shirts, I saw from the corner of my eye that Sahu was cringing. Serves you right, I thought. He must have realised it could get awkward if she was allowed to go on.

'Come, come, I'll show you around,' he said, steering me away. 'Our things are all over the place. It's more than a month since we moved, but we haven't yet settled in. Of course, I don't believe in housewarming rituals or anything of that kind. This is an excuse to get friends together.' He led me through the rooms.

The house was spread over two floors. Steel for the structure had come from scrapped railway tracks. Doors had been fashioned from repurposed iron sheets. The rooms were painted in bright colours that one normally avoided for interiors. A skylight in the roof, a small garden in the yard. Sahu had given so many tours that he touched upon the salient features with great economy.

'The windows are all second-hand. They're from demolished houses. We couldn't get uniform sizes, but you can't tell because they're in different rooms. These are hollow bricks from Kerala to keep the house cool. All the stone is from old buildings. Only when it comes to the bathrooms did we not compromise.'

'Beautiful. Who's the architect?'

'A friend, Sudesh. He's here.'

Sahu took me into the backyard where a group of his friends had gathered. The air was filled with Bengali chatter. A middle-aged man in jeans and a brown kurta was holding forth on the design.

'This is Sudesh Goswami. We are standing in his creation.'

He introduced me: 'Mr Manmohan, my boss, but more importantly, a famous Kannada short-story writer.' I listened for any trace of sarcasm. He went on. 'It's unusual to find someone with his sensibilities in a workplace like ours. He's passionate about art as well. We created a small art gallery in the office at his sole instigation.'

Though he was being somewhat theatrical the others appeared to listen in earnest. Their subsequent demeanour indicated they thought I was a person of some importance. It was unclear if that was because of my interest in art and literature, or because, as stated, I was Sahu's boss. An elderly gent among them named Sen began: 'What kind of stories do you write? I mean, are they about social issues? Science fiction? Detective stories?'

I recognised his level at once. It's always people like this who latch on at parties and never let go. 'Well,' I said, 'if you've heard of literary fiction . . .'

He did not get the sarcasm in my tone. Sahu did. 'Arre, dada, Manmohan's writing is different. You may call it intellectual. He has read a lot of literature. He heads the audit division in our company.'

I didn't like the description one bit but this wasn't the right time to correct him. Sometimes the opinions we seek to keep to ourselves tumble out even as we grope for the right words. This was one such instance, I thought.

Just then Sahu saw new arrivals and rushed off to greet them, leaving me with Sen, who was not done yet.

'Wonderful, wonderful. Have your stories been translated into English?'

'Some of them.'

'You must tell me the titles of your books. I'm sure they're available in Bangalore?'

'No books in English, I'm afraid. Just a few stories in magazines and anthologies.'

'Then maybe you could send them to me. I'll return them, of course.' He pressed a visiting card with his address into my hand. 'I used to be in the central excise department. When I retired I was posted here. I said to myself, well, home is wherever one happens to be. I can speak a little Kannada, but don't read it at all. You know, people like you should write in English.'

'Oh, there are enough people writing in English. Kannada is fine for me.'

'But you could reach so many more people with English. It's the best way to spread local culture. People like me could then read your work. Am I not right? What do you say?' He laughed as if he had won the exchange.

'Everyone is entitled to their opinion,' I said. He waited, thinking I was going to say more. I let him wait and looked about.

The others around us had been silent. I thought I'd end the conversation. I turned to the fellow beside me. 'Have you eaten?' I asked.

'No. Come, let's get something,' he said, rescuing me.

There was upma, mixture, Mysore pak and coffee. Simple and tasty. 'South Indian menu,' I heard Sahu's wife say several times to her Bengali guests. Some were discussing how to make coffee as the South Indians did. I took my plate and drifted over to a group of people from the office. The conversation meandered on through generalities – the lure of money and comfort that made us endure injustices; the absence of camaraderie in the workplace; the apathy that ensured an employee only raised his voice when the axe was about to fall on him.

Soon, the group dissolved. I chatted with a few people, finished eating and got ready to leave.

Guests were still coming in as I made my exit. Sahu had a wide circle of friends outside the office. Collapsed in a chair, his wife was fanning herself with the edge of her sari. She waved goodbye without trying to get up.

Sahu stepped out to see me off. A black car parked next to mine was preparing to depart, its doors wide open. I waited for it to leave. Six young men and women proceeded to stuff themselves in. A young woman was left outside peering through various doors to see if she might somehow squeeze in. Her body language suggested she was not a part of the group.

Sahu called out to her. 'Let them go. I'll find someone to drop you home.'

The doors were closed with some effort and the car left.

As I walked to my car, I said to Sahu, 'Where does she need to go?'

She heard me and said, 'Anywhere in the city will do.'

'Come then, I can drop you,' I said, unlocking the car.

She was wearing blue jeans and an orange T-shirt. She said 'Thanks,' opened the other door and got in next to me.

I introduced myself as we drove off.

'Hi! I am Shami,' she said. 'Samir Uncle is a friend of my mother's. She was busy so I came instead.'

She spoke confidently. Her English was easy and self-assured.

'Where do you have to go? I'm headed towards Lalbagh,' I told her.

'Oh, great. I'm not too far then – Basavanagudi. You know the J.R. Bakery? Three crosses from there.'

No matter how much I compose myself, I become flustered in the presence of a young woman. My gestures are stiff, my words sound unnatural, I am overly self-conscious. It didn't help that her perfume had begun to waft over to me.

Driving from the new layout towards the main road, I turned my head quickly to look at her. Straight hair falling loose to her shoulders. Narrow face. I was unsure if I should talk to her as an equal or as I would with someone younger. I said nothing.

She must have noticed my glance. She asked, 'So, what did you think of the house?'

'I liked it,' I said. 'These days people like to stuff their homes with knick-knacks until it looks like a handicrafts emporium. I liked the simplicity of this one.'

'Oh, Samir Uncle has taste. The salvaged window frames were really such a nice touch.'

I wondered just how close Sahu was to her.

After a while, she said, 'I overheard Samir Uncle say you are a writer?'

'Yes, I write,' I said. 'But more than that, I read. It's the only thing I do in my free time.' I sensed her turn and look at me. I took my eyes off the road for a moment and smiled at her in the car's twilight, relaxing a little.

She said, 'I love reading. But there's just so much to read! It kind of feels like a huge mountain that can't be climbed.'

'You could finish climbing a mountain, but there's no end to literature,' I said. 'It's something to take pleasure in all through one's life.'

After a pause, she asked, 'What are you reading at the moment?'

'I'm revisiting Conrad's *The Secret Agent*. This morning I had to stop with thirty pages left, or I would have been late for work. Sometimes I'm envious of people who take up literature full-time.' I'd surprised myself by being so forthcoming with a person I had only just met.

'Oh, I've read it!' she said. 'What's his name . . . Verloc. Scary book. How can a regular guy like that make a plan that involves killing his own family member? Revolution and all that is fine, but we can't throw away our moral compass.'

'Absolutely right! You've put it wonderfully,' I said, not stinting on the praise. 'You must have read the book very deeply.' I was so moved by my own generosity that my eyes welled up a little. I didn't consider whether the opinion was her own, or whether she had lifted it from somewhere.

She said nothing. I glanced at her and saw the hint of a smile. My words had pleased her as well as made her coy. In a flash I understood who she was. She wanted to be seen as someone who was precocious, and was trying, perhaps without her own knowledge, to convey this to me. She was a young woman, a girl even, but she liked to be thought of as evolved and sophisticated.

Once we got into the city, traffic slowed us down. At a signal where shop signboards illuminated the car, I saw that she had a leather bag in her lap and was playing with its clasp. She wore a thin spiral ring on her right index finger. The car's air conditioning cut us off from the vehicles and noise outside and made for an artificial solitude.

It was she who broke the silences in our conversation. I learned that she was currently working in an art gallery. It had been two years since she finished college. As a child she had lived in a house in the Cantonment area, but the city's growth had swallowed it up, leaving no trace. Sahu had given her Tolstoy's stories for her eighteenth birthday, and she was only reading them now.

'Tolstoy is great, isn't he?' she said.

'The greatest.'

We were approaching Basavanagudi and I could think of nothing to say. Driving along the Lalbagh compound wall, I reached for an old legend: 'There's a tower inside, built by Kempegowda when he was founding the city. He predicted that Bangalore wouldn't survive if it grew beyond this point. Looks like he was right.'

'Oh, apparently that story is not true. There's a watchtower built by Kempegowda, but it wasn't meant to mark the city's limits or anything. I heard this from a historian. We tend to believe any story as long as it's told well.'

'Maybe,' I said, annoyed with myself. 'But look at Bangalore these days, that story feels relevant. You have to tell me the way to your house.'

'Keep going straight. I'll tell you where to turn right.'

When I turned, it was into a wide, empty dead-end street lined by tall trees.

'What a beautiful area,' I said. 'Hard to believe there are still places like this.'

'No traffic during the day either. Here, to the left,' she said. We stopped.

I got out of the car with her.

The house was set inside a large compound enclosed by walls that must have been eight feet high. Three large trees on the footpath outside, a few more inside. An iron gate that rose to the height of the wall was fitted with a pale blue fibreglass sheet that cut off the view. A dog began to bark as soon as she touched the latch. When she opened the gate, it bounded up in welcome and clambered all over her. It barked louder when it saw she wasn't paying attention. 'Bee! Quiet!' she commanded, grabbing its collar. It whimpered and went silent. I could see a dense garden through the partly open gate.

'Please come in,' she said, as a formality. I made my excuses.

'Thanks for the ride, and for the conversation. I'm travelling for a week, but I'll call when I'm back. Maybe we could get a beer one evening when you're free?'

'Sure,' I said, though I was startled. She waited outside while I reversed and waved goodbye.

I didn't mention Shami to my wife, I am not sure why. Maybe, deep down, I wanted to keep her a secret from Shalini.

She would call in a week she had said. I turned her words over in my head, wondering if she had meant exactly a week or roughly a week. It struck me that I hadn't given her my phone number. I told myself it wouldn't do to make too much of something said so casually. The daily grind took over and before long it had escaped my mind.

She called in the afternoon, precisely a week later. The first thing I said was, 'How did you get my number?'

'Where there's a will, there's a way.'

'I thought that was our first and last meeting. There was no sign of you.'

'I said I would call in a week. I was out of town but I am back today. Are you free to meet this evening?'

'Sure. Where?'

'How about Grant Book House and then we go somewhere?'

'I could get there by six thirty. Is that okay?'

'Great. I'll be on the second floor. See you.'

Half an hour before leaving the office I called Shalini and said I might be a little late. She was never one to ask for details. I told myself I was going to meet Shami with nothing more than the anticipation of getting to know someone new. And so it didn't particularly trouble me that I did not tell Shalini everything.

I was ten minutes late by the time I parked and walked to Grant Book House. Feeling too impatient to wait for the lift, I rushed up the stairs to the literature section on the second floor. I was out of breath when I got there. Under the shop's fan, the nape of my neck felt cool. I had broken into a slight sweat. As I stood there, looking around for her, a boy from the shop came up. 'Sir?' I sent him away and took in the space more slowly. There she was on a stool in a corner, flipping through a book. She saw me as I walked up and got to her feet.

She was wearing jeans today as well. Sleeves rolled up, a white shirt through which I could discern the outline of her bra. Silky hair left untied in deliberate disarray. Her face shone without make-up. I was unnerved by the splendour of her youth. I sucked in my stomach, stood tall, ran a hand over my hair and tried to compose myself. I had driven her home last week in near-darkness, and I realised at once how different it was to see her face-to-face in bright light. Just as it takes sickness to appreciate good health, it is only those who are past it that can recognise the glow of youth.

'Finished buying your books?' I asked.

'Wasn't planning to,' she said. 'Just thought this a good spot to meet. I like browsing.' She began to put books back on the shelves. 'Just a minute, I want to show you something.'

She went to a shelf on the other side of the shop, pulled out a book with a yellow cover and came back. When she placed it in my hands, it was Conrad's *The Secret Agent*.

'Oh! I have the same edition,' I said, thrilled. The book somehow seemed to connect us. I gave it back to her, smiling. 'Where should we go?'

'First let's get out of here. Then we decide,' she said. She put the Conrad back on its shelf and we left.

'I know a place, not very far,' I said.

'Anywhere, as long as we can sit down and have a conversation.'

We walked to my car and drove to Airways Garden Restaurant. It was a short distance, but it took ten minutes in the evening traffic. I struggled to find something meaningful to say. By the time we were at the restaurant my account of a friend who tripped on uneven paving on a footpath with disastrous consequences had been completed, and I had finished lamenting the sorry situation with citizens' rights.

It was past dusk when we parked outside Airways. We entered the large open-air courtyard, tables laid out neatly amid trees and plants. It felt heady to walk in with her. I must have strutted as if I had won a victory of some sort. Without having to look I could sense eyes turn towards us. I picked a table in the corner and we sat down opposite each other. I was filled with a strange emotion resembling pride, something perhaps only men around my age would understand.

The tables were spread about the garden in small gazebos lit by lamps hanging from tiled roofs. A waiter materialised as soon as we were seated and placed a worn sheaf of thick paper sheets in front of us. I took a cursory look through the menu. 'I'll have a beer.'

'Same here,' Shami said.

The instant she spoke, it struck me that I had flouted etiquette. I was mortified. 'It should be ladies first, right? I don't like to be formal with friends. But still.'

'Oh, don't worry about it,' she said.

'I like this place because there's a sense of privacy even among so many people. And they have the coldest beer in Bangalore. The hariyali kabab is quite good too.'

'You come here often?'

'No. But this is where I meet old friends.'

It was windier than usual. The rustling of leaves was loud enough to almost drown out the conversations around us and the noise of traffic outside. The waiter brought a bottle of beer and two tall glasses. He filled the glasses and asked, 'Anything else?'

'One hariyali kabab,' I said, glancing at Shami. I explained: 'This is a vegetarian restaurant, so it's a kabab in name only. Hope you don't mind.'

'No, I'm fine with veg,' she said.

The beer beckoned, golden in the dim light. We raised our glasses and wordlessly said cheers with a blink. I took a gulp, placed my glass on the table and let out a long sigh that released the accumulated weariness of the day. I immediately rued my folly. It was perfectly fine to do this while drinking with other middle-aged men, but to let off sighs like a pressure cooker while in the company of a young lady was shameful. My facade of refinement had collapsed.

There was a moment of silence. I thought the sigh would linger through the evening if I didn't say something quickly.

'I went to the office early today since I didn't sleep much last night. I was at a yakshagana performance. Three hours. I used to watch these shows all night when I was a boy,' I said.

'Oh, I'm sorry! Maybe I should not have called you today.'

'No, nothing like that. It's good to go out when you're tired.'

'You know,' she said, 'I only learned about yakshagana recently. From someone who came to inaugurate a show at our gallery. I had to look it up on the internet. That's the thing about growing up in Bangalore – you could spend all your life without coming into contact with Kannada.'

Now the conversation had turned to yakshagana I prepared to recount my memories: easy chairs in the show tent; the smell of roasting peanuts; gas lanterns hissing in tea stalls; the strange exhilaration that seizes me when I hear the beating of drums; all those varied characters with their tendencies reflected in the design of their armlets and headdresses. Long ago, there was that one and only time that I donned a costume and danced. On the day after a performance, it would be hard to play in the field because our feet kept finding the holes left by the tent poles. A dull oil stain would mark the spot where the generator had been.

I wanted to tell her all of this, but while I was worrying if I would find the right words in English, she had embarked on a story about how the rent was hiked at her art gallery. I wasn't really interested, but I listened anyway.

We talked in a rush, as if resuming an old conversation. She asked no personal questions. Neither did I. She was eager to keep it flowing by saying the first thing that came to her. Equally, I was happy to listen to whatever she had to say. Then she surprised me by asking, 'Is Samir Sahu a close friend?'

I hesitated to answer without knowing what had prompted it. 'Depends,' I said.

'He's friends with my mother,' she said, as if she understood. 'He has some interesting things to say about labour unions in Bengal. And he has heard these really powerful stories of the Naxalbari uprising from people who were involved. I used to make him repeat them all the time.' After a pause, she said, 'But how does someone who feels so strongly about society and justice end up in this city, working at a job like that? Pressures of life, I guess.' She bent forward slightly. A few strands of hair drifted onto her cheek.

I sat back and took her in. Toned shoulders. There was poise and a certain ease with which she held her glass of beer and drank from it. She wore a sleek, silver ring on one of her fingers. Her laughs began with a flash of teeth. Green gemstones dangled from her ears.

I had drifted away for a moment. I gathered myself. 'Sahu and I, when we sit for lunch at the same table, no one wants to join us. We talk about democracy, communism, the role of communists in our independence struggle, the wheel of history, and so on. Our colleagues can't make head nor tail of what we are saying.'

Shami leaned into her chair and pushed her hair back with both hands. It looked like she would be doing this at intervals through the evening. Sahu had emerged as a competitor out of nowhere. I too would need to raise the sickle of revolution. But it would have to be done subtly.

'Did you say Sahu used to share Naxal stories he had heard? What a time it was. I had a friend who was a revolutionary. You could even say I joined in, in a small way. Feels like another life.'

'Really? What did you do?'

She had opened her mouth wide and invited me to lower a hook. I took a swig and obliged.

'Nothing is achieved when people like me raise a few slogans only to go home to sleep,' I said. 'Look, it is not enough to want to do something. You need the right opportunities. I used to have a friend whose name was Chandu. Those slogans, the *rasta rokos*, the endless talk of revolution all sound so romantic. But in the end it's only the lower-middle class who are truly committed to a revolution. They walk, we talk.'

A little self-deprecation goes a long way.

The waiter appeared to ask if he should bring another beer. I said yes. I was slightly embarrassed to have got through my glass so quickly. Hers was still three-quarters full.

Shami looked entirely at ease, as if our being there was well within the bounds of propriety and convention, as if the nature of our conversation was perfectly ordinary. As for me, I hadn't yet come to terms with the fact that I was here, drinking in the company of a young woman. I had to make an effort to suppress the throb of exhilaration I felt.

'Back when we were students in the hostel, we had no money. But what experiences we had! As the bank balance grows we have more to lose. Our risk appetite goes down. It's people who have nothing that get to change the world.'

'Very true. What kind of activism did you and your friend get into?'

'Oh, I would have to go on all night,' I took a sip of beer, 'if I started talking about Chandu and Chirag.' The moisture beaded on the outside of the glass formed a drop and fell on my shirt. I felt a damp coldness on my stomach. 'My own role is very boring.'

'I'm sure that's not true. Lived experience is always fascinating,' she said, smiling in encouragement.

There was no doubt that I had a willing audience. And liquid courage. I launched into my slum eviction story. Some of the details would be hard for me to describe in English. But when there's a young woman sitting wide-eyed in front of you, what does it matter which parts are true and which are not. Stories deserve to be told with a little recklessness. Even as I was telling it, it began to feel like someone else's story.

About the time I had finished college and come to Bangalore to find work, the city corporation demolished a large slum. I was then staying with relatives. It had been arranged that I would occupy a room on the terrace and go down for breakfast and dinner. My father was paying for all this, but they still insisted I be back home by eight every evening.

'I didn't know boys had curfews too,' Shami said, smiling.

That morning my friend Chandu had showed up at half past eight while I was finishing breakfast. By the time I went out to greet him, he was hopping with impatience. He asked, 'Did you hear about the slum?'

I had. It was on the front page of every newspaper. 'Let's go,' Chandu said, and scowled when I asked where.

We reached the spot around ten. Complete chaos. It was swarming with policemen struggling to control the crowd of onlookers. On one side of the road that cut through, the slum was finished off.

Only the previous day, the place had been packed with tiny homes. All gone, leaving behind a wasteland of tin sheets and broken walls. It was near the end of summer, and the sun was particularly bright. Secrets that had been hidden indoors now lay strewn about in the day's glare. Boxes of talcum powder. Glinting fragments of mirror. Cooking utensils, grimy clothes and bedsheets. Plates.

'Oh God,' Shami said, softly. I glowed with satisfaction.

When Chandu and I talked to the residents, the women of the slum repeated their story from the beginning each time. They had told it so often that it had become mechanical for them. But every time they told it, it felt like a new detail caught them unawares and made them break down.

Residents had been forced to evacuate their houses the previous night before the bulldozers started their work. One man had been so drunk that he would not wake up. He had been lifted physically from his bed and put down outside. A photograph of him sleeping on the road was in several newspapers. He was still out cold when we went. A large group hovered over him, some looking alternately at him and his photograph in the newspapers they held.

In the middle of this a woman shouted that there was water in the tap at the end of the road. They had all just lost their homes, but even so they rummaged among their possessions and ran with pots and buckets to fill with water. In an instant they had formed a queue. I still marvel at how their daily routine could take over despite the dire circumstances.

Chandu and I spent the day there. I had not informed anyone at home and didn't want them to worry if I wasn't back by dinner time. When I said as much, Chandu said, 'Revolution is not something one does as a hobby. It demands total dedication. You will understand this if you meet Chirag. He may even come here today.'

Shami was looking at me intently. I said, 'When I think of the path my life has taken, I can't believe that person at the slum was me. It's so strange to find myself in a corporate job.'

I put my beer down and looked into her eyes.

'So did you meet this Chirag?' she asked.

'It's a long story, but yes. When Chirag was in hiding he once wanted a pamphlet translated from English to Kannada. So Chandu brought him to my place late at night. We worked on the text for a few hours and they sneaked off early in the morning. Chirag was a really intense person. Fully committed to the cause.'

The tables had filled up as the night set in. The buzz of conversations surrounded us. A stiff breeze suggested the possibility of unseasonal rain. I had got through three glasses while I told my story. She had been sitting with her half-full glass for an hour. I wanted to order more, but I stopped myself, thinking I would come across as a drunkard at our first proper meeting.

'I'll just be a moment,' she said, and got up to look for the toilets.

I sensed I would soon be troubled by questions about my motives. I thought of home, my wife, my son. Was I really sitting here slobbering and wagging my tail to impress a girl? My mind raced through the evening's conversation. No doubt, I had given it my best. Casual talk of revolution, stories of fighting the good fight, in a tone that suggested my present wealth and position were entirely by chance. Anyway, there had been nothing that could lead astray an eager young mind. If I had spiced things up a little, that was simply the nature of all storytelling.

When she had returned and sat down in her chair, she said, 'Thank you. I don't think I could ever forget this evening.' There was more. 'You know what? My mother doesn't like me working. She says she would give me twice my salary if I quit. All I want is to leave home and live by myself. But to get a job that will support me I need some experience first.' Clearly these were things that had been weighing on her mind. I nodded.

The waiter came to our table and lingered. Her glass was not empty. Out of politeness I asked if she wanted anything else. She shook her head. I called for the bill.

'One minute,' I excused myself, and got up. Before going I told her, 'Look up Chirag Hamsa on the internet.'

Walking to the toilets, I realised I was a little tipsy, and it wasn't only the beer.

When I returned and sat down, she said at once, 'Oh God. Chirag was a big Naxal leader. He was in your room a whole night?'

'I've told very few people. Keep it to yourself.'

'Of course. You know, hearing about the things you've done, it's like I'm wasting my time. I should be out there risking new experiences.'

'He was a very bright fellow. They said he died in an encounter, but it was actually murder.'

The bill arrived. 'Let me get it,' she said.

'Certainly not. Youngsters shouldn't pay. Not when I am here.'

'You sound like my mother,' she said. 'You must meet her sometime.'

'Definitely,' I said.

I left a generous tip and leaned forward and to one side to stuff my wallet into my back pocket. Then it struck me how typical this movement was for middle-aged men with bulging wallets, and I felt self-conscious.

'Shall we leave?' I asked with my eyes. I walked close to her as we made our way through the now-crowded restaurant. In the car, I asked, 'Did you like the place?'

'It's wonderful.'

The traffic had eased. We drove in silence. She seemed to be in a sort of reverie. I heard her say 'Oh God' under her breath again.

I understood why. She was lost for words. When Chandu told me about Chirag, the age I was then, revolution had a seductive quality that lent its glow to everything it touched. Chandu soared in my esteem for having these connections. I felt a little bit like a revolutionary myself only from knowing him. Chirag had shunned his family wealth to join the comrades. A few hours with him and I began to feel as if part of his sacrifice was somehow mine too. I have used that night in my room, translating a pamphlet for him, to build myself up in my own eyes. It is how I atone for any guilt I might feel about thinking of myself as an idealist while having done nothing about it.

'At the time I had no idea how dangerous it was to have him in my room,' I said. 'Experiences don't come with a preview, right? We don't know what their significance in the future will be.'

'Like today,' she said. 'I didn't expect to hear any of this. There's so much out there that I know nothing about. I've never met anyone with a direct connection to people like Chirag Hamsa. You must tell me more.'

'Best to leave it at that. Saying more won't be good for either of us.'

A little mysteriousness can be irresistible to the imagination. My words were bound to have fired up her curiosity.

There was hardly any traffic at that time of the night. Before long we were at her house. 'Thanks for such a lovely evening. I'll call tomorrow,' she said. After she had waited a while in front of the gate, it was opened from within. Her dog bounded out to welcome her. I waved goodbye.

It was ten when I got home. I had never been that late without notice. I worried that Shalini would be furious, but she was not. Seema, an old friend, had called and they had gossiped for an hour about their classmates from college. Even as I was at the door, she began a litany of others' woes: 'That Shyamala's husband has Aids it seems,' 'Ragini has been posted to Gulbarga and her husband has been sent off to a village in Madhya Pradesh.' She had found plenty of reasons to believe she was better off than the rest, and this seemed to have put her in a good mood.

As I sat down to take off my shoes, she said: 'Thoo, I smell hooch.'

'Just a little beer.'

'It's all the same. Your son has gone to sleep. I have eaten.'

On the way to our bedroom, I saw Ajit was fast asleep in his room, the door slightly ajar. I wanted to be alone. 'A quick shower and I'll come for dinner. Tell me everything then,' I said.

She'd asked nothing about where I had gone or with whom. She must have assumed I was returning from one of our office parties. I stepped out after a cold shower.

'That Suhas is still not married. You know who I'm talking about? We did our training together.'

'Why not? Isn't this the guy who'd write long letters to you?' I noticed a greater than usual softness towards her creeping into my speech and grew cautious lest she suspect anything. I carried out a plate of food, switched on the TV. A discussion of some sort was on. Talking heads were confidently proposing solutions to fix the country.

'Yes, yes, the same fellow. She ran into him last month at a movie theatre.'

'You seem to have gathered a lot of news today,' I said.

I twice considered telling her where I had been, then felt it would make no difference. How would I put it, anyway? That I had made a new woman friend? That I had met someone over a shared interest in literature? How would I say these things with any conviction when I didn't believe them myself?

I finished dinner, switched off the TV and put the plate in the sink. As I was getting ready for bed, I said, 'I met a friend of Sahu's today, called Shami. We were in Airways having a beer. That's why I was late.'

She was distracted and not really listening. What I had said caused me a twinge of shame. I had implied that Sahu was present without actually saying so. I mused for a time on the uses we have for grammar and construction. And then I fell asleep. ■

മലയാളം

In everyday Malayalam, the word *shraddha* means attention or care. You might hear it from a teacher who corrects your carelessness in class – *shraddikkoo!* (pay attention!). Or from a stranger warning you about a pothole hidden by the gushing rainwater of a monsoon – *shraddikkane!* (take care!). I still remember hearing the word as a child, when Kerala was lusher than it is today. The roads were surrounded by paddy fields back then, and in every monsoon, water brought to life thousands of water lilies on the roadsides. We kids, mesmerised by the flowers, would forget about the water snakes and other creatures that loved the lilies too, and passers-by would have to call out to us – *shraddikkedaa kallappillaare!* (watch it, you scamps!).

Borrowed from Sanskrit, the word shraddha has a long cultural and philosophical history. In religious contexts, it means 'faith' or 'observances of faith, earnestly made'. In the Vedanta school of Indian philosophy, it means to bear faith in what you may not see, the ultimate reward of which is a glimpse, at least, of what you have reposed your faith in. In Buddhism, shraddha refers to the powers of devotion and concentration that develop as the student of the Buddha's teachings traverses the path of learning diligently, experiencing it closely. In everyday Malayalam, though, it no longer has a religious or sacred meaning. Shraddha is almost entirely secular.

The eminent literary editor Mini Krishnan once described translation as the act of sending an arrow through the eye of the clay bird for a second time. The allusion, of course, is to the warrior Arjuna, one of the heroes of the Mahabharata. A peerless archer, he establishes his prowess by sending one arrow after another through the minuscule hole, declaring that all he could see at that moment was the bird's eye. As a literary translator working between Malayalam and English, I have returned often to the word shraddha to describe my vocation, because it names, more clearly than any word I know, the kind of focus that translation demands. In my experience, the process calls for three distinct kinds of shraddha.

The first kind suggests the careful eye of a jeweller. The translator's task is like that of someone loosening a precious stone from an ornament in one metal and setting it in another. It requires delicacy. The aim is to ensure that the reset stone catches the same light. Sometimes it even catches better light in the new metal. In rare moments, I have felt this to be the case: for example, when I read Balachandran Chullikkad's translation of Neruda's love poems. As someone able to read both English and Malayalam, it seemed to me that the anguish of lost love – its almost physical tenderness – was conveyed more powerfully in Malayalam.

The second kind of shraddha is attention to sound – not only to the texture of the source language, but to the cadences which gesture to its social life. In recent years, as the commercial interest in Indian-language literature has grown, translation has too often meant pulling a text into a standardised global English, legible to transnational elites and non-resident Indians. I take issue with this. Translation, I believe, must sometimes push back against this current.

In literary translation, regional dialects and demotic usages – for example, Malayalam as it is spoken in the south-eastern districts of Kerala – are most often turned into standardised English. This standardisation can flatten language. In Malayalam literature itself, there is now a movement that seeks to revive demotic speech and dialects, bringing them back into print to challenge the growing ubiquity and elitism of standardised Malayalam. The same flattening recurs in translation: even dialect-rich work is presented in standardised English.

Literary translators might take their cue from Indian cinema music directors, who have long transported tunes from one region to the other, remaking them without erasing their origins. Salil Chowdhury, the famous Bangla composer, brought folk-inflected Bengali melodies into Malayalam film songs. These were loved not only because they fitted the contexts, but because they left behind a

മലയാളം

sweet tinge of the unfamiliar in the listener's ear.

The third form of shraddha is the ability to recognise and preserve the layers within a text – these may be historical, social or cultural. Translation is about more than literary pleasure. It allows communication across time and cultures. This kind of shraddha is mostly found in scholarly and academic work, where a text may be approached as a repository of memory, a monument of power, or trace of resistance – each layered, contradictory and, at times, unruly.

Many philosophers consider love and justice as opposing poles, but the three forms of shraddha mentioned involve developing a careful balance of the two. Shraddha, in Malayalam, describes a kind of tender discipline. And that, I think, is what translation ultimately demands: care, alertness, a commitment to let something live.

Of course, shraddha is not just a literary value or the ethic of an intellectual life. It is the everyday business of kindness, the slow work that sustains life. In Kerala today, shaped by neoliberalism and a predatory capitalism, there is less space for shraddha. And yet, you will still stumble upon it. I did this year during an ongoing strike by health workers – all women – who keep Kerala's public health going. On the side of a busy main road, surrounded by police, huddled together against the rain, a group of women sat hard at work. They were compiling health records for their respective wards, calling pregnant women whose check-ups were due, talking to elderly, bed-ridden patients they visit every month to deliver medicines and offer company to alleviate the loneliness of old age. Seeing me watching, one of them turned and said, 'Madam, we are on strike, but all these people rely on us – we cannot drop our shraddha.' ■

Saturday writing club

A space to write, a place to belong

Join Arvon's free monthly online writing club

Arvon • The Home of Creative Writing since 1968
Residential Courses • Online Masterclasses • Writing Retreats

Sign up here

ARVON

ARTS COUNCIL
ENGLAND

Supported using public funding by

LOTTERY FUNDED

SOHRAB HURA
2013
Magnum Photos

I AM MY MOTHER'S OLDER BROTHER

Sujatha Gidla

For a long time it was my fervent wish that my parents would come live with me after their retirement. But my father died, and my mother refused. She insisted on living entirely on her own terms. Only when she became completely dependent, in every way, did my wish come true.

I am my mother's eldest, the one who first gave her the experience of childbirth and of being a mother. All her ideas of how to raise children with care and a scientific temperament she put into practice on me. By the time my sister and brother came along, idealism had given way to practicality.

When I was five years old her older brother – who was also her father, mother, and best friend – went underground to organize landless peasants to take up arms against landlords. It was a great loss to my mother. She needed to talk about him, and in me she found a rapt and sympathetic listener. In this way, she transmitted to me his ideals, which she shared – justice, equality, solidarity with the poor and oppressed.

Growing up in the small South Indian town of Kakinada, I was keenly sensitive to my mother's troubles in life. She was burdened every morning with the drudgery of cleaning dishes, washing clothes, cooking. Then hurrying off to college to give lectures in history. When she returned late in the evening, again she had to cook and clean.

In her appearance, she was extremely modest, partly because we had little to spend and partly because she had no time to think of clothes or jewelry. Her personality was a curious mix. To almost everyone, friend or stranger, she was pleasing to a fault. But when it came to confronting social evils, as when she stood up in public meetings to make a speech, she was fierce. Many people admired her: neighbors, her students, my father's students, my teachers, my classmates, their parents, activists of all kinds. They came to her for solace and advice, and she would always go out of her way to help them.

The year after my mother retired, my father died. She was then fifty-nine years old, and for the first time in her life she was alone. I flew home from New York to be with her. For once, she wasn't all smiles when I met her, glowing with delight, saying endearing things, giving me news of relatives and friends, cooking specially for me, boiling water for my bath. She was not the helper and consoler but the one in need of support.

After a few months, I returned to New York. And she prepared to go off to the distant industrial township where my brother was working as a chemical engineer to live with him and his family, as Indian widows traditionally do. Before long, I got news that she had left and gone back to Kakinada. Some minor incident had made her feel unwelcome. She went away with her suitcase in the middle of the night and, since there wasn't any transport from the township at that hour, sat at a bus stop till morning.

She decided to live on her own in the apartment my parents had bought for their retirement. It was a world in itself. There were five families, two maids, and a watchman. She would tell me all about them on the phone. Though her depression lingered, once she settled back in Kakinada she was more or less her old self. Pleasant, compassionate, gregarious, socially active. In fact, she seemed to be thriving now that she had full control of her own finances – her and my father's pension. No longer did she have to worry about money, and she spent it as she liked – mostly by giving it away to all and sundry. In India, women live in the shadow of fathers before marriage, in the shadow of husbands and in-laws after marriage, and in the shadow of sons when their spouses die. My mother was a rare exception, and other women envied her for it.

But when, in the years after my father's death, she came to visit me and my sister in America, she would behave as though we looked down on her. She would take offense over nothing and stop talking for days. And when I went to see her in India, she guarded her independence zealously. She would never let me spend money, never let me help with cooking or cleaning or do anything for her. Whenever we went out, she had to be in charge of where we were going and how to get there. When I bought her an air conditioner, she threw a shocking tantrum. She was cutting onions when I brought it home, and she flung the knife on the floor in a rage.

I blamed my mother's new circumstances for the changes I observed in her. And when for the first time a serious strain was put on our relationship, I blamed the social and cultural gap that came from my moving to America. I myself had gone from taking pride in my innocence and over-politeness to being firmer and more street-smart, even assuming a typical New York impatience. Also, having left India in search of a freer life – both as an untouchable in a caste society and as a woman in a patriarchal one – I had adopted the American norms of dating and living with boyfriends, which are not common even in big cities in India. Perhaps naively, I never imagined my mother would have any objection. But when she visited New York for the first time it was over my living arrangements that we had our first big row. She left New York as abruptly as she had my brother's house and went off to spend the rest of her trip with my sister in Florida.

Otherwise, the special bond we had always shared remained intact. We talked for hours on the phone. One time, when I casually asked her a question about our caste status and where it had come from, she started telling me stories I had never heard before. I started taping these conversations – over a hundred hours of them – which I transcribed for my own interest and later used as the basis for a book.

I was shocked to learn we had not always belonged to the mainstream of Indian civilization. My great-grandparents lived as hunters and gatherers in a remote forest. They were forced out onto the plains by British economic policies and there, being latecomers, entered Hindu society at the very bottom, as untouchables. If not for the help of Canadian missionaries, who offered them education, medical care, and jobs, they would have gone on living in utter misery.

Having tasted literacy, and not having any other means for advancement, my great-grandparents were keen to have their children educated at mission schools. My mother and her brothers, in their turn, grew up at the time of the independence struggle, when there was a short-lived effort to unify the nation against colonial rule. Unlike today, when there is more open discrimination and untouchables are forced to rely on 'reservations', or government quotas, it was a time of openness in employment and higher education for the few untouchables lucky enough to have been spared from farm labor and sent to school. My mother told me all this, and how her brother became a Congress activist and later a communist militant and guerrilla leader, as well as a famous poet. She became a college lecturer, which is not as distinguished or well paid a profession as it is (or used to be) in the West, and struggled to raise us three children, especially when separated for a long period from my father due to transfers to colleges in far-off towns.

Work on the book brought us closer. But between finishing the manuscript in 2013 and its publication four years later, our connection started to fray in ways I could not understand. There were bitter fights over her plans for dividing her savings. The amounts were small enough, and I did not need anything from her, but I objected when she said she wanted my brother to handle everything when she died and take the largest share. I was offended by the favoritism. After all, she had raised me to oppose discrimination against women.

When I visited her several years later, I arrived at her apartment to find a large banner hanging over the front door with a hand-drawn picture of my author photo at one end and at the other a bunch of roses. On top it said in big letters: WELCOME HOME, SUJA. Underneath, in smaller print: CONGRATULATIONS ON YOUR ACHIEVEMENT. LOVE, AMMA, BABU, ANITHA.

We sat together, and as usual she began talking. She had always observed the world with a keen eye, and she loved to share what she noticed in her amusing and articulate fashion. When she was growing up it was her brother who listened and listened while she talked and talked, then it was my father, and since his death it had been only me. But this time she was talking too fast and going on too long, her own narrative skill leaving her breathless. She finally said, 'I think it would be dangerous for me to go on talking.'

We got ready for bed. When I am with my mother, I sleep no more than three feet from her. She was very happy to have me near and said, 'I have three children, and I will divide whatever I have into three equal portions. Why should it be anything but equal?'

So she had decided to stop favoring my brother. I said nothing, having promised myself not to respond if this matter came up.

She proceeded to say, 'But I will give Babu more.'

I was amused. 'How can it be equal and yet he gets more?'

She said, 'It is equal.'

'But you also said more.'

'That is because he spends a lot of money visiting me every year. You girls don't.'

'How can you say that? I visit you every year. And when you were eighty, I flew to India just to be with you on your birthday. That year I visited you twice.'

'No, you visit only rarely. Besides, Babu bought the air conditioner for me.'

'But that was me!'

'No, it was Babu.'

'Don't you remember, you threw a tantrum and chucked the knife on the floor?'

'That was Babu.'

We turned off the lights and went to sleep. But in the morning and the days that followed it rankled me to hear her shamelessly lie just to torment me. 'You know there is a record of how many times I visited you,' I told her. 'In my passport.'

'Then show me your passport.'

But I had forgotten I had recently renewed my passport, and so there was only one entry stamp – the one for that very visit. 'You are a liar,' she said. 'It's proven.'

One morning she put on a sari to go out and started looking for some papers in her safe. Only she couldn't find what she was looking for. She was getting more and more worked up: 'No, I kept it here. How can it have gone?' I could not help but feel sorry for her.

Finally, she set out. 'Where are you going?'

'I have some business.'

She went to a branch of the State Bank of India on the main road and I followed her. They gave her some information she couldn't grasp and some instructions she couldn't follow. I explained to her what they had said. It seemed that, earlier that day, she had been to another branch some miles off, whose clerks had sent her here, and now they were sending her back.

I followed her to the other branch. More complicated instructions from the bank manager there. She was in a state of extreme agitation. I could see her blood pressure rising. I took the papers and helped her do some calculations. Only then did I realize she was trying to liquidate her savings and transfer the money she had long been vaguely promising to give me to my account in New York.

I told her I didn't want the money. It was her lies and insults that I objected to. But she refused to listen. She was determined to prove she was not biased and I was greedy. It was turning into a scene. So I let her transfer the money with the bank manager's help, telling her I would send it back once I got home.

When I was leaving for New York, she accompanied me to the railway station, but we didn't speak. I didn't accomplish much of what I hoped to in that visit. My intention to discuss plans for when she could no longer live on her own had come to nothing. But I had managed to get her to sign a couple of papers, a green card application and an application that would allow me to request leave from my job for the sake of her care. She was reluctant and suspicious but she signed.

When I reached New York, I called as I always did to let her know I had arrived safely, and this time also in the hope of hearing she felt remorse for how she had treated me. To my shock, she accused me of stealing her money. I reminded her it was she who insisted I accept it. She said I had threatened her and made her sign over her power of attorney against her will.

'What power of attorney? When?'

'You had me sign those papers.'

'That was for your green card and my family leave, all for your sake.'

'I know what they are. You had me sign the power of attorney by force.'

I slammed the phone down.

I was bitter. At the same time, I began to worry. She was old. She was frail. She lived alone. When the pandemic began in 2020, I got back in touch. She was in the highest risk group. I sent her letters listing precautions to take. No reply.

I decided to travel to India as soon as restrictions were lifted. My idea was to settle her in a place set up for a woman her age, whether it was her own apartment with hired help or a suitable old age home. When I called her to let her know my plans, she forbade me to come.

In Kakinada, I rented an apartment that I hoped to persuade my mother to move into, one hundred times better than hers. I planned to hire help to look after her there once I was ready to go home. This place would be much more comfortable than any old-age home.

I imagined my mother sitting on the balcony, sipping tea, reading a newspaper.

Weeks went by and my mother wouldn't speak to me. I tried sending her some snacks. She sent them back with a message saying she could never forgive me. I was there six months before I got my chance. An annual memorial was held for my uncle. She could not fail to attend, nor could she stop me from coming too. I prepared for the day with hope and anxiety. I dressed well and neatly combed my hair as she always urged and as I ordinarily would never do. I entered the meeting hall and spotted her sitting with some people. She was frailer than ever. I knelt before her and held her hand. She allowed me to sit with her during the meeting and stayed to eat dinner with me. I saw her off as she got into a car.

Now that I was allowed to visit her, I could see she was living a disorderly life. She did only what she felt like doing. Sometimes she watched news or cricket matches on TV, but mostly she read. Newspapers, magazines, books. Unlike in the West, college lecturers in India need not be scholars, and typically are not. Many lecturers in small towns like ours lack a basic understanding of their subject. My mother was not one of those. She had genuine interest not only in her subject – modern European and American history – but many things outside of it as well. She always read newspapers and magazines regularly, but she never had time for books until after her retirement. Now I saw she was reading a huge volume on the rise of Nazism in Germany. She made notes, she dog-eared pages, she underlined passages. She read the hell out of that book. Then she started on a book I gave her about the Indian independence movement. She would read all day, fighting off sleep until four or five in the morning.

She was not taking care of herself or the apartment. It was filthy, but she refused all help. She would clean it herself, she insisted, but nothing ever got done. When I challenged her one day, she tucked the hem of her sari into her waist and, gathering brooms and dusters, worked day and night for three days. But all her effort was somehow ineffectual, and I never saw any difference.

She came to visit the apartment I was renting. She lay down on a couch and read a newspaper, then left. I tried to get her to come back – if not to live there with me, then at least for another visit. This made her fear I would hold her captive there. She wouldn't come. She said the floors were shiny like mirrors. If she set foot on them, she said, she would get confused and fall down. Instead, she asked me to come eat lunch with her every day.

My mother was speaking with me now, but not about the issues I had come to India to resolve. Months passed and progress was very slow. And then, in a moment, we were back where we started. We had a small disagreement, and again she said I stole her money. Now she added new accusations. She said I stole her watches and took her gold bangles. To taunt me, or so I thought at the time, she even acted out how I supposedly approached her, grabbed hold of her arms, and yanked the bangles off her wrists.

Eventually, I had to return to New York. Three weeks later a cousin called. My mother was not doing well. She was not cooking for herself and wouldn't let anyone send her food. She lived on fruits and sweets brought by visitors. Her apartment was unlivable. There were dead rats hanging from curtains, rat nests in pots. Some fetid liquid coming out of the refrigerator. My cousin told me he stepped inside, gagged from the stink, and had to get out right away.

I flew back the next day. There was no time to waste on coaxing her to see a doctor. She would never listen to me. I enlisted the help of her doctor along with friends, relatives, activists, prominent people in Kakinada. On their advice, I tried various schemes to get her into the doctor's office. I sent confederates to urge her to seek care and even to slip her a sedative. Everything backfired.

In the end, I went myself, together with the woman who cooked for me and the watchman of my building, who had his own auto-rickshaw. When we arrived, my mother was just going out to the bank. She let me in to ask after her health. We got up to leave, and she walked us to the gate. Just as we reached it, the cook and I put our arms around her waist and tried to steer her toward the auto. My mother realized she was being ambushed and started screaming. She dropped to the ground and lay stiff, making it impossible to lift her to her feet. The watchman came and, taking her by the shoulders, dragged her into the auto. She shouted out to people on the street that she was being kidnapped. She was losing her independence, and she resisted like a wild horse refusing to be broken. The coconut seller in front of the house and all the neighbors gathered to gawk in horror at the spectacle.

At the clinic run by her doctor, she begged him to call the police. The nurses drew her blood, and the tests came back in no time. She had a severe urinary tract infection. Septicemia. She needed to be admitted immediately.

The doctor phoned a psychiatrist, who rushed over and spent an hour with her in her room. When he came out, I was told she had dementia.

For a week straight, she did not stop ranting. She even threatened the doctor that she would report him. She told the nurses to piss off. She wouldn't eat. She kept urging strangers passing by her room to call her other daughter and her son and let them know she was being held prisoner.

It was fifteen days before she was discharged. We got into an auto. When she saw it wasn't going in the direction of her building, she resented the fact but did not resist. She would never return to her apartment, her sanctuary, her pride.

The angry, willful, suspicious woman I had been dealing with on and off for the past few years disappeared. Now she panicked when I was out of sight. She apologized for the things she had done to me, the particulars of which she could not recall. She even told me she was no longer concerned about social expectations and I should live my life the way I wanted to. She who once called me a thief and a bully now marveled at what a generous and all-knowing person I was.

Gradually, I was disabused of the idea that I could settle my mother there and go back to New York. It was necessary for me to stay and care for her full-time. Having exhausted all my savings, I managed to get access to my mother's account where her pension was deposited every month. I hired a cook, two aides, and a physical therapist.

When I flew back to New York for a few weeks, however, my mother reverted to the state she was in when she was first brought to the clinic. She shouted abuse all day and made dark threats. Only the sight of me on a video call would soothe her. I could not look after someone on a separate continent. And so, I decided to move her to New York.

In her condition, she could not fly economy. I emptied her account and bought two business-class tickets. Throughout the flight, I was surprised to see my mother sitting relaxed and comfortable as though in an easy chair in her own living room. Until she asked a flight attendant for something and was told, 'Why, we are going to be landing in New York in fifteen minutes.' That was when she turned to me with a look of astonishment. 'Why have you brought me to New York? Why didn't you tell me you were bringing me here?' She was disturbed. 'My brothers will be looking for me. They will be worried.' As the horror of her abduction sunk in, she faced it bravely: 'Just tell me how you intend to dispose of me.' Her unhappiness lasted a few minutes.

For years, I had explained the changes in my mother's behavior in various ways. I would tell myself they were due to her living alone after my father's death. Or to the cultural gap that had opened between us. Or a patriarchal streak I had never noticed. Or else a nasty side of her personality, previously hidden from view, had unexpectedly come to the surface and slowly taken possession of her.

When I was first told she had dementia, I was happy to learn she was not evil but merely sick. And yet I could not accept that her condition was as severe or as permanent as I was told by the psychiatrist at the clinic. After her discharge, I saw unmistakable signs of a decline in her faculties. But I still didn't trust the doctor's assessments. I decided to restore her cognitive health with proper nutrition, medications, and supplements. I bought her sensory toys, coloring books, small puzzles. It was several months after her first hospitalization that I accepted that my mother had dementia.

As I took care of her, I had many questions. She would get agitated in the late afternoon and restlessly sit down, stand up, sit down again, and again stand up. What should I do? And how could I stop her talking endlessly? I turned for answers to social media forums for dementia caregivers. I found many people facing the same difficulties, including some who were themselves in the early stages of the illness. Each post would get hundreds of replies offering advice and support.

The problems addressed in these forums were not limited to the needs of the loved ones. As a caregiver, I have experienced symptoms myself, including total neglect of my own needs, bursting into loud sobs when talking to her doctor, not wanting to go out or meet people or even answer phone calls. Fear of what I will do with my life when I am no longer caring for my mother.

Dementia is a vicious disease that has a cascading effect on many lives. It can spoil relationships and break up families. And of course, it destroys careers and ruins finances. In India, I had the benefit of residing in a poor country dominated by imperialism where medical services and domestic help are, for better or worse, dirt cheap. The aides I employed in Kakinada were allowed only one day off a year by the agency that sent them. Even with the extra time off I gave them (never as much as they asked for or needed), I could afford to care for my mother on her modest monthly pension.

For all its costs and troubles, caring for my mother has been a source of fulfillment. I spend nearly every hour of the day or night at her side. Ever since she came home from the hospital, she has called me Annayya, 'dear older brother'. For some time, I would laugh and try to remind her I was not her brother, but she persisted. Once I asked her why, and she replied with perfect lucidity that it made her heart brim with contentment to utter that word. And when she does, I love to hear it. I know she is calling me her protector.

Sometimes now, when she gets upset, I explain to her how she came to forget so many things. I tell her how she began having problems with her memory and difficulty taking care of herself, and how I came to India to help her. I tell her the whole story I have related here, and she listens quietly like a wide-eyed child hearing a bedtime story.

It is like going back in time, but with the roles reversed. My mother, whose own mother died when she was only four, now has for a mother her daughter who chose never to have children.

No wonder she is confused. Last night I asked her, 'Who am I to you?'

When questioned like that, she often suspects a trick. 'It depends on the context.'

'What context?'

'From a sociological point of view, you are my husband's daughter.'

'What other point of view?'

'There is the scientific point of view.'

'Who am I to you from a scientific point of view?'

'You are my mother.'

'No, no . . .'

'You are my mother,' she insisted. ∎

ਪੰਜਾਬੀ

Each morning in my childhood home began the same way, with the lilting voice of the kirtan singer Bhai Tarlochan Singh reciting the 'Japji Sahib', the first hymn of the *Guru Granth Sahib*. The song flowed from my father's tape recorder – thirty-eight metred stanzas, composed by the founder of Sikhism, Guru Nanak. I couldn't understand most of the words, yet I was carried away by the music. The Punjabi of the 'Japji Sahib' – formal, ancient, and yet familiar, like kinfolk pausing at a caravanserai – sounded very different from the Punjabi I spoke at home. Many words stirred me, but one in particular held me fast: *hukam*, the fulcrum of Guru Nanak's poetics.

I still remember the first time I came upon a lived experience of hukam – though it was much later that I would understand it as such. As children, my playmates and I often found ourselves playing in front of a house whose quiet attracted us. Walking with a stick to the front door, a lean man in a peach-coloured turban, kurta and dhoti would wave us inside. His silky white beard flowed down to his stomach, and his eyes smiled from behind round-rimmed glasses. He'd laugh when we came running in and ask his cook to bring us biscuits. We called him Babaji. Now and then he teased us with nicknames, but otherwise he was as quiet as his house. All we knew about him was that he was very, very old – as old as one could get.

One morning, my mother woke me up to tell me that Babaji had not woken up. I still remember the four words she spoke: '*Babaji poorey ho gaye.*' Babaji has become complete. I was seven, and Babaji was seven years shy of becoming a supercentenarian. This was how I made my first acquaintance with a universal law: what is born must die. Hukam.

At first blush, the Punjabi word – derived from the Arabic *hukm* – means command or decree. But this definition makes it seem too rigid and conventional. In Sikh theology, it represents the divine order that originates from a singular source, the Akal Purakh or Timeless Being. Again and again, Guru Nanak returns to this cosmic law in his poems: '*Hukmi hovan jeea.*' By hukam, beings come to be.

Birth and death are only one aspect of hukam, applicable not just to beings but also to the cosmos. Life begins, then ends. So does the universe. Whenever I think of that word now, the memory of Babaji arises with all its poised radiance. And with it comes a tacit love for Punjabi, because a language that equates death with completion must be beautiful. It carries a fragrance of gratitude.

When I was younger, I could not see why the Guru laid such emphasis on bowing to an authority, even an ineffable One. Ever an iconoclast, Nanak was not given to unquestioning belief, but pushed back against what he saw as the dogma, ritual and empty aestheticism of late-fifteenth-century Punjab. In time, however, I have come to realise that for Nanak, hukam is not an external authority's decree to which one should submit, but the cosmic order to which one must attune for inner peace. It is not a surrender of freedom but its ultimate fulfilment through realisation, a quiet calibration of one's will with the divine will.

What comes before and what remains after? '*Arbad narbad dhundhukara*,' says the Guru, '*dharan na gagana hukam apara*':

For billions of aeons and beyond
it was pitch dark
There was no earth   no sky
only hukam beyond bounds

I was on vacation earlier this year with my family when I heard about the sudden hospitalisation of my uncle, my father's sister's husband. Within hours of his arrival at the hospital, he was placed on life support. I decided to drive back to Delhi with my family, but with two hundred kilometres still to go, I became uneasy. I pulled over near a restaurant and called my uncle's older son. His phone was busy, so I called his younger son. '*Phuphaji?*' I said. '*Phuphaji poorey ho gaye*,' he said. He had become complete. It was the same phrase, word for word, four decades on. Hukam. ∎

COME RAIN, COME DOWN

Yash Sheth

Introduction by Ruchir Joshi

Come rain, come down, I'll give you a penny!
Oh this penny is fake, but you've come anyway!
Come rain, come down, fill my pot with water!
Oh the rain's come down, swept my pots into the flood!
— Traditional Marathi nursery rhyme

I was visiting Bombay in late September 2005, well after the monsoon season gets over in the city, when some dark clouds occupied a small corner of the sky. Around me everyone began to panic. In the streets, people kept glancing up anxiously; pavement shops began to cover goods with plastic sheets; people got on their mobile phones, yelling shrill instructions to kith and kin to get home quickly. Inside homes, refrigerators were checked for supplies and windows were shut tight. The clouds passed after a while, perhaps there was light drizzle in some places, but it took until late evening for things to come back to normal.

It took me a few minutes to understand that this panic was triggered by what had happened several months earlier. In July, the city had been hammered with 944 mm of rain in twenty-four hours, then 644 mm the following day, with the heavy rain continuing over the next week. The previous twenty-four-hour high in Bombay's recorded history was in 1974, when the coastal metropolis had been hit by a monstrous 575 mm of water. On 26 July 2005, the rain started at 2 p.m. and within half an hour the city's local train network had been shut down – something that happens only rarely, and usually only after week-long downpours. This increased traffic on the already crowded roads. As the onslaught continued, the flow of the city's sewage pipes – all opening out into the Arabian Sea – was reversed, as the rain sent high-tide seawater jetting through the system and into the maze of streets and shanty towns. People caught in the unmoving traffic jam had no idea what was coming. As the filthy water rose around many of their air-conditioned cars, it reportedly disabled the cars' electronically operated windows; as the vehicles went under, the windows stayed up, while water pressure made it impossible to open the doors. People drowned in many different ways across the city; others were electrocuted or buried under collapsing buildings. The downpour across those two days in July caused the deaths of around a thousand people. In September, millions were still terrified at the sight of the smallest raincloud.

Along with Madras, Calcutta and Karachi, Bombay is one of the four great subcontinental cities that grew out of trading posts established by early British colonialists. While Calcutta is on a river, the other three cities are coastal ports in regular hard negotiations with the sea. Bombay has been culled from the Arabian Sea in stages over the centuries: the rivulet-cut jigsaw of seven islands initially came Britain's way via a royal dowry from Portugal, and over the centuries it was joined together by man-made pieces of reclamation, a process that still continues.

Today, traversing the sprawl, it often feels like different pieces of the city have never really fitted properly, that the right kind of pressure could quickly break them apart. Rather than geological, this pressure would most likely come from some mix of ethnic, economic and environmental strife. For all the vibrancy you feel when you're immersed in the exhaust of Bombay traffic, the whiff of tension and friction is never far from the nostrils. Monsoon season or not, Bombay exists under a constant shower of binaries: some of the richest people in the world live here, next to millions of the poorest; it's the most cosmopolitan city of the Indian subcontinent, ruled by the most regressively parochial ethno-jingoists; it's a city where Indian women arguably have the most freedom, and yet the violence against them is constant and horrendous.

From its inception this place has always been a site of transaction and tussle, and it's unsurprising that even its many names are now in competition with each other. One unreliable story says the Portuguese called the cluster of islands Bom Bahia, referring to the great natural harbour offered by the biggest island. The British name Bombay seems to have coalesced from variations of this, and for most of the city's history this is what the world and many people in India have called it. The current official name – Mumbai – is the one used earlier only by the Marathi, Gujarati and Konkani communities; the story attached to this – also contested – refers to the goddess Mumba Devi, the chief deity of the Koli fishermen who settled here from Gujarat, centuries before the Europeans arrived. Bambai, an amalgamation of the first two, is what people from north India have always called it, and the name used by the generations of north Indian labourers who built the city.

Yash Sheth lives in Bhayandar, in what south Bombay snobs would consider a far-flung, downmarket suburb in the north-east of Greater Mumbai. In 2005 – the year of that terrible flood – he was ten years old, and he watched the TV with horror as the city was carpet-bombed by rain. 'Where we live wasn't much affected,' he remembers. 'It was mostly in the city part.' There has always been this division between 'the city part' and the suburbs, between what is 'town' and what is not, and it stems from the 'white town' and 'black town' of the East India Company's initial trading post. As Bombay-Mumbai spread northwards and eastwards, gobbling up coconut grove, swamp, hillside and beach, this suburb frontier has shifted, in sequence, from Worli to Dadar and Sion, to Bandra, Andheri,

Borivali, Vasai, Virar, Powai, Mulund and now Thane, which was not long ago considered a separate town. The Mumbai Metropolitan Region is now one of the biggest urban agglomerations in the world, packed with a population of about 23 million people.

There is a weather-radar app that tells you exactly where and when it's going to rain in this city state. On most mornings during the monsoons, Yash Sheth checks the app and heads out of his home, chasing the rain, catching up with it on Uttan Beach, Reay Road or Chor Bazaar. He chooses not to own a vehicle and to use public transport, and this shows in his photographs. Bombay-Mumbai is one of the most highly photographed places in the world but a majority of these images fall into familiar clichéd clusters: the Gateway of India; the curve of Marine Drive; the crowds celebrating the immersion of huge statues of Ganesh, the elephant god, at the end of the rains; film stars at shoots; the *dabbawallas*, the Indigenous lunch-delivery people. The people in Sheth's pictures are mostly from the less-photographed Mumbai: labourers and shanty-dwellers in their daily environments, commuters, people walking the beach, and what the Indian media likes to call 'the lower-middle class' – those who are above the poverty line but very far from the comfort of the country's top 3 per cent, of which the city has far more than its share.

The constant movement in these monsoon photos comes from two directions, sometimes three – the rain constantly whipping down from above, the sideways press and jostle of the crowd, and, from below, the bite of water rising around the knees. The raindrops seem to come horizontally, spitting into the lens, the flash often turning them into surreal snowflakes floating over a tropical city, as ubiquitous and unlikely as the thousands of small Chinese-made statues of Ganesh that appear in the street stalls at the start of every monsoon. These are images made by someone who shares with those he photographs a sense of the wet, fungoid daily grind of the endless rainy season, someone who's as used to the smell of engine fumes, shit, piss and petrol-streaked seawater.

Whenever he does attend to the usual Bombay scenes, Sheth manages to defamiliarise them: three flash-ghosted kids on a beach, as though they've been cut out of the picture and kidnapped; a woman walking away after having quietly crucified Christ, her work done for the evening; two weirdly suited aliens scouting the Malabar Hill skyline as the rain-sea smashes into the parapet on Marine Drive, possibly the only moving creatures in an abandoned metropolis; a low-level company executive transplanted from a Wong Kar-Wai film set in 1960s Hong Kong, his tie soaring up into the grove of high-rise buildings.

Looking at Sheth, looking at the people, looking at the sea, you can immediately sense the relief that the rain-stitched expanse offers, a brief escape from the claustrophobia of the city. Then you turn back and you're back in the cage formed by streams of warm grey water, back in the roiling wet traffic, the ground slippery under your feet, or disappeared under the street-rivers winding through the narrow marketplaces.

Traditionally there are many soft notions about rain, and especially rain in Bombay-Mumbai. Rain itself comes with many names, the Hindi-Sanskrit *varsha* and *varsha ritu* (for the season), the Hindustani *baarish*, the Marathi *paus*, the Gujarati *varsaad*. Besides being a season for replenishment and rest, the monsoon period is also supposed to be the season for love, for romance and for erotic exchange; Bombay cinema is replete with rain-drenched song sequences, which range from sweet, meet-cute scenarios to steamier entanglements. Viewing Yash Sheth's photographs, it feels as though Bombay has invented rain for itself, that it has the first full use of it before it ruthlessly licenses it to other places for a price. ∎

You won't want to miss a word.

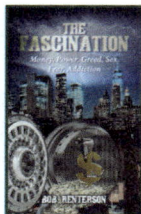

The Fascination
Money, Power, Greed, Sex, Fear, Addiction
Bob Renterson

Bill, a recovering alcoholic who now spends his days as a freelance insurance investigator, is led on a dangerous quest to get to the bottom of a series of mysterious deaths.

£15.95 paperback
978-1-7283-8721-5
also available in ebook
www.authorhouse.co.uk

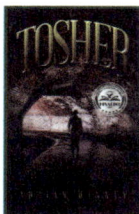

Tosher
Adrian Winney

In the dark, grimy sewers of Victorian London, a helpless baby, abandoned and left to fate, found an unlikely savior in the form of Jack Tanner, a compassionate Tosher.

£17.56 paperback
978-1-6655-8898-0
also available in ebook
www.authorhouse.co.uk

Dragon's Eye - A Fantasy.
J. M. Clay

Two teenagers Gwyl and Liz are drawn into a timewarp and join the denizens of the other-world in the constant battle between the powers of the Light and the Dark.

£13.99 paperback
979-8-8230-8295-2
also available in ebook
www.authorhouse.co.uk

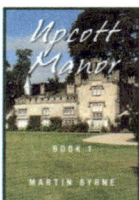

Upcott Manor
Book 1
Martin Byrne

Lord Godfrey inherited a neglected estate in 1815. Over the next 100 years, he, his wife, and the generations to come made Upcott Manor and Estate significant.

£36.99 paperback
979-8-8230-9137-4
also available in ebook
www.authorhouse.co.uk

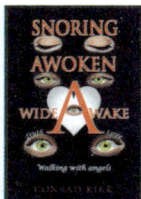

Snoring Awoken Wide Awake
Walking With Angels
Conrad Kirk

Conrad Kirk shares his personal story of awakening, inspiring readers to unravel the inner child that has been trapped deep within their consciousness.

£17.99 paperback
979-8-8230-9030-8
also available in hardcover, ebook & audiobook
www.authorhouse.co.uk

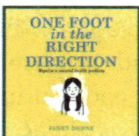

One Foot in the Right Direction
Bipolar a mental health problem
Janet Dunne

Join Janet Dunne on a transformative journey of hope and healing. Discover laughter, resilience, and the unwavering belief that you can reclaim your life from bipolar struggles.

£16.99 paperback
979-8-8230-9008-7
also available in ebook & audiobook
www.authorhouse.co.uk

authorHOUSE®

Real Authors, Real Impact

Visit us on Facebook & Twitter

ગુજરાતી

The word *vyavhaar* – વ્યવહાર in Gujarati – exists in many Indian languages and has one basic meaning across them all: 'conduct' or 'behaviour'. This consensus is misleading; the separate regions and their communities make certain words mean many – and sometimes different – things. Vyavhaar, in Gujarati, has absorbed the region's association with commerce and mercantilism, and the word now has multiple, untranslatable meanings that reflect Gujarat's world view.

Friendship and business in Gujarat intertwine and become almost inseparable, so vyavhaar can, at times, mean a measurable economic transaction within social events, such as a marriage. To ask 'How much vyavhaar do we have to do for this wedding?' is essentially asking, 'How much money do we need to give to the bride and groom?' The question is an implicit clarification of how this relationship is defined socially, and what its literal financial value is. Vyavhaar is also therefore a give and take: just as it values social interactions, it can also function as a term that makes economic transactions legible as social events. It is not uncommon to do business with someone who can be trusted in his vyavhaar – as in his dealings with other traders and business are clean and governed by the social and economic protocols of both the society and market. This usage does not occlude vyavhaar's official definition of behaviour or conduct, but instead it becomes pregnant with protocols of a mercantile community that sees good vyavhaar as good business.

This concept of vyavhaar as representative of a world structured around negotiations and transactions, where actions are reciprocal and systems of give and take are maintained, is also sometimes opposed by *parmaarth*: a more spiritual world, where every action directs towards a divine spiritual goal. In *Angaliyat* by Joseph Macwan, a Dalit novel I translated from Gujarati, Bhavaan Bhagat, the oldest and wisest man in the community, strives for parmaarth by detaching from the world of vyavhaar: he refuses to attend social functions or to arbitrate disputes and simply goes away on a pilgrimage when he feels like it. When one of the young men in the community is murdered violently by the upper castes, the old man decides that the Dalit community cannot afford to be otherworldly before they can set right their world of vyavhaar – this world. The word vyavhaar occurs several times in the novel, using every dimension of its meaning: sometimes as a social relation, sometimes as conduct and sometimes as a negotiation in highly intricate and caste-based relations.

Vyavhaar is not entirely absent of spiritual meaning, though – its quotidian notions of exchange and trade have potential to lead to the spiritual. In Jainism, it can refer to sacred periods of discipline that, through small everyday actions, shape the soul and prepare it for liberation. In Vedanta it refers to the everyday words and concepts that are used as stepping stones that expand to arrive at new, more spiritual meanings.

My first learning of vyavhaar was in the context of caste, where it is so embedded that it doesn't even need to be spelled out. The matrix of caste is sustained by knowledge of who belongs to which caste, which then determines the kind of vyavhaar that must be employed to maintain the caste ecology: when an upper-caste member finds out (by sleight of speech or gesture) that the person they are talking to belongs to the so-called lower caste, the vyavhaar of eating together, inviting someone home, accepting food from that person, is revised silently. It becomes clear that the quotidian vyavhaar is also a word that keeps status quo and power relations intact, under the guide of mere 'good manners'. ■

REG INNELL
Salman Rushdie, 1984
Getty Images

RECLAIMING THE TERRITORY

Interview with Salman Rushdie

S alman Rushdie was among the foremost early writers for *Granta*, when it was still published out of a single room at the University of Cambridge. He has enjoyed a long association with the magazine, and has contributed fiction, reportage, poetry, memoir, and literary essays to its pages. This spring, the editor of *Granta* visited Rushdie at his place in Manhattan. They spoke for an hour about his dealings with the magazine, the course of Indian fiction, and his brushes with Indian politics. Part of their chat was recorded on the editor's phone, and has been lightly edited for clarity.

EDITOR: Bill Buford, the first editor of *Granta*, tells a funny story: he was reading *Midnight's Children* on a train, an early galley, and fell in love with the book before he knew you or met you, and then ran an excerpt of it, without your permission, in this magazine.

SALMAN RUSHDIE: In *Granta* 3.

EDITOR: In *Granta* 3.

RUSHDIE: I learned about that at a party. Jonathan Cape used to have this very grand authors' party every year, around Christmas, which was, in those days, extra grand because they wouldn't invite any journalists, only writers. *Midnight's Children* hadn't been published – this was December 1980 – but there had probably been a galley. I was the new kid on the block, going to the Cape party, surrounded by Doris Lessing, John Fowles – anybody you could think of. Martin [Amis] was there – I met him there.

EDITOR: That's where you first met Amis?

RUSHDIE: Yes. But then Bill Buford arrived, and I'd never met him, and he said, 'I have something to show you.' And he took me down to the front of the building where he'd left his briefcase and produced a copy of *Granta* 3. He said, 'Look, there's the first chapter of *Midnight's Children*.'

I asked, 'How exactly does this come to be here?' And then he said that he had asked Tom Maschler, the publisher of Cape, and Tom Maschler had said 'okay'. But nobody ever told me.

EDITOR: You never signed anything?

RUSHDIE: No. I said, 'You know, the question of payment arises.'

EDITOR: We can settle that debt here and now.

RUSHDIE: I think they paid me something like £40, after the fact.

EDITOR: It seems like you took this in your stride.

RUSHDIE: Well, there it was, it already existed. I mean, *Granta* 3 is very interesting. That's where the magazine began to find its rhythm. Angela Carter and Russell Hoban and all sorts of very good people were in the issue. The company was excellent.

I remember when *Midnight's Children* came out, *Granta* was still being published out of an upstairs room in Cambridge, above an art gallery. Bill invited me up to do a reading and it was the first book reading I'd done in my life.

Bill and I immediately got on very well. I was kind of irritated by what I believed to be bullshit (because Maschler had never confirmed to me that he'd given Bill permission and there was nothing in writing, which there should be) but I just thought, you know, it's good.

EDITOR: Buford describes himself in that period as a hustler. But isn't that what you need to be, with a little magazine, no?

RUSHDIE: Yeah. The more I learned about him . . . For *Granta* 1, he just wrote to every living great American writer and said, 'I want something good from you.' Amazingly, quite a lot of them sent him stuff.

★

EDITOR: It seems there are multiple ways of looking at your work in the 1980s. One would be 'He's come out of Bombay' and there's Saadat Hasan Manto in the background. Another way would be, for lack of a better word, 'world literature', a sort of 'Oh, this is Marquez, but for India'. But there's another way of looking at it too, which is that you were part of a generation in London, with close relationships with Ian McEwan and Martin Amis. How do you think about that generation now?

RUSHDIE: All of those ways are true. As far as the generation thing is concerned, at the time, everybody tried to make us a generation.

EDITOR: Including *Granta*, not least of all.

RUSHDIE: Martin and Ian and Julian [Barnes] and Ish [Kazuo Ishiguro] and Angela. Some of us got on very well. Some of us didn't really know each other. Some of us didn't even like each other's work. Each of us, I think, resisted the idea of calling us a generation. And we didn't have a project, right? We were all very unlike each other.

EDITOR: But there are certain commonalities. For instance, not every novelist of that period or the generation before or after you was reckoning with historical problems the way yours was. Whereas in your 'generation', you're addressing India's Partition. McEwan has an early novel about Germany, the Second World War. Amis didn't start off that way so much, but he certainly went in for that when he got older, taking on the Nazis and Stalin. Ishiguro does it in the background of his novels.

RUSHDIE: I came out of a country which had just been born. And the subject of empire was quite present, at that time. I had also had a very bad English public-school experience and then a very good university experience. So I had learned England the hard way.

EDITOR: Have you ever talked to Ishiguro about the fact that you both have a hinterland? He left very early, but he still often comes back to it, in various ways.

RUSHDIE: I don't want to speak for him. I get the sense that the Japan subject is less present for him than it used to be. These big successes of his later writing, like *Never Let Me Go* (2005), really have moved on from the subject of origins. I haven't detached quite in that way. I find it almost impossible to have a central character who's not of Indian origin.

EDITOR: One has the sense, though, in that early 1980s moment, that you actually are expressing a kind of love for the lost India of your childhood, or are trying to recreate it in your own mind.

RUSHDIE: By the time I started writing *Midnight's Children*, which was the mid-1970s, I'd been not living in India for quite some time, and my parents had – kind of disappointingly – moved to Pakistan, which I wasn't attracted to. So I had this worry of losing touch, losing contact with where I came from, and I decided that I'd better write a book that tried to reclaim it. I always thought of *Midnight's Children* as the book that reclaimed that territory for myself.

EDITOR: You wrote a funny piece for *Granta* 11 (1984) about the Raj and its depictions – I think it was the year Paul Scott's *Raj Quartet* (1966–75) was televised. One of the things that comes out in it is that you're up against an enormous industry that runs from E.M. Forster to Scott, to TV, to pop culture. You had to compete with something working on a very large scale.

RUSHDIE: When I finished *Midnight's Children*, I wasn't actually certain that anybody would want to publish it, because it was very long, it was written in a weird English and had almost no white characters in it, and it wasn't about the British experience of India, which everything else was. Of course there's *A Passage to India* (1924), there was *Heat and Dust* (1975) – that kind of book. It was a big gamble to write that book and, well, I guess it came off.

EDITOR: Something that people in my generation often forget is that *Midnight's Children* came up against the Indian state well before Ayatollah Khomeini issued the fatwa against *The Satanic Verses* (1988).

RUSHDIE: Indira Gandhi sued me. There was a lawsuit about one sentence in which I talked about her relationship with Sanjay Gandhi. She didn't like it because I said that he held her responsible for his father's early death, because of their separation, a story which is well known in India. It had been published many times. But she decided to use that to sue me. And the problem was that it was a lawsuit about three people, two of whom were dead, and the third was suing me.

EDITOR: How did that shake out?

RUSHDIE: She got assassinated. You can't libel the dead. In the end, it was a very non-aggressive lawsuit. All she wanted was for us to remove the sentence. Not even to withdraw books already in print. I had said, 'Well, look, if we really have to do it, it's not even a very important sentence, so we'll take it out, but the book needs reprinting.' But then she got killed. So.

EDITOR: A definitive outcome. But the lawsuit still must have put you under some pressure.

RUSHDIE: I mean, it was awful to get sued by the prime minister of India. I had some very strange conversations with lawyers. Tom Maschler, and me, and lawyers. I remember asking some very heavyweight lawyer that Cape had employed, 'So, what's the defense?' And he said, 'Well, to be found guilty of having defamed somebody, the person you're defaming has to be a person of good character. So if you can explain to me why the prime minister of India is not a person of good character, then you have a defense.' And I said, 'Okay, well, that means we can try the Emergency in an English court.'

Tom Maschler's face went very pale.

EDITOR: Trying the Emergency: that would have been extraordinary.

RUSHDIE: Yeah. Though, obviously, a super-high-risk route. And Cape, certainly, were not eager to go down that route. But I thought it would be amazing to have judges that she couldn't bend, examining the atrocities of the Emergency.

EDITOR: But that gets into something I'm curious about, which is that you've sort of been in permanent opposition when it comes to India.

RUSHDIE: I've always been on the wrong side. Rajiv Gandhi was the person who banned *The Satanic Verses*.

EDITOR: Before the fatwa.

RUSHDIE: Before the fatwa. Because he got some protests from a couple of Muslim MPs. Block vote politics.

And when *Shame* (1983) came out, it got banned in Pakistan because of Zia-ul-Haq. I guess if you're going to write a novel which satirizes a Pakistani dictator, and there happens to be a Pakistani dictator in power at the time . . .

★

EDITOR: When you look at Indian writing before *Midnight's Children* and then after, one has the sense that that novel created its own genre, and that many Indian writers, perhaps too many, got caught up in its wake. And this was all just in English. In 1997 you write that introduction to an anthology of Indian writing, *Mirrorwork*. And you say there – it reads even more polemically now than it did then – that the vernacular languages of India can be interesting, there are certainly stories there, but they're essentially going to be provincial and that the real action is in Indian writing in English. In fact, if I recall, the only vernacular writer you included in that collection was Manto.

RUSHDIE: I got into so much trouble.

EDITOR: But let's just say you were right. What do you think has happened since that moment? Because it now seems like the opposite.

You talk to the publishers in Delhi or Mumbai, and it's all about translation. There's a real chase for authenticity. Prize committees are completely in thrall to it.

RUSHDIE: I think what's happened is three things. One is that the actual publishing industry in India is much more established. It's on a bigger scale than it ever used to be. The second thing is, yes, they're beginning to translate. One of the big problems in India was always translating between Indian languages; if you were writing in Bengali, nobody could read you in Hindi, which included Tagore. The translations that existed were often not very good. All that has improved a lot, so people are no longer in the same way confined to the language area – they can cross borders in the way that English crosses borders. And the third thing is that writing in English has proliferated into so many forms; it's not just literary novels. Now there's pulp fiction, there's romantic fiction, there's erotic fiction, so it's become a much broader spectrum of publishing, which is healthier. I think young writers starting out in India now might not feel what I felt, which is that I couldn't actually start out there, because there wasn't a literary world. Now there is a literary world.

EDITOR: So you think a writer in Calcutta, writing in Bengali, has a better chance today of being translated into, say, Gujarati?

RUSHDIE: That's still the problem – translation between different regions. Also, translating from English into Indian languages. But that's happening. You know, it was a long time before anything I wrote was being published in Hindi. But now, I get published in several Indian languages: Malayalam, Hindi, Bengali, Marathi, et cetera. So all of this is a really healthy development. I think *Midnight's Children* did do something which you might describe as kicking open the door. It allowed Indian writers in English to feel that they could be heard, that they didn't have to imitate Western writing. They could find their own voices.

EDITOR: So, despite being written in English, you mean it kicked open what became a succession of doors that got us basically to where we are now, where you can be an Indian writer in a vernacular language and still find an international audience? You point out in your introduction that film was a completely different story. Because of the medium. A director like Satyajit Ray could become a giant, on his own terms, in his own language.

RUSHDIE: But he was still badly treated in India. The Bollywood folks didn't like it. Ray was criticized by a lot of big stars for producing negative images of India for Western consumption. The biggest movie star in India, Nargis, who was the star of *Mother India* (1957), attacked him for that. She said, 'Why doesn't he make films about positive achievements in India, such as the building of dams?'

EDITOR: A Ray film about dams. I would watch that.

RUSHDIE: When Ray, once in his life, tried to go into the Hindi market with his film *The Chess Players* (1977) – which was made in Hindi using Hindi movie stars – the Bombay film industry tried very hard to block its distribution. And with some success. Although the film was made to broaden his audience, it was very nearly prevented from doing so.

EDITOR: It seems that many of the vernacular languages may have paradoxically benefited from the Modi era, in that as much as Delhi backs the proliferation of Hindi, this in turn encourages more concerted countering from local languages in other Indian states.

RUSHDIE: And it all makes them get more international attention, you know. The International Booker has recently gone to two Indian books not originally in English [*Tomb of Sand* by Geetanjali Shree (English translation from Hindi by Daisy Rockwell, 2021) and *Heart*

Lamp by Banu Mushtaq (English translation from Kannada by Deepa Bhasthi, 2025)]. That kind of thing would never have been possible in the early 1980s.

EDITOR: You and Naipaul are both interpreters of the Indian experience, in both fiction and non-fiction. But, certainly on the historical plane, you're very far apart.

RUSHDIE: When I was writing *Victory City* (2023), one of the things I was writing against was Naipaul's portrait of the Vijayanagara empire, where he, basically, uses the idea of 'Muslims, bad; Hindus, good'. Vijayanagara destroyed by Muslim armies is a metaphor for the wounded civilization. Whereas, if you look at the history of that period, that's not what's happening. Actually, the Muslim caliphates and the Vijayanagara empire were much more interpenetrated than that. They were intermarrying. There were Hindu generals in the Vijayanagara army. They were Muslim generals in the Golconda armies. It wasn't about religion. It was about power and regional command, regional control.

The Hindutva people have also picked up on that idea of using Vijayanagara as a metaphor. And I thought this needs to be undone.

Everybody's trying to rewrite the history of India. And very often they want to rewrite it to downplay the Muslim contribution to it, and enlarge the non-Muslim contribution. One of the things that was strange about Naipaul was that when he first started going to India, when it actually was in much better shape, politically and culturally, he didn't like it at all. And the more Hindu it got, the more he bought into it.

EDITOR: In *India: A Million Mutinies Now* (1990) he seems to be getting back in touch with the Hinduism of his childhood in Trinidad, where a kind of protestantized, fundamentalist version of the religion still thrived.

RUSHDIE: Vidia and me, we didn't agree much, you know. We didn't know each other very well. We only met each other maybe half a dozen times. But it's one of those strange things, I disagreed with him politically in almost everything, but I like reading him.

It's not surprising to say that I really like *A House for Mr. Biswas* (1961) the best. Because, I think as he got older, his writing lost human warmth.

A Bend in the River (1979) is a fantastic novel, but it's very icy in its attitudes. The Indian non-fiction books I don't like. Actually, I like *An Area of Darkness* (1964) more than the other two because it feels more truthful. The return of the native discovering that the glorious homeland is not that glorious. I thought it was actually quite an honest book.

Anyway, I don't think Vidia ever wrote for *Granta*, did he?

EDITOR: Ian Jack published some of his Bombay notebooks in *Granta* 57. Naipaul published one short story in the *Paris Review*, and he wrote a lot for the *New York Review of Books*. He was close with the then co-editor, Robert Silvers, who famously sent him into the fire of Reaganism for a piece about the 1984 Republican National Convention called 'Among the Republicans'. I think Naipaul was very taken with the New York intellectuals, like my old neighbor Elizabeth Hardwick –

RUSHDIE: And grand elitism.

EDITOR: And he was amused by Norman Mailer.

RUSHDIE: Guess how many times I've been published in the *New York Review of Books*?

EDITOR: Zero? Really?

RUSHDIE: Bob Silvers had his 'Indian'.

In my younger days, there was a moment when we would send something I'd written to the *New York Review* and it would come back so quickly that it was clear the envelope hadn't been opened. After that, we just stopped sending.

EDITOR: One of your deepest forays into what would become *Granta*-style reportage was your Nicaragua book, *The Jaguar Smile* (1987).

RUSHDIE: Yeah, that's in 1986. I was in the middle of writing *The Satanic Verses*, and I was kind of stuck. That book had problems that I didn't know quite what to do with. Then I had this invitation [from the Sandinista Association of Cultural Workers] to go to Managua, and I just thought, let me get out of my own head and go and look at some people with actual problems. And so that book intervened. I had to write it, and then go back to writing *The Satanic Verses*. It's the one really extensive piece of hard journalism I've ever done.

EDITOR: You must have produced it quickly.

RUSHDIE: Very fast, very fast. Because I thought, you know, there's a war on. And if it's going to happen, it needs to happen now. And actually, Sonny Mehta, my editor at Knopf, was fantastic for saying, 'Okay, we'll publish it immediately.' It came out a few months after I was in Nicaragua. And a bit of it came out in *Granta*. That chapter about eating the eggs of love.

EDITOR: For this *Granta* issue on India, I've been reading through Indian literature from the 1980s and 1990s. There are writers such as Vikram Seth, who, now, when I read him, seems almost to write in reaction, or at least in response, to you. *A Suitable Boy* (1993) feels like: 'Let's go the opposite direction, full pedal to the metal into realism.' It reads like a patient, loving, heavily detailed portrait of the crummy, provincial, northern Indian bourgeoisie.

RUSHDIE: It is like an opposite direction, yes, but that was probably a good thing.

EDITOR: Seth's *The Golden Gate* (1986) only gets better with time. It's such a beguiling and unusual offering.

RUSHDIE: To use that Eugene Onegin meter.

EDITOR: It's wild and great.

RUSHDIE: I haven't looked at it for a long time, but I remember really, really liking it. And I like the Ladakh book as well, *From Heaven Lake* (1983). And now you know, today, there might be a war.

EDITOR: Fingers are back on the trigger.

RUSHDIE: There was just a terrorist attack in Pahalgam, a beautiful mountain village in Kashmir. In my childhood, we would go to Kashmir for the holidays, and so I spent a lot of my life there. Just outside Pahalgam, there's a mountain meadow. This incredibly beautiful meadow up high called Baisaran, and that's where these tourists were, that's where the jihadis came and killed them. I used to play in that meadow when I was a kid, and now it's just somewhere that people get murdered.

EDITOR: When were you last in Kashmir?

RUSHDIE: A long time ago. Somewhere in the 1980s. Now, unfortunately, because of Islamist radicalism and all that, it's probably not good for me to go.

EDITOR: You would need a bodyguard, no?

RUSHDIE: The Indian military behaves so badly in Kashmir anyway, that I kind of don't want that. But if I don't want that, other people behave badly. My family is Kashmiri. It's a real loss. ∎

DAVID MONTGOMERY
Salman Rushdie, 1988
Getty Images

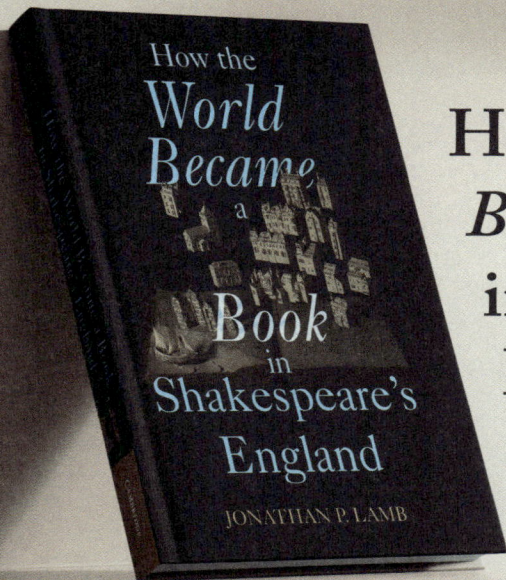

How the *World Became* a *Book* in Shakespeare's England

JONATHAN P. LAMB

"If the world were indeed a book you'd want it to be written by Jonathan Lamb"
EMMA SMITH, Professor of Shakespeare Studies, Hertford College Oxford

"Lamb's book is teeming with examples from writers familiar and little known, and Lamb writes with verve, wit and clarity."
ADAM SMYTH, Professor of English and the History of the Book, Balliol College, Oxford University

"This is a book that will be read and re-read by anyone interested in Renaissance books and their readers."
ZACHARY LESSER, Edward W. Kane Professor of English, University of Pennsylvania

"Jonathan Lamb provides an enthusiastic and insightful survey of how Shakespeare and other writers describe the world as a book."
BRIAN CUMMINGS FBA, Anniversary Professor of English, University of York

"Entertainingly readable and endlessly illuminating."
LAURIE MAGUIRE, Professor of English Literature, Magdalen College Oxford

cambridge.org/worldtobook

CAMBRIDGE UNIVERSITY PRESS

VASANTHA YOGANANTHAN
Young Warriors, 2015
Sitamarhi, Uttar Pradesh

TRANSFORMATIONS

Umesh Solanki

TRANSLATED FROM THE GUJARATI BY GOPIKA JADEJA

I woke at four in the morning. Two hours earlier than I should have. I was very hungry. There was some milk left over from the night before. I smelled it – it hadn't curdled. I took a bowlful of fada from the container and poured the split wheat into the pressure cooker. I added the right portions of milk, cardamom and sugar. I cooked the fada until the first whistle then turned the stove off. After ten minutes I scooped the split-wheat porridge into a bowl and began to eat it with a spoon.

I started reading the text messages from my friend the philosopher. After I began I felt compelled to read them all again. I was drawn to an old message: 'When the company we keep dominates us, it colours everything we do.' I put the fada aside, sat at the computer, and began to write.

At the time I must have been fifteen years old. Right next to our vaas, the quarter of the untouchables, was the vaas where the scavenging Valmiki community lived. In the Valmiki vaas, Kachro Doho – Old Man Kachro – was on his deathbed, only he refused to die. His ageing wife, Dahi Dohi, kept thinking, 'It would be good if the old man finally dies.' His sons, his sons' wives, his sons-in-law, everyone else kept thinking: 'It would be good if the old man dies.' But the old man would not die. The doctors said he wasn't sick. The Bhuvo said no threads or spells were necessary. So what now?

Everyone was tense. People came and went from the house, but the old man would say nothing to them. Relatives came and bhagats came – devout men. They performed a Satyanarayan puja ritual, and organised devotional bhajan singing. There was only one motive behind all this activity – to let the old man's jeev, his life spirit, leave his body. But every effort was in vain.

Four days passed. Kachro Doho drank water, but he would not leave the water, would not let go of his life. Slowly, people began to think that the old man must have some unfulfilled wish that was holding him back. But no one knew what that wish was, and the old man would not tell. Is it that you want to eat a sweet patasu? Or that you want sukhdi? Do you want to eat surmu? Drink some daru, some alcohol? Or do you want to visit the shrine of the mother goddess for her darshan? They asked many questions, but the old man would not say what he wanted. And so they worried all the more.

Petha Kaka lived at the far end of the vaas. He was Kachro Doho's best friend. They'd spent their childhood together, grown old together, become community elders and gossips together. They'd fight and make up. Only the last time they fought they did not get together again. It wasn't until the fifth day that Kachro Doho lay dying that Petha Kaka came to his house. He went to Kachro Doho and brought his ear close to the old man's lips. Kachro Doho said something. When Petha Kaka heard what he had to say, he cleared everyone out of the house and called Dahi Dohi inside. He whispered Kachro Doho's words into Dahi Dohi's ear. Dahi Dohi smacked her palm against her forehead and laughed softly. Petha Kaka left the house and Dahi Dohi shut the doors. After twenty minutes she opened the doors again. Everyone went into the house and they said, 'Doha's jeev has left; the old man has died.'

It did not remain a secret that Kachro Doho's dying wish was to have sex with his wife: word spread across the vaas. On everyone's lips the same phrase: 'Kachro Doho turned out to be a *harvaryo haap*, a wriggly snake.' When Kachro Doho's funeral procession went through the village children laughed softly, and the young and the old laughed softly. While Kachro Doho's pyre burned the wind laughed softly. Kachro Doho's pyre burned amid soft laughter. Kachro Doho's barmu, the twelfth day of mourning, passed amid soft laughter. Kachro Doho was forgotten but the label *harvario haap*, wriggly snake, stuck to his youngest great-grandson Jivo. He was in my class at school. I knew Jivo by name and by his excellent schoolwork.

I t was a holiday. Everyone was playing with marbles. I didn't know how to play, so I stood by watching quietly. Jivo was about to win when Punjiyo arrived, tall as a palm. Punjiyo had a bad habit. He could vomit whenever he liked. He'd stretch himself up on his toes and pull at his ears. Just like that: vomit out. Vomit is usually nasty, but Punjiyo's vomit was especially nasty. Punjiyo spewed his yellow vomit all over the marbles arranged in a circle. Everyone cried out, 'Aieeee!'

Jivo was furious. He jumped up and told Punjiyo he had to wash off the marbles. It was strange, since Jivo was usually so quiet.

'Shut up and scram,' said Punjiyo.

'Wash the marbles,' Jivo repeated.

'And what'll you do if I don't, huh?'

'I'll break your head.'

'Fuck your mother!' Punjiyo caught hold of Jiva's collar and shoved a finger into his throat. Then he pulled at his cheeks. 'You puny thing! *You* think you can break *my* head?' He shoved him so hard that Jivo fell down. As soon as Jivo was on the ground Punjiyo began spitting on him, thu thu thu.

Jivo vomited. Looked at his vomit, started to cry. When Punjiyo saw Jivo crying, he ran off like a camel. Everyone got together and poured sand over the marbles. They rubbed the marbles with their feet to clean them off. The game started again. Jivo cried while he played.

That evening, Jivo came over to my place to eat dinner. I was alone. I was in a playful mood and teased him: 'No one at home, *harvariya haap!*' When he heard that phrase his face dropped, and I felt bad.

'I'll never say that again.'

Jivo smiled. As he smiled, tears ran down his cheeks and fell onto his plate.

After that, Jivo always smiled when we met. And I smiled too. Over time our smiles became words and the words friendship. We'd meet at school, play in the field behind the house. We didn't go to each other's houses. We would talk, and sometimes Jivo would walk with me to my house. He would stand in the courtyard. He never sat on the string cot. He never asked for water and I never offered him water. If my mother was home, she'd give Jivo water. Bai, mother, would bring him a pot of water and he would cup his palms, waiting for her to pour it from above. She would wave his cupped palms away and hand him the pot. Jivo started pouring the water from the pot, careful to keep his mouth away from the rim, but Bai told him to just put it to his lips. Finally she convinced him.

I never felt like going to Jivo's house. I used to think, 'A Bhangya's house, the house of the lowest of untouchables, is dirty.' I don't remember why, but one day I had to go to his house, and I was surprised when I saw how clean it was. It was much cleaner than ours. When he saw me, Jivo filled a brass tumbler with water and handed it to me. I couldn't refuse. I began to drink. For a moment I felt like I might vomit. Then I drank the rest of the water quickly. I asked for more water. This time when I drank I didn't feel like vomiting at all. Our friendship became stronger. When Jivo came to our house, I'd give him water. When I went to his place, I asked for water.

Jivo was good at school. He excelled in maths, science and English. I was weak at maths and science. English I couldn't understand at all. When we did our homework together at Jivo's he'd say, 'You'll learn, I'll teach you.'

Jivo started tutoring me. At first I was bored, but then it became fun. My one goal was to pass the term exams. When they came I passed science for the first time. I failed maths by one point. English I failed outright. After that we studied harder.

The second round of exams came, and I passed every subject for the first time in my life. I placed seventeenth in the class, and it seemed as if everything had changed. The village was different. The way my blood ran through my veins, the blinking of my eyes, the way I spoke, the rise and fall of certain words – everything seemed to move to a new beat.

'Let's get some milk pedo,' said my brother Jasu, and he took me to Suhkadiya's sweet shop. We ate halwo dripping in ghee instead of a pedo. I snuck a bit into my pocket when Jasu wasn't looking. We ate the rest and went our separate ways. Immediately I started to run, ran so fast I almost hit a bicycle at one point. I went to Jivo's. Took the bit of halwo out of my pocket and offered it to him. He ate it with relish. My shorts were stained with ghee and sugar, but I knew Bai wouldn't say anything.

The results of the final exams were posted. I passed, and placed fifth in the class. Jivo, who was usually first in class, came second. The results inspired in me a hunger to study, and to know more. To satisfy that hunger I began reading. I read whatever I could find. Before the next school year began I read my way through all the books for Class 8. When I came across a scrap of writing, I'd read it. If I found a newspaper, I'd read the whole thing. I became a member of the public library in the village. Slowly, this flood of reading gave way to a smaller but steady stream.

On Shravani Poonam, the full moon day in the month of Shravan, Jivo, Vikram, and I went to Khedbrahma to the shrine of Mataji, the mother goddess, for darshan. Vikram was Jivo's neighbour, and was in Class 9. Vikram and Jivo had money, I didn't. I told my brother Jasu we were going to Khedbrahma, and he immediately gave me two ten-rupee notes. I was thrilled. We went for darshan, sought her blessings. Ate prasad of sakariya, candied groundnuts, and dried coconut. Ate another helping of the prasad, then a third. We drank orange sharbat at the bus stand. As we drank our sharbat we decided to go and watch a film, the first show. There was a huge crowd at Aradhana Cinema House. Vikram did something sneaky – he slipped through the crowd, took a few blows from the watchman's stick on his way, and cut through the queue to get us tickets. It was a violent film, all action. Jivo really liked it. I enjoyed it too. Afterwards Vikram kept sticking out his butt, repeating dialogue from the film as he farted: 'If you've drunk your mother's milk, then come and fight! Dhichkiyan! Dhichkiyan!' We laughed.

We were hanging on to the rails of the jeep driving us back to Vadali. Two other people were clinging to the rails with us. At Shyamnagar they got down. The jeep started again and gained speed. Vikram was in his element.

'If you've drunk your mother's milk, then come out and fight! Dhichkiyan! Dhichkiyan!'

He hung on to the rail of the jeep with one hand and made the shape of a pistol with the other, reciting the dialogue. We all laughed. Vikram thought of a new game. He released his grip on the rail, which he was holding with both hands, and then gripped it again. He let go of the rail then grabbed it again, did it three or four times. He told me to do it. I did it twice. He asked Jivo to do it. Jivo refused.

'Jivo, if you've drunk your mother's milk, then let go of the rail and show me!' Vikram said.

Jivo was angry. He let go of the rail then grabbed it again. We began to take turns playing this game. Vikram would repeat the dialogue from the film and we'd let go of the rail for a moment, one after the other.

It was Jivo's turn. Vikram said the line. Jivo released his grip on the rail. At the same time, Vikram added, 'Dhichkiyan . . . Dhichkiyan . . .' I had to laugh at the way he said it – 'Dhichkiyan . . . Dhichkiyan . . .' Jivo laughed too. The jeep was going at speed. Jivo's laugh and the jeep's rattling were in sync. The distance between Jivo's hands and the jeep's rail grew. Jivo couldn't grab the rail again. My eyes were on him. The back of Jivo's head hit the road, then his body was dragged by the jeep, before it bounced and crashed against the trunk of a Baval tree by the roadside. Vikram shouted, 'Stop the jeep!' I couldn't speak. The jeep stopped. I got down from the jeep with my head spinning and fell, unconscious. When I opened my eyes again I was in hospital. There I learned that Jivo was no more.

I stared at the computer screen, listless. My blood cooled in my body, slowed. I turned off the computer and looked at the clock. Still an hour and a half left before work. I covered the fada, locked my room and went outside. Sat on a bench at the railway station.

It was morning. The birds were singing. People passed by. The animals were playful. There was so much to enjoy, but I felt as if there was a solid iron wall between the world outside and the atmosphere within me. My insides swallowed the tree, swallowed the birds, swallowed the animals, swallowed the whole scene. From afar I saw a ten-year-old boy selling peanuts. My insides swallowed the boy, pulled him down almost to my navel. Suddenly, someone shook me. 'Sayeb, sayeb!' I was startled. When I looked up there was the peanut seller. 'Sayeb, peanuts?' I bought ten rupees' worth. The boy went away. I put a few peanuts into my mouth, but something was wrong. My insides had swallowed the flavour. I got up from the bench and scattered the peanuts around the trunk of an Ambli tree. ■

తెలుగు

I n Mexico City recently, I heard someone say, '*Eso me da ñáñaras.*'
When I asked, a friend explained that ñáñaras describes a bodily
unease, like when you shiver with the creeps. Or when we say
something is 'cringe'. The strange word, which felt like a jar on the
nerves, delighted me. Another friend compared it to the heebie-
jeebies. We started talking about words that wake our senses and
ripple through our bodies, and I offered one from my first language.

In Telugu dictionaries you will find the word వంకర టింకర romanised
in a number of ways including *vankaratinkara* or *wankara-tinkara*
(the letter వ serves as both *v* and *w*). It sounds like *wunker-tinker*, with
the first word pronounced like bunker, and a straightforward English
equivalent might be 'crooked'. A *vanka* is a crooked stick for threshing
corn, or a rivulet. *Nelavanka*, literally the month's curve, is a crescent
moon. *Vankaya* is the crooked vegetable we know as eggplant. Vanka
also works figuratively suggesting something twisted or warped, often
signalling fault or blame. Someone speaking dishonestly might be
said to speak *vanka maatalu*, or crooked words; *vanka pettadam*, to
throw vanka, is to criticise.

I feel sufficiently studious when I explain the word wunker
in isolation, but wunker-tinker fills me with glee. It can describe
someone's shaky handwriting or the zigzag parting in one's hair.
It might describe the way a drunkard walks or how a kid with their
first bicycle careens this way and that through the streets. One of
my favourite ways of thinking of wunker-tinker is 'chaotic'. But even
when wunker-tinker is used to chastise someone, it retains a comedic,
exuberant effect. When you call someone chaotic, or better yet, a hot
mess, you might disapprove, but there's no denying they possess
some allure.

Part of wunker-tinker's appeal lies in its awkward sound. Tinker
makes the word *feel* crooked: as if wunker were heading in one
direction, and then tinker pulled it in another. Wunker is a word in its
own right, but tinker has no meaning on its own. It follows along like

a hype man – echoing and amplifying wunker, without changing its meaning.

Wunker-tinker is an example of what are called *janta padalu* or echo words – a form of linguistic reduplication. Most languages employ reduplication, whether exact (bye-bye), partial (flip-flop) or in echo words (higgledy-piggledy). In South-Asian languages, reduplication is especially common and can alter meaning – by intensifying a word (*thondera thonderaga ra*, come fast fast!), for example, or signalling duration (*appudu*, meaning at a certain time, *appudappudu* meaning sometimes). But its primary function is aesthetic, expressive, and inventive; it sharpens the tongue and enlivens the language. In echo words, the second part rhymes with or partially replicates the first word but may not have an independent meaning. For instance: *illu gillu*. Someone asks if you own a house and you snap back, *Illu ledu, gillu ledu!* I don't have a house, I don't have a schmouse!

Telugu makes ample, generative use of repetition, especially with words that appeal to the senses: *gala-gala* – the jingling of coins; *tapa-tapa* – small fruit falling; *misa-misa* – shining like a fish; *gusa-gusa* – someone is whispering rumours; *kasa-kasa* – they are chewing an unripe fruit; *ghuma-ghuma* – the fragrant smell wafting in from the kitchen; *kutha-kutha* – the crackling of rice as it finishes cooking; *pitha-pitha* – stickiness, the rice has been overcooked.

Such words and the rhythms and sensations they produce do not translate well between Telugu and English. I don't mean to distinguish the particular music of Telugu – a vowel-heavy language – from that of English. I mean rather an affective relationship to sound and rhythm itself. Wunker-tinker and all manner of reduplicated words reveal the strictures of good taste in English. English has its share of such words: willy-nilly, namby-pamby, hokey-pokey. But these tend to be perceived as childish or indecorous, testing the boundaries of English decorum.

తెలుగు

When English reduplications originate in other languages, the words often undergo a devaluation. Mumbo-jumbo is a prime example. 'Maamajomboo' likely referred to a ritual figure in the Mandinka language of West Africa, but as it entered English, the term became shorthand for nonsensical, suspect speech. Similarly, *Hobson Jobson*, the foundational dictionary of Anglo-Indian terms, takes its title from colonial mimicry of the sound patterns English officials heard in India. The Shia mourning chant, 'Ya Hassan! Ya Hussein!' took on a pejorative cast and eventually mutated into 'Hobson Jobson'.

The colonial attitude towards the rhythms of Indian languages is not surprising: English embarrasses quickly around reduplication. The primary English form of improvisational reduplication, is the schm-, which comes from Yiddish. We can say Joe Schmo or fancy-schmancy, but also improvise: morning-schmorning or yellow-schmellow. Yet even here, the schm- can sound overly dramatic and, well, schmaltzy.

In Telugu, reduplication *can* be theatrical, but isn't necessarily so. Echo words don't feel déclassé, as they often do in English. Peppered through ordinary speech, they are also to be found in the highest literature. In contemporary English, rhyme can sit uneasy. Imagine a conversation in which a friend tells you that their morning was super-duper, or that their workday was easy-peasy: a word that might come to your own mind in response is 'cringe'. Or even ñáñaras, a word with a sense of botheration about it. Whenever I said the word to someone in Mexico, a smile would flicker across their face. Like wunker-tinker, it produces an off-key enjoyment, a fleeting, complicit pleasure. ■

FALMOUTH
UNIVERSITY

STUDY FLEXIBLY ONLINE

BREAK COMEDY BOUNDARIES WITH AN ONLINE MASTER'S FROM FALMOUTH.

There's a great industry need right now for new television and audio comedy writers. Throughout our Comedy Writing master's programme, developed by award-winning BBC comedy producer Simon Nicholls, you'll benefit from career guidance masterclasses from the very best in the industry.

- Gain the skills, tools and industry insights to push your projects to the top of the commissioning editor's pile and get your comedy script green-lit
- Study the work of renowned comedy writers, reflect on professional trends and learn how to seize market opportunities
- Learn how to write sketches, sitcoms and comedy dramas, developing a body of work for multiple platforms including television, audio and online

**Harness our expertise in a way that works for you.
Start in January, May or September.**

**Discover Comedy
Writing MA (Online)**

"I finished the course with an industry-ready portfolio I'm proud of and a peer network of fellow writers and performers that I couldn't have got anywhere else."

Nicky Roberts, graduate

falmouth.ac.uk/online

WILFREDO LEE
Neptune Memorial Reef, Florida
Alamy

UNDER THE RUINS

Raghu Karnad

In February last year, the prime minister of India boarded a boat in the seaside town of Dwarka, where the Gulf of Kutch meets the Arabian Sea. He wore a saffron outfit with a belt of gilded fabric, and held a fan of peacock feathers in his hand. Away from the shore, Narendra Modi, seventy-three, had a spherical aquatic helmet placed over his head. He was lowered into the waves.

Underwater, in the safe company of navy divers, Modi assumed poses of prayer and meditation. The gold lamé of his belt caught the light from the surface, shining against his vestments. All around him swirled the grainy teal of the littoral waters. If you could see past the bubble helmet, the navy scuba team – and the fact that, from Modi's perspective, he was facing multiple cameras – it was a classic image of *tapasya*, or yogic austerity: the superhuman yogi lost in meditation, underwater.

I was watching on TV, feeling queasy. I'd been following headlines about the Archaeological Survey of India (ASI), a government department established more than 150 years ago, digging up mythic cities. These were places named in the epic poem, the Mahabharata. Some of the excavations were new; others were older but drawing fresh attention. Modi was on a pilgrimage to one under the sea.

Back on dry land after his performance, the prime minister gave a speech. 'Ancient Dwarka, which is said to have been settled by the Lord Sri Krishna himself . . . today it is submerged in the sea,' he said, speaking in Hindi. 'It was my great fortune to go into the deep sea, and at that sunken city, to present myself and do puja to Sri Krishna.'

'Archaeologists have written a great deal about that submerged city,' Modi went on. 'Our ancient verses speak of it too.' He then recited from the Harivamsa, an epilogue to the Mahabharata:

> Bhavishyati puri ramya sudvara praarya-torana
> Chayaattalak keyura pruthivyam kakudopama
>
> It will be a radiant city, with splendid gates and archways,
> With lofty pavilions like armlets worn by the earth, rising like the hump of a bull above the land.

In the Mahabharata, Krishna – a living king and an incarnation of Vishnu – establishes a new capital on ground offered up to him by the Sea. This city, called Dwarka, is laid out by a celestial architect, with 'prosperous courtyards, high edifices struck by the clouds' and palaces that 'cover even the sky'. Later, after the epic's final battle, after Krishna too has been killed, the Sea comes to reclaim its gift and Dwarka disappears in the waves.

For decades, archaeologists have been intrigued by modern Dwarka and the evidence of ruined structures beyond its shore. The footage of Modi's dive, however, only shows the submerged prime minister; nothing of the submerged city. Google News led me to a view of the ruins: a sea floor littered with pavilions and pillars, whole temples that had defied the pull of time and tide. A monumental stone wheel, covered in intricate carvings, glowed in the green and slanting light.

I was amazed, for a moment, and then annoyed. The images were AI-generated. '*Representative pic*', I read in a tiny font, though they weren't that either. Other photos, presented as pictures of the Dwarka seabed, turned out to be from an Atlantis-themed novelty reef in Key Biscayne, Florida. What the images actually represented was the distance between the real and imaginative dimensions of the Archaeological Survey's project – between archaeology as research and archaeology as wish fulfilment.

People used to say that it was dangerous to keep the entire text of the Mahabharata in your home – that it could set the house on fire. You didn't need to, anyway. Its tales of warring heroes, gods, queens, demons and sages have radiated through Indian art and storytelling for centuries. The main narrative, about a rivalry among the Kuru princes that builds into an apocalyptic war, is continuously reworked today into airport novels and lyric poetry; movement theatre and festive stage spectaculars; tempera murals and acrylic on canvas; movies, memes. The familiarity of the epic's themes has never receded: the anthropologist Irawati Karve noted in *Yuganta*, a commentary on the Mahabharata published in 1967, that the story is 'one familiar to most Indians: the struggle for property in a joint family.'

Along with the Ramayana, the Mahabharata is often compared with Homer's epics. Unlike in the Iliad and the Odyssey, however, the divine characters of the Sanskrit epics – Rama and Krishna in particular – likely have more worshippers today than they did in the past. The coverage of the ASI's 'Mahabharata sites' – locations in the epic poem supposedly corresponding with points in the landscape – which appeared in newspapers and on TV, nodded towards that congregation. '7 Mind-Blowing Proofs that Mahabharata was Real', read the headline of the *Daily News & Analysis*. Other outlets jumbled mythic and scientific phrases: *survey conclusively prove divine sample palace concrete evidence sacred Lord*. As I opened new tabs, my heart sank. I'd seen all this happen before.

Archaeologists first took interest in the Mahabharata in the 1950s, and they treated the epic as a tool. The problem they wanted to solve was the mystery of the 'Dark Age' of ancient India.

This was a roughly 1,500-year blank in the historical data between the decline of the Indus Valley Civilization and the first chronicles of the reign of Ashoka, in the third century BCE. 'How to bridge this vast gap . . . has been one of the most baffling problems of Indian archaeology,' wrote a young officer of the ASI, Braj Basi Lal. His solution was to use the 'literary evidence' from the epics, which had evidently been composed in that interval.

Lal had a simple hypothesis. In the vicinity of Delhi, and further east on the Gangetic plain, a number of towns and villages had names that were the same as, or similar to, places in the Mahabharata. There was a Hastinapura (the capital city from which the Kuru clan ruled); a Barnawa (a colloquialised Varanavata, the town where the Pandava heroes are lured into a deathtrap, the Palace of Lac); and a Kurukshetra (the final battlefield). Within Delhi itself, there was an area known to locals as 'Indraprastha', the radiant city built by the Pandavas for their new wife, Draupadi. A dozen other north Indian sites shared the names of minor locations in the poem. At these sites there was often a raised mound of earth, a few hundred metres around, indicating past settlements and archaeological remains.

In 1954, Lal led a series of surveys and excavations of the mounds. When archaeologists dig, they identify distinct layers, or strata, of human artefacts held in the soil. The basic principle of stratigraphy is that activity over one period of time forms a layer, and the period that follows puts a layer down above it – layer rising above layer, up to the surface.

Lal began at Hastinapura. There, he and his team found deposits of a distinctive ceramic pottery in the lower layers of the mounds. They had a light, ashy colour and a smooth texture. The fragments, or 'potsherds', were often decorated with patterns in black pigment: criss-cross strokes or concentric circles, spiral shapes and dots and dashes. This was called Painted Grey Ware, or PGW, and dated to the centuries around 1000 BCE. Within its strata, the grey ware itself was relatively rare. It was found alongside rougher ceramics like terracotta, and objects made of copper, ivory, iron and bone. The rarity and finesse of the PGW suggests that it was likely restricted to the ruling class, and the society that produced it was called the Painted Grey Ware Culture.

It was a modest clue, one that appeared to point the way to the milieu of the Mahabharata kings. But in these grey potsherds, Lal had found his legacy, or even his legend. These sites, he said – selected by names recorded in myth, and revealing a shared, archaic material culture – situated the events of the Mahabharata in real time and space. The names of these sites were not coincidence, but transmissions of an ancient past.

After Lal, the archaeology of the epic became equated with the PGW 'horizon' – a term with roughly the same meaning as layer or deposit, but with the added, useful connotation of a limit to how far we can see. Many historians have been uneasy with Lal's hypothesis, given the thinness of the evidence. The director general of the ASI, Amalananda Ghosh, wrote in the organisation's journal of the year 1954–55 that 'a word of caution is necessary, lest the impression is left on the unwary reader that . . . [Lal's] excavation has yielded archaeological evidence about the truth of the story of the Mahabharata.' He warned against Lal's argument being taken full circle: details from the myth may have helped validate the archaeologists' inquiry, but that did not mean that the archaeology had validated the myth. 'Caution is necessary,' Ghosh wrote, 'that fancy does not fly ahead of facts.'

As Lal's hypothesis passed into the hands of laymen, eccentrics and, later, the very-online, it took on a life of its own. It was absorbed into a common belief that the epic was a Hindu form of history, a genre that was otherwise scarce in ancient Indian literature. Today, when I search online for an explanation of the 'Mahabharata era', many of the top results are from BeerBiceps, a winsome former weightlifter who is now one of India's most successful YouTubers. In a typical video, titled 'Must Watch – Mahabharata's Scientifically Proven Proof', the guest (a chemical engineer by training) gives 5561 BCE as the definite date of the war. BeerBiceps nods along, wide-eyed.

In another episode, BeerBiceps suggests that the epic originates in a high-technology culture that was destroyed by natural disaster about twelve thousand years ago. Each of these videos has been viewed millions of times.

Online, the Mahabharata grows larger in scale as it moves further back into the past. Two tendencies converge in all of this excitement. The first is the cult of esoteric knowledge, of secret cities and civilisations. The other is the doctrine of India's new ruling establishment: Hindu nationalism.

The old story of Indian civilisation I'd grown up with – sanctioned by the Congress, and still prevailing in the 1990s – was one of gain. Every past era had added to the cultural wealth of the subcontinent, and each newly arriving influence had been absorbed by the Indian genius for syncretism. This binding vision of the past had carried the national movement, and after 1947, lent justification to a republic in which every community could make an equal claim of belonging.

Hindu nationalism, or Hindutva, presents a counter-narrative: from the start of time, the subcontinent has been the cradle and homeland of a single civilisation, one that draws its identity from Sanskrit texts – first the Vedas, later the Ramayana and Mahabharata. Untold centuries of sacred continuity were shattered by successive Muslim invasions starting around 1000 CE. Then comes a thousand-year history of loss – the loss of battles, of gold, of women; the loss of face, and eventually, of self – all of it symbolised by the loss of temples.

A serious problem for this story is the evidence that early Sanskrit-speakers were a migrant population themselves. These 'Aryans' originated in the Caucasus, and only made their way to northern India by the second millennium BCE, during the Dark Age. Other migrants originating from the same archaic culture settled around the Aegean – so the Mahabharata and the Iliad both share a foreign ancestry. Among scholars, the Aryan Migration Theory is a largely settled consensus based on numerous linguistic, archaeological and genetic studies. For Hindu nationalists, it is heresy.

The historicisation of the Mahabharata became a way to spread a vision of a supremely ancient, Sanskritic world over the murky dawn of Indian history. The vision subsumes any academic disputes about the Dark Age or the deeper past. Ghosh, the ASI director general, warned against the circular logic that could lead to conjuring the epic, and its supernatural milieu, into the country's idea of actual history. For nationalists, that is exactly the point: the sanctioned account of original, warlike Hindu ancestors who inhabited great palaces is meant to grant legitimacy to latter-day warlike Hindu nationhood.

For most of my life, a focal point of India's politics and culture wars has been a few acres of ruined masonry in a town in Uttar Pradesh called Ayodhya. In the Ramayana, Ayodhya is the name of the birthplace and capital of Prince Rama's kingdom. Some Hindus believed that the two were the same, and that the precise location of Rama's birth had been marked by an ancient temple – until the sixteenth century, when a Mughal general sacked the temple and built a mosque in its place.

In 1980, a new political party – the Bharatiya Janata Party (BJP) – committed itself to setting right this injustice to Lord Rama. Using a murky combination of archaeology, appeals to faith and physical violence, the BJP fed the belief that ruins of a temple had been found at the site in Ayodhya. Hindus, the BJP claimed, could not rest until they had restored a temple where the mosque now stood. In December 1992, thousands of Hindutva diehards stormed the mosque and tore it down. The provocation set off riots and killings across the rest of India. From that year on, the opposing lines of India's culture wars would be: *Masjid ya Mandir* – Mosque or Temple?

Until the Ayodhya movement, most Hindus were content to worship Rama in his immanence. They recognised the landscape of the Ramayana in their own backyards. Now he had an exact physical address. Worse, he was becoming a subject of history – not just in the sense of being forced into the chronological record, but also of being made a stakeholder in a dismal argument over the past. Specifically, it was about what Muslims had done in India in the past, and what they were still doing in India today.

Rama also became a litigant in court. In 1989, the lawsuit concerning the 'disputed site' came to include the deity himself. Using an old colonial precedent, a far-right organisation had entered Ram Lalla, or the Child Rama – as manifest in an idol they had placed on the site – as a physical party to the lawsuit. For the next three decades, the BJP used the missing temple to lash Hindus into one political bloc, and to make them vote for the party that promised to redress their grievance. In 2019, party leader Narendra Modi was elected prime minister for a second time. In that air of fait accompli, India's Supreme Court ruled in favour of Ram Lalla and his temple. It was surreal to witness; it amounted to a twenty-first century hierophany: the divine Rama was presented as a litigant, and left as a landowner.

The inauguration of the new temple was scheduled just before the next national election. It was a media spectacle of unprecedented scale and Modi had the starring human role, opposite Ram Lalla. On the morning of 22 January 2024, the prime minister performed the idol's *pran pratishtha*, the rituals meant to 'bring it to life'. I was still recovering from the coverage when, five weeks later, Modi went diving for Dwarka in the Gulf of Kutch.

In the epic, Kurukshetra is where the armies meet for their final, epoch-ending battle. Modern-day Kurukshetra is a pilgrimage city in Haryana, on the crowded agricultural plain north of Delhi. I came across an essay on Medium by a young man from Kurukshetra. He wrote with warmth and quiet feeling about what it meant to grow up there, with a sense of a mythic past beneath his feet. The author, whom I'll call Abhimanyu, lived in Thanesar, the historical part of town, right by the monumental tomb of Sheikh Chilli – 'a Mughal marvel,' he called it, 'its Persian architecture a testament to that era's grandeur'. Thanesar was also where the archaeological mounds were located, in which Lal found a layer of PGW. 'I'd wonder about the pottery and relics uncovered here . . .' Abhimanyu wrote. 'These findings aren't just artefacts to me – they're proof that Kurukshetra's story isn't myth alone. The red soil I kicked up as a boy playing cricket might've once soaked up the blood of warriors, a thought that still gives me chills.'

There was something rare about the essay: it felt expansive, and free of prejudice. 'Kurukshetra's history didn't end with the Mahabharata,' Abhimanyu wrote. That ancient tradition was layered with Buddhist and Jain heritage, 'lingering in forgotten stupas and tales,' and then an Islamic one. At Sheikh Chilli's Tomb, 'where I spent lazy afternoons, I could feel the layers of time,' he wrote. 'Each ruler left something behind, shaping the Kurukshetra I know.'

I scrounged around online until I found a way to contact Abhimanyu. He messaged me back. I told him how touched I was by what he had written, and its lack of chauvinism, despite the obvious pride he had in his home town. He made it seem natural to acknowledge the potency of a mythic past while reaffirming later traditions; to 'feel the layers of time' and to celebrate them.

'It almost made me want to go to Kurukshetra myself,' I told him.

'Sure,' he replied. 'You should come.'

'Ha ha.'

'If you take the train, I'll pick you up and show you around,' he said. 'If you don't mind riding pillion.'

My impulse was to refuse. It was June, and the temperature was crossing forty degrees Celsius every afternoon.

Travelling last year in Greece, I'd been more than ready to embrace the epic landscape: to accept that the heroes' homelands listed in the Iliad – Athens, Sparta or Corinth – corresponded to real city states of antiquity, and to the modern municipalities and resort towns of the present. Troy, the walled city in the forefront of the myth, was long believed to be a Homeric invention. Since 1870, though, it has been identified with a site in Anatolia called Hisarlik.

There, Heinrich Schliemann had excavated a layer of artefacts that seemed to correspond to the epic period itself. Was the ASI's quest so different from Schliemann's? But it was only the epic places closer to Delhi, where I lived, that I felt I had to deny. To gain a historical Mahabharata might mean losing the mythological one – to stop seeing it as a shared fiction, and fix it instead as a set of facts.

Rejecting the archaeologists' discoveries, however, didn't do much to protect the myth. It only ceded one more piece of the landscape to Hindu nationalism. Buried under the layers of my refusal was a bead of envy, for the simple thrill I too might have felt at encountering the legend in the real landscape around me. It was a two-hour trip from New Delhi railway station to Kurukshetra; the trains ran through the day. I had a guide. I could just go.

I went first to the village of Barnawa, midway between Delhi and Kurukshetra. This was the place Lal associated with Varanavata, where the Kauravas had built a Palace of Lac, and 'induced their cousins to live in it, with a view to burning them to death'. Lal had found a mound where, he wrote, 'the Painted Grey Ware can be picked up in abundance'.

I've known the story of the Palace of Lac for what seems like my whole life. It's popular in children's books. I never quite knew what lac was, but I've now learned that it is a resin-like material secreted by the lac insect. Lacquer is extracted from it. It catches fire easily. The word derives from the Sanskrit 'laksha'. The story goes like this: early in their lives, the Pandava princes and their mother, Kunti, are sent off to visit a festival in the town of Varanavata. Their wicked Kaurava cousins build a palace of lac, a Lakshagriha, and urge them to stay there. Our heroes have suspicions. The place is designed to go up in flames as they sleep. They turn the tables, escaping through a tunnel and setting fire to the palace themselves, while their enemies' cronies are still inside. The ashy bones of the victims pass as the Pandavas' own remains, and the Kauravas are tricked into believing their trap worked.

The story really gets moving after this failed deathtrap. The Pandavas, alive but incognito, travel on to a kingdom whose princess, Draupadi, is about to choose a husband. Arjuna – the middle brother, and their best warrior – passes an impossible test of archery and wins her hand. She consents (then learns she has to marry all five of them).

Despite the famous legend and Lal's survey, the ASI did not excavate the Barnawa mound until 2018. In February of 2024, it leapt back into the news. In the weeks after Modi's temple spectacle at Ayodhya, a local court wrapped up a fifty-year-long dispute over the mound, ruling, of course, for the 'Hindu' side – a *gurukul*, or traditional-style school – and rejecting the opposing claim that a Sufi tomb and graveyard had occupied parts of the mound. For a few days, newsmen trooped around with cameras, broadcasting segments that I watched before my visit. On screen, news banners read, 'Ancient Lakshagriha – Eternal Heritage' or 'For the First Time, the Pandavas' Palace of Lac on Camera!' The filmed visuals made much of a pair of low tunnels that opened into the side of the mound.

Apparently these were the very tunnels the Pandavas had used to escape the burning palace. Fantastic! Reporters took turns crouching in the tunnel's mouth, venting into their microphones. 'When you go and see the Lakshagriha for yourself,' one of them said, seeming to address me directly, 'You will find all kinds of evidence from the Mahabharata era. Historians and local elders will acquaint you with signs and symbols.' The soundtrack over his voice was like thunder, or war drums.

It was quieter when I got there, on a mid-morning at the height of summer. The ancient mound is on the edge of modern Barnawa, a brick-built village lost in the web of highways and choked canals that surround the National Capital Region. The mound is roughly fifty feet high and covers several acres. I found I could drive right to the top of it, where I parked beside the overbuilt institutional compound of the *gurukul*. Its ruins will one day make a good addition to the mound.

I'd come here hoping the place would feel monumental, or even mystical; send up shivers from three millennia deep. Looking out from the mound's edge over modern Barnawa, I thought the low, blocky outlines and brick walls might pass, in the white-out sun, as a city from an early civilisation. But from the mound beneath me I felt nothing. Maybe in the tunnels! They were nearby, at the bottom of a stairway that began at the edge of the mound.

Heading down the steps I heard laughter. I found the first tunnel with three slender bottoms poking out of it into the sun. A family was on a picnic. By this point – the temperature now forty-one degrees Celsius – even the women, a bit wary at first, had ducked into its cool darkness. I bent down next to them.

Inside, the tunnel was sandy and round, like the burrow of a large, tidy animal. 'It turns this way and that,' said the older woman beside me, gesturing into the darkness. A little girl was clutching her hand, doing a nervous jig. Then the men came scuttling back from the depths, and it was my turn to go in. I made it around three or four bends, navigating by mobile flashlight, before my rib cage started to contract with panic. 'The Pandavas made this tunnel,' the woman called, as I reappeared. 'Don't be scared, it won't fall before you come out.'

Back at the tunnel's mouth, I searched the pitted earthen walls for the promised signs and symbols. But this was just plain mud. From my seat in the dirt, I made a phone call to Disha Ahluwalia, an archaeologist who specialises in PGW and who had helped supervise the 2018 dig. No, she said, the tunnels had nothing to do with the Mahabharata. The PGW horizon here was below ground level, that is to say at the bottom of the mound. The tunnels were well above that level. They had been dug much later, into soil that was already a matrix of the remains of later habitation.

The bulk of the Barnawa mound turned out to have been a brick fortress of the Kushan period, the first to third centuries CE. The curious visitors and reporters from Delhi had had other expectations. In the first month of the dig, she told me, crowds gathered 'hoping to get a glimpse of the Lakshagriha. But they were met with potsherds, and they were like, *Okay, so you've found broken vessels? We can find those at home.*'

The project ended abruptly when a senior ASI official was transferred to another region. Ahluwalia's team was given a week to pack up and fill in the trenches they'd made over months of diligent labour. The work has not been resumed.

Nationalists and archaeologists are not always natural allies. In the past decade, the ASI – which also looks after India's historical monuments – has spent less than 1 per cent of its budget on excavations. A fifth of that outlay, since 2020, has been devoted to a single location: Vadnagar, Modi's home town. Everywhere else the budgets are minimal and permissions capricious. Ahluwalia told me that she isn't surprised when ASI officials sensationalise their finds, telling TV channels that they've found historical proof of the Mahabharata; it's a bid for attention, but also for funding. 'It's an actual temptation,' she told me. 'It's easy to fall into that trap.'

At the train station of modern Kurukshetra, Abhimanyu was waiting for me. I got on his scooter, and we rode across town and onto the highway. Abhimanyu was twenty-eight and soft-spoken, with lank hair and dark stubble, a peaceable smile. Given the confidence of his writing, he seemed coy in person, or maybe just dreamy. I learned that he worked from home, and had gotten a distance-learning degree from Kurukshetra University, despite living in town. I asked if we could begin at Jyotisar, where the story of the war began. In the poem, on the dawn of battle, Arjuna has a crisis of conscience. His chariot is pulled by white horses, and Krishna has offered to serve as his charioteer. Together they ride to the centre of the battlefield. The poem describes eighteen divisions, each – *each* – with 20,000 war elephants and equal numbers of chariots, 100,000 men on horseback and another lakh on foot. On both sides, Arjuna sees friends and family. He says:

> *Krishna, seeing my own kinsmen arrayed for battle here and intent on killing each other, my limbs are giving way and my mouth is dry. My bow, the Gandiva, is slipping from my hand ... I do not see how any good can come from killing my own kinsmen in battle.*
>
> *Speaking thus, Arjuna cast aside his bow and arrows, and sank into the seat of his chariot, overwhelmed with grief.*

Krishna replies with a holy sermon about war and duty, in the course of which he reveals himself in his vast and terrifying cosmic form. This dialogue, called the Bhagavad Gita – or just the Gita – is now regarded as one of the great articulations of Indian metaphysics and morals. It gets Arjuna back on his feet to carry out his duty, which right then is carnage.

The Jyotisar lake, locals say, is the place where the Gita was spoken. Along one bank, a platform of white marble is surrounded by shrines. Three banyans grow from the centre of the platform, covering the area in shade. Beneath them is a modest figurine – also of white marble – of horses and chariot, Arjuna and Krishna, their dialogue underway. Pilgrims were being led up to a newer statue, installed in 2021. This was Krishna not as charioteer, but as the full-blown godhead revealed during the Gita. The statue, huge and literalistic, stood out in the sun, coursing with excess detail – with the attempt to engrave god's terrible infinitude, not on the mind, but on thirty-five tonnes of copper alloy.

We stayed under the banyans, where, according to his posts, Abhimanyu liked to sit 'imagining Krishna's words echoing through time'. I tried to elicit in person some of these reflections. He demurred. Back on his bike, we moved on to the mound at Thanesar, another of Lal's PGW sites, which I found landscaped into a city park. A few excavated trenches were preserved for what appeared to be purely picturesque reasons.

Abhimanyu took me to his home for lunch and a rest. The electricity was out. He opened up a bit as he talked about AI, and about creating content on AI platforms, which he published on other platforms, filling his CV with diverse achievements (two novels, a podcast, a free-access course on digital marketing). I was on his couch and dozing off. I sat up as it hit me that his posts were AI too.

The salient thing about Abhimanyu, it turned out, was not that he was a native of this mythic landscape, but that he was a native of the AI-enabled web and devoted to its generative powers. Reticence left him as he told me, for an hour, about his years using AI, which began long before ChatGPT, when he had learned to use tools like QuillBot to write papers for students at American universities.

There was a great contrast between Abhimanyu's two worlds, between the tight confines of the family home in an Indian B-town and the pearly horizon of gratification online. The fact that he wrote his posts with ChatGPT was a technicality to Abhimanyu. 'Earlier, people wrote with pen,' he told me. 'You prefer to type on a keyboard. I can't even think about writing on a keyboard – word by word. I write with AI. It's like the same thing.' I couldn't condone the analogy, but it was true that without AI's mediation, I would never have met him, nor felt invited to see Kurukshetra. I would have to accept this strange act of translation.

His post on Medium was, in his eyes, a genuine creation: perhaps the most genuine of his prolific career. He was moved to create it after seeing, on Wikipedia, that Kurukshetra had several separate pages: one about the district, one about historical Thanesar, another about the mythological war. 'I wanted to show what unites them, for the people who live here,' he said. To do so, he used Gemini's Deep Research tool and then ChatGPT, to add a personable tone and a few details from his own life: the lazy afternoons he passed at Sheikh Chilli's tomb; skipping school to wander around with friends during the Gita Festival. 'I've watched it grow, balancing its ancient soul with modern dreams,' his essay concludes, 'and I hope you'll see it through my eyes.'

After lunch we said goodbye.

A. K. Ramanujan once wrote that no Hindu ever reads the Mahabharata for the first time. In fact few people ever read it at all, in any language, let alone Sanskrit. It's too long. The whole text runs to two hundred thousand lines, which qualifies it as humanity's longest extant ancient epic.

To even write down the Mahabharata, legend has it, Vyasa had to enrol the elephant-headed god Ganesha as his amanuensis. Ganesha's quills wore away so fast that he yanked out his left tusk to use as a pen. Whether or not this part is true: the written transmission of the Sanskrit epics only seems to have begun between 300 BCE and 300 CE. Like the Greek epics, they began as heroic plays recited by bards. Later they took on canonical form, and were ascribed to a single poet. The poets – Vyasa, Valmiki or Homer – have become numinous, half-mythic figures.

The oldest manuscripts of the Mahabharata to reach modern scholars are from no earlier than 700 CE. In every century, authors added new names and legends, along with new grammar and concepts that couldn't have been there before. Certain battle formations, and the Bhagavad Gita itself, only became part of the war story well into the Common Era.

The resultant text is less a record of a moment in history than a process of history. It mainly telescopes the transformation of early Iron-Age clans – herders and raiders of cattle, governed by codes of kinship – into settled kingdoms governed by laws of caste. This explains the archeological finds. The PGW culture is meant to reveal an Epic Age, but in material terms it is a picture of simplicity. Instead of palaces that 'cover the sky', there is scant evidence of any architecture at all. That society seems to have built with wattle and daub, or later, mud brick and thatch. It left behind no golden maces, breastplates or crowns. It left no inscriptions. That's because it probably had neither writing nor coinage. In the sea by Dwarka, what has actually been found are not sunken temples, but blocks of masonry and crude stone anchors.

The paradox of India's epic archaeology is that the society it reveals is a modest one. It is only imagination, with visual culture chasing behind it, that has ever managed to realise the sublime hyperbole of the epic. In the present, Mahabharata prompts are constantly fed into AI engines. I recently watched a teaser for *Mahabharat: An Eternal War*, a 'completely AI-generated cinematic masterpiece'. The gigantism of its palaces and armies, the high-fantasy pomp, seems wrong, but also right. Online, swole heroes are cut down again and again, each time in new ways, in a new war. ■

मराठी

*R*e (rhymes with bay) is a small word. Just a single letter – ₹ – but it carries a weight that belies its size. This single syllable does a lot of work in Marathi. It is a familiar and informal form of address, used mostly with men. It's hard to explain what it means because it doesn't translate cleanly into English. Its tone and intent shift. It can convey exasperation, affection, irritation, even teasing; it all depends on the context. You might hear:

'No, re, you can't go out today.'

Here, re acts as a pacifier, softening the ban.

'Why are you behaving like that, re?'

Now re signals closeness but also a mild rebuke.

In Konkani, the language of my native Goa, we have something close: *reh* (it rhymes with care). But reh is gentler, softer in tone, and doesn't carry the same intent or directness as re in Marathi. There is no re in English – not even Indian English.

While translating my first book out of Marathi – *Cobalt Blue* by Sachin Kundalkar – I encountered re many times in the text. The book is set in a middle-class household, where re is used frequently. How was I to translate it into English?

At first I thought of a word from my own childhood: *men*. In Mumbai, we used it a bit like New Yorkers might use 'dude'. You'd say, 'No, men, I didn't take your pencil,' or, 'You're mad or what, men!' It was common in the anglophone Goan community I grew up in, but by the time I was translating *Cobalt Blue*, it had receded. Young people, brought up on American television, said dude instead. I remember a student once writing 'dood' in an essay – he had only ever heard the word spoken by the Teenage Mutant Ninja Turtles.

I couldn't use dude or men in the translation. Neither sounded right. *Cobalt Blue* centres on a middle-class Brahmin narrator who knows he's gay but remains in the closet. It would take something away from him to use either word – it would turn him into someone else.

The words we put into the mouths of our characters reveal them to the world. In *Cobalt Blue*, the family takes in a mysterious male boarder, who refuses early in the novel to reveal his last name. This is a growing movement in India, where dropping one's surname can erase one's caste. But it is a sticky thing, caste. Even small linguistic signals can reveal much. At dinner, the boarder uses the word *poli* rather than *chappati*. Poli is a word favoured by Brahmins. The mother hears this and relaxes: now she can be sure that her boarder is not violating their insular caste stronghold. It is hard to capture a moment like that in English because language is caste-complexioned in India.

My second translation – *Baluta* by Daya Pawar – was the first Dalit autobiography written in Marathi. Here, the challenge was the title itself. *Baluta* refers to a caste practice in which Dalit communities in Maharashtra were not paid wages for their work, a practice that continued well into the twentieth century. Instead, they received a small share of village produce. This share was called *baluta* – the wages of slavery, that is, no wages at all. I considered translating the title as 'The Wages of Slavery' but I felt this would present the book as a misery memoir, when it has so much more, with wonderful riffs on sexual politics, food habits, and the differences between rural and urban India. Eventually, I left the title alone. *Baluta*, it would be, in English too. If Indian readers could figure out *Bonjour Tristesse* and *Ndima Ndima*, they could handle *Baluta*.

In his book, Pawar warns his readers that they might not understand some of the words that he uses because they deal with parts of the cow once it has been butchered for beef – the animal being divided according to a system known as *gudsa*. He tells his Marathi readers that the word will not mean much if they don't eat beef. Some words move quietly within castes, never written down, words fresh to the world of print.

In India, to translate is to be aware of these layers – religion, caste, class, region, gender. It's a country where four major religions were born, where Christianity arrived before it reached Rome, and where the third-largest Muslim population in the world lives. You start with a single letter – र – and end up navigating caste, class and belonging. ∎

Preparing for a launch at the Thumba Rocket Equatorial Launching Station, 1966
Fondation Henri Cartier-Bresson / Magnum Photos

INDIA IN THE HEAVENS

Srinath Perur

R ocket launches in Thumba, a fishing-village-turned-rocket-facility on the south-western coast of India, take place on the third Wednesday of every month. On the day I visited, about a thousand people had gathered, mostly busloads of school students, a few employees of the space centre with visiting parents, a batch of interns from the nearby Indian Institute of Space Science and Technology. They were all crowded into a high-roofed viewing shed by the beach, set amid coconut palms and Kerala greenery freshly rinsed by a monsoon shower. 'This is nothing,' a guard told me. 'Usually we have three or four times the number.'

As rockets go this one was small – a roughly twelve-foot long RH-200 sounding rocket developed by the Indian Space Research Organisation (ISRO). 'Sounding' because it was meant to study – sound out – the atmosphere, here, where the Earth's magnetic equator cuts through the tip of southern India. A band of charged particles called the equatorial electrojet flows some 100 kilometres above, affecting radio communication and navigation systems. This favourable location for studying atmospheric and cosmic phenomena, and a bout of inspired scientific diplomacy, was what convinced the UN to underwrite the operation of India's first rocket facility in Thumba in the 1960s. Member countries supplied equipment and expertise. India provided personnel and the special geography.

Thumba is where the first modern rocket was launched from India, in 1963. An engineer at the facility told me the first sounding rocket had been launched from the exact same spot. He turned out to be a civil engineer. 'You need every kind of engineer for space,' he explained. Not far away was the workshop where that rocket was assembled – a former church once consecrated to St Mary Magdalene, which is now dedicated to space.

A loudspeaker in the middle of the viewing area relayed the terse chatter of subsystem teams. Each team reported their okays, the mission director declared the launch on. The countdown began. The crowd shouted out the last ten seconds in concert with the loudspeaker. Zero. A small pocket of silence torn by the roar of a flaming plume. The rocket was visible for only a few seconds as it arced high over the sea and out of sight.

In 1978, my mother joined the then nine-year-old ISRO. She and a friend had been the first women at the engineering college in her small town in the Indian state of Karnataka. For the next thirty-two years, she worked at the satellite centre in Bengaluru, specialising in ground station systems and mission planning. The little plaques and models she brought home to commemorate the latest launches gave us a sense of pride in the work she was doing. And though she was long retired by 2023, when Chandrayaan-3 became India's first craft to land on the Moon, she and her peers celebrated the moment as something to which they had contributed. They used their WhatsApp group to coordinate a bulk purchase of models of the spacecraft.

Something I have always found bemusing about my mother is her ability to keep her scientific self distinct from the rest of the world she inhabits. A traditional belief in India has it that eclipses are generally inauspicious and bad for health. So she might tell a pregnant family member to avoid going out during an eclipse and, when asked why, mumble something about harmful rays. But in another context you might find her explaining to her granddaughter the orbital alignments that cause eclipses. Having designed antennae for satellite communication, she knows exactly what rays are out there. Her two ways of thinking somehow coexist, each affording the other its own integrity.

She is not alone. There is an element of faith in ISRO's pre-launch rituals for satellites and rockets. Staff have been known to perform Hindu puja ceremonies before moving material to the launch sites. Coconuts are broken open to grant auspices to important pieces of equipment. Before major launches, senior officials of the Indian space programme take models of the spacecraft to be blessed by Lord Venkateswara, a form of the Hindu deity Vishnu. 'On the day of the launch,' writes retired ISRO space engineer Ramabhadran Aravamudan, 'everyone would troop to the temple in Sriharikota and pray for its success.'

ISRO officials have in recent years been photographed and interviewed in the Tirupati Venkateswara temple complex, looking like any of the other supplicants. In 2014, one photograph showing women employees of ISRO celebrating the success of the Mars Orbiter Mission went viral. The striking thing about the photo was its very ordinariness – how relatable the women seemed, dressed in saris, wearing bindis, thumbs up and flashing Vs. It seemed to remind the public that the staff of ISRO were visibly no better or worse than any other Indian. It made their accomplishments indistinguishable from the nation's.

National space programmes tend to project a country's self-image into the heavens. The first Indian in space, Rakesh Sharma, went up in 1984 on a Soviet spacecraft, and became the first person to practise yoga in orbit. Prime minister Indira Gandhi asked him on a call what India looked like from up there. Sharma replied with words from a Hindi patriotic song: '*Sare Jahan se Accha*' – 'Better than all the world.'

But what made the Indian space programme different to that of the US or the USSR was the humbleness of its beginnings. The Soviet and the American programmes were expressions of each country's economic bounty, part of their bid for global supremacy and prowess in the Cold War. By contrast, when Henri Cartier-Bresson documented the Indian rocket launching facility in 1966, he photographed a rocket cone being wheeled along on a bicycle. The radical juxtaposition of Indian technology and Indian poverty has never gone away. When the MP Karti Chidambaram spoke in Parliament after a lunar exploration mission in 2023, he said it was 'baffling' that when India was landing spacecrafts on the Moon, at home the practise of manual scavenging, in which people clean human excreta from sewers and drains without protective equipment still went on. 'How can we as a people have this contrast?' he asked. 'There is something seriously wrong in our society if we can't leverage the scientific advancements we are making.'

In saying this, Chidambaram was reviving an old argument. In its infancy, the Indian space programme was never intended to be a glamorous deflection from the country's economic destitution. Instead, it was a central part of an inspired, developmentalist vision for the improvement of the lives of everyone in the country. Space not as a symbol of the country's technological prowess, but as a practical means of social uplift.

Every national space programme has had a 'father'. There was Korolev in the Soviet Union, von Braun in the United States, Qian Xuesen in China. In India, the father was Vikram Sarabhai. Born in 1919 in Ahmedabad into one of the country's wealthiest families, Sarabhai went to the most private of schools – one that existed only within the family's compound and was meant solely for its children. It was equipped with its own physics and chemistry laboratories, and when a young Sarabhai showed an aptitude for the mechanical, a workshop was put in. As a boy he often encountered Gandhi, a family friend, and in 1937 he went to Cambridge following a recommendation from India's first Nobel laureate Rabindranath Tagore. By all accounts, Sarabhai was a rare bundle of charm, means, connections, idealism, and ferocious industriousness.

At the end of the 1950s, as the US–USSR space race heated up, Sarabhai dreamed of a programme with a different set of goals. He wasn't interested in space exploration. What he wanted was to use space research to address India's needs on the ground. The population was poor, largely illiterate and spread across some half a million villages, many of which were unconnected by roads and lacked schools. They would, he proposed, be saved from the skies. As Asif Siddiqi, a historian of science and technology, told me, 'People would ask, "Why should India have a space programme if it's so poor?" Sarabhai's way was to think: India needs a space programme precisely because it is poor.'

A word Sarabhai was particularly fond of was 'leapfrogging'. Advanced technologies, he believed, could create shortcuts to socioeconomic development. He envisaged satellites beaming down coursework to community television sets in far-flung villages. Images from space would warn farmers of crop diseases and weather disturbances. 'We do not expect to send a man to the Moon or put elephants white, pink or black into orbit around the Earth,' Sarabhai said, taking a sly dig at the Soviets and Americans, who had respectively shot a dog and a chimpanzee into space.

Sarabhai formed a body for space research called the Indian National Committee for Space Research in 1962. He was the one who convinced the UN to fund India's first rocket facility in Thumba, and he was there in 1967 to witness the launch of the first Indian-designed rocket – the RH-75. Before his death in 1971, Sarabhai's team had begun developing an indigenously made satellite launch vehicle, called the SLV-3, that could place a small satellite into orbit.

Sarabhai planned to launch satellites into a geosynchronous orbit by the end of the decade. The distance between the satellite and the Earth was crucial. The further a satellite is from the Earth, the slower it needs to go to maintain orbit, until at around 36,000 kilometres it matches the Earth's rotation. It then appears to be fixed in the sky. The sci-fi writer Arthur C. Clarke had proposed in 1945 that such satellites could be used to reflect television transmissions or telephone calls. This is what Sarabhai had in mind.

Before the Indian launch vehicle was ready, the Soviet Union stepped in with an offer to put the first Indian satellite into orbit, which meant the newly consolidated ISRO could focus on building it. A team led by U.R. Rao constructed a 360-kilo satellite in Bangalore, designing it to conduct scientific experiments in X-ray astronomy, aeronomics and solar physics once in space. Prime minister Indira Gandhi named it Aryabhata, after the sixth-century Indian mathematician and astronomer. It went up in 1975 as part of the Interkosmos programme. Within months, the 26-sided polyhedron of Aryabhata appeared on Indian postage stamps and currency notes. For the first time, India had an object orbiting the Earth.

The possibility of using space for widespread socioeconomic uplift arrived the same year. This time ISRO partnered with NASA, who were keen to test out their latest telecommunications satellite, on the Satellite Instructional Television Experiment (SITE), which took direct TV broadcasting to some 2,400 villages in six states of India. ISRO supplied village community centres with television sets equipped with an antenna and receiver to catch SITE programming, and developed content for educating rural Indians on agriculture, sanitation, family planning and the basics of science.

The technology worked, and press reports were rhapsodic: a number of farmers had saved their crops because of SITE programming; villagers had mobbed a medical centre asking to be inoculated against smallpox; having television to watch in the evening had made the toddy shop less popular and reduced instances of drunk and disorderly behaviour. Midway through the SITE pilot, the multi-purpose Indian National Satellite System (INSAT) project was approved. The INSAT satellites, which one researcher described as 'a crowded Indian bus shot into space', were intentionally constructed to combine multiple disparate functions – more complex to make, but far cheaper to launch than two or three separate satellites. First launched in 1982, the INSAT satellites were equipped with modules for TV broadcasting, telecommunications, meteorology and remote sensing. The average Indian in the 1980s and 1990s made long distance calls via INSAT, watched the national news through it, and received weather alerts based on its cloud images.

With the INSAT system deployed, the percentage of India's population receiving television coverage went from 26 per cent in 1983 to 90 per cent in 2005. Two cyclones of similar intensity struck the state of Andhra Pradesh in 1977 and 1990, before and after INSAT's imaging allowed such weather events to be tracked. Around ten thousand lives were lost in the first, and fewer than a thousand in the second.

ISRO now has over twenty Earth observation satellites in orbit, used for a variety of applications across the country – from agriculture, forestry, weather forecasting, urban planning, and mineral exploration to water resource management. Sarabhai's vision, it might seem, was on its way to being realised.

In recent years, though, India's ambitions for its space programme have prioritised exploration over application. ISRO launched its first lunar orbiter mission, Chandrayaan-1, in 2008, subsequently finding signs of water on the Moon. In 2014 it put an orbiter around Mars. A journalist who has been covering the Indian space programme for decades recalls hearing a senior ISRO official say about the shift: 'We've done the bread and butter. Now we do the jam.'

In 2018, Prime minister Modi announced the *Gaganyaan* mission, a new ISRO programme devoted to human spaceflight. The aim was to launch a new set of Indian astronauts into space by 2022, to coincide with seventy-five years of Indian independence. Delays have pushed the launch of that mission back to 2027, and the project is currently set to cost $2.3 billion. (In comparison, ISRO's Mars Orbiter Mission cost around $74 million.) The government has since set out an even larger vision for ISRO, which now includes having a wholly Indian space station operational by 2035, and putting an Indian on the Moon by 2040.

Are the benefits from such missions worth the expense? These are complex and costly projects, designed to enhance national prestige without necessarily breaking new scientific ground or contributing to socioeconomic development. A broad set of indigenous capabilities in space, however, may be vital for a future in which countries look beyond the Earth for energy and resources. A clue to Sarabhai's thoughts on the matter might be found in an article he wrote titled 'Space Activity for Developing Countries': 'There is a real danger that developing nations may adopt a space program largely for . . . glamour, devoting resources not through a recognition of the values of which we are talking about here, but from a desire to create a sham image nationally and internationally.'

The BJP-led government had image firmly in mind when it declared the date of the Chandrayaan-3 Moon landing – 23 August 2023 – National Space Day. New textbook modules were promptly issued for school courses across the country. One linked India's ancient past with the modern space programme by listing examples of various flying vehicles mentioned in the Vedas and epics. This ancient evidence, the modules claim, 'reveals our civilisation had the knowledge of flying vehicles in those days', alongside 'details of construction, working of engines and the gyroscopic systems'. The achievements of the Indian space programme signalled nothing less than the revival of a thwarted civilisation.

Currently, ISRO has two operational launchpads at Sriharikota, and a new spaceport is being developed in Tamil Nadu for small satellite launches. But its ability to put satellites into space is limited, since it is only able to undertake about a dozen major launches a year. It has not yet developed a true heavy-lift launch vehicle capable of carrying twenty tonnes or more into low Earth orbit. By comparison, SpaceX can manage something like a hundred launches a year, and has rockets that are several times more powerful than ISRO.

The cheap satellite market is firmly dominated by the US and private enterprises like SpaceX. Still, India is determined to compete. In 2023, ISRO released a new space policy that creates a framework for private space companies to participate in the Indian space programme. ISRO will be the primary agency for research and exploration activities in space. Its commercial arm – NewSpace India Limited (NSIL) – will transfer technology to private players for commercial launches and satellite building. Around 250 start-ups already operate in the space sector, though it's early days yet. With the continuing involvement of private entities, ISRO hopes to quadruple the Indian share of the space economy by 2033.

India's intended future path in space is beginning to feel no different to that of other countries.

Nineteenth April 2025 marked the fiftieth anniversary of the launch of Aryabhata. I attended the commemorative event at Bengaluru's Jawaharlal Nehru Planetarium, where an auditorium was packed with schoolchildren. M. Sankaran, the director of U.R. Rao Satellite Centre, delivered the inaugural address.

Standing at a lectern in front of a rotating model of Aryabhata, Sankaran spoke about the plight of the nation in the 1960s and early 1970s. There was recurrent food shortage, and grain was being brought in through foreign aid. Three events, he said, deeply affected the psyche of young people in the decade that followed, and contributed to the subsequent rise of India. The first was the Bangladesh liberation war of 1971, in which India decisively routed US-backed Pakistan. The second was the country's first successful test of a nuclear weapon in 1974. The third was the launch of the Aryabhata in 1975. These were symbols, Sankaran said, 'of a rising power which dares to imagine that we can get rid of our shackles of poverty and work towards high economic prosperity as well as technological superiority'.

A.S. Kiran Kumar, a former ISRO chairman, began tossing out

questions to the crowd during his speech. The schoolkids certainly seemed to have their facts in order.

He asked if they knew when the first satellite was put into space. 'Which was the year?'

'Nineteen fifty-seven,' came the scattered response.

'How many years after our independence?'

'Ten.' Stronger this time.

Kiran Kumar reminded the audience that India was the only country to start a space programme for non-military activities. 'Why was India doing this? It is because, as was pointed out, it was trying to regain its position, which was . . .' he waited for the audience to respond.

'In the early millennia, where do you think India was? Was it at the top of the table or the bottom of the table?'

'Top.'

'From the top of the table it had come down, but it resumed its journey after independence. And now today you are the – *dash* – largest economy?'

'Fourth.'

'Very soon you want to become?'

This response was an easy chorus: 'First!' ■

BLANK.

BECAUSE WE LIKE TO LEAVE THE
SPOTLIGHT TO TALENTED AUTHORS.

INDIAN ORBITS

Keerthana Kunnath

Introduction by Granta

JERWOOD PHOTOGRAPHY COMMISSIONS

India's first satellite, Aryabhata, went up in 1975 on a Soviet rocket. It blinked in and out of contact over four days before eventually losing signal, more a proof of concept than a machine of profit. By the time it crashed back into the Earth's atmosphere in 1992, it was best known for gracing the ₹2 banknote. The satellite industry in India today is, by contrast, a big business. In under a decade, the country's space economy is expected to grow to $44 billion.

This summer, the photographer Keerthana Kunnath travelled to the new sites of India's interstellar ambition. She captured the people and places assembling the country's second space age. Dhruva Space, based in Hyderabad, makes modular satellites for commercial, defence and scientific missions. AgniKul Cosmos, in Chennai, is wagering on customisable rockets built with 3D-printed engines, a bid to give India its own quick-turn launch capacity. Pixxel, founded by two engineers in their twenties, is building a series of advanced imaging satellites, promising to precisely map the Earth's skin through hundreds of spectral bands. ∎

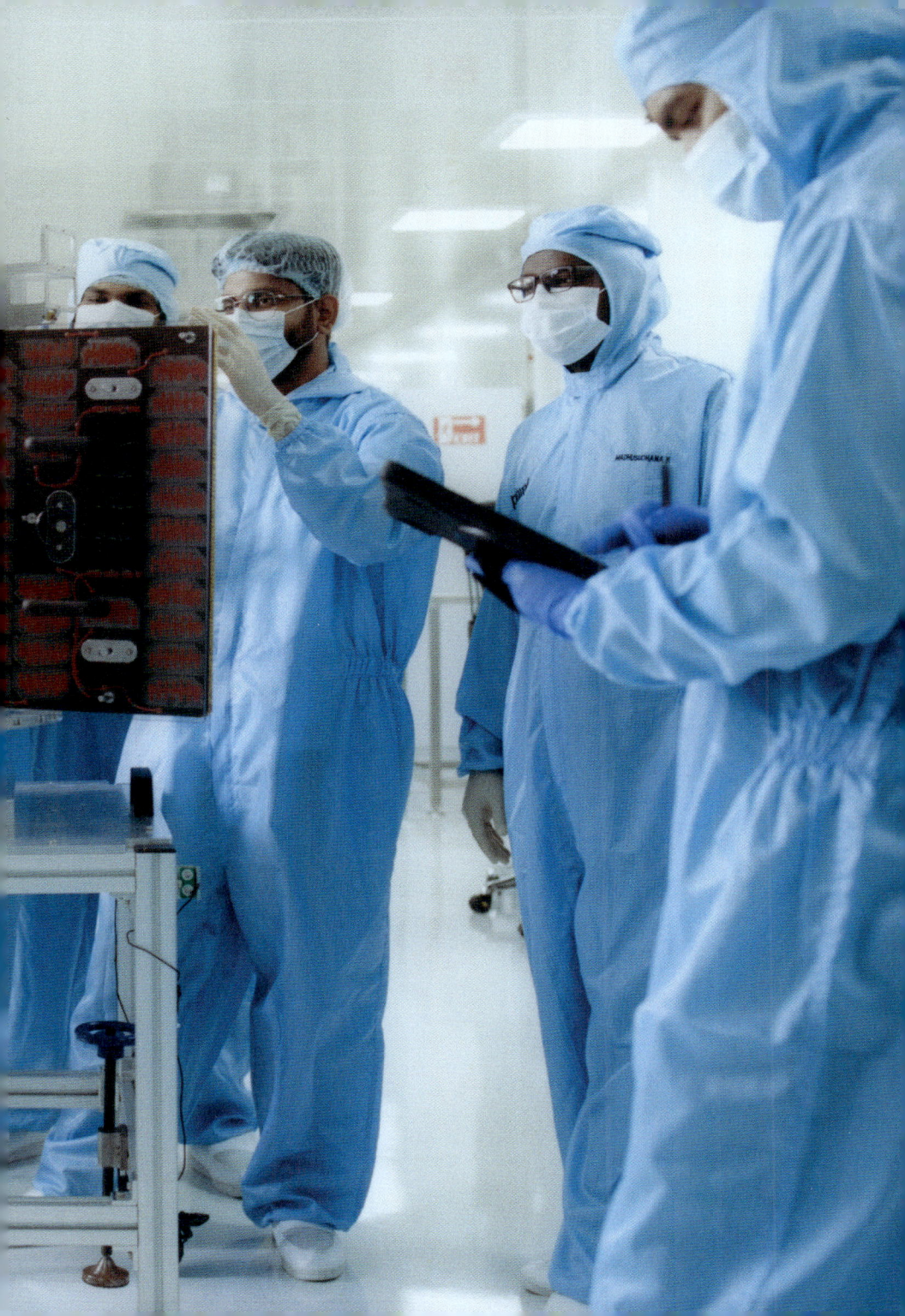

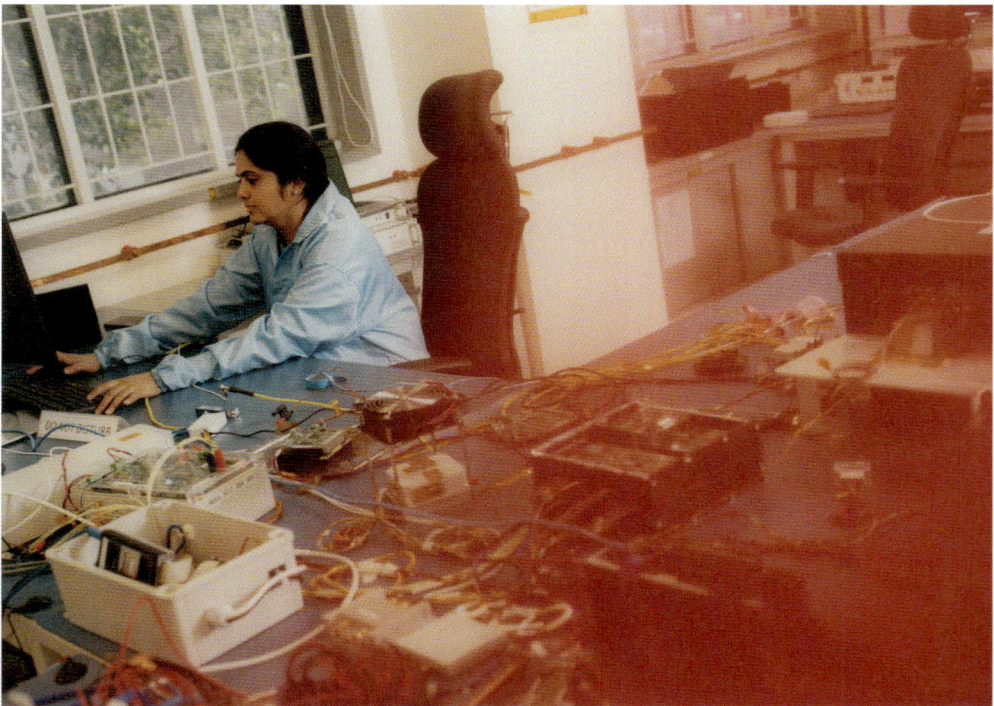

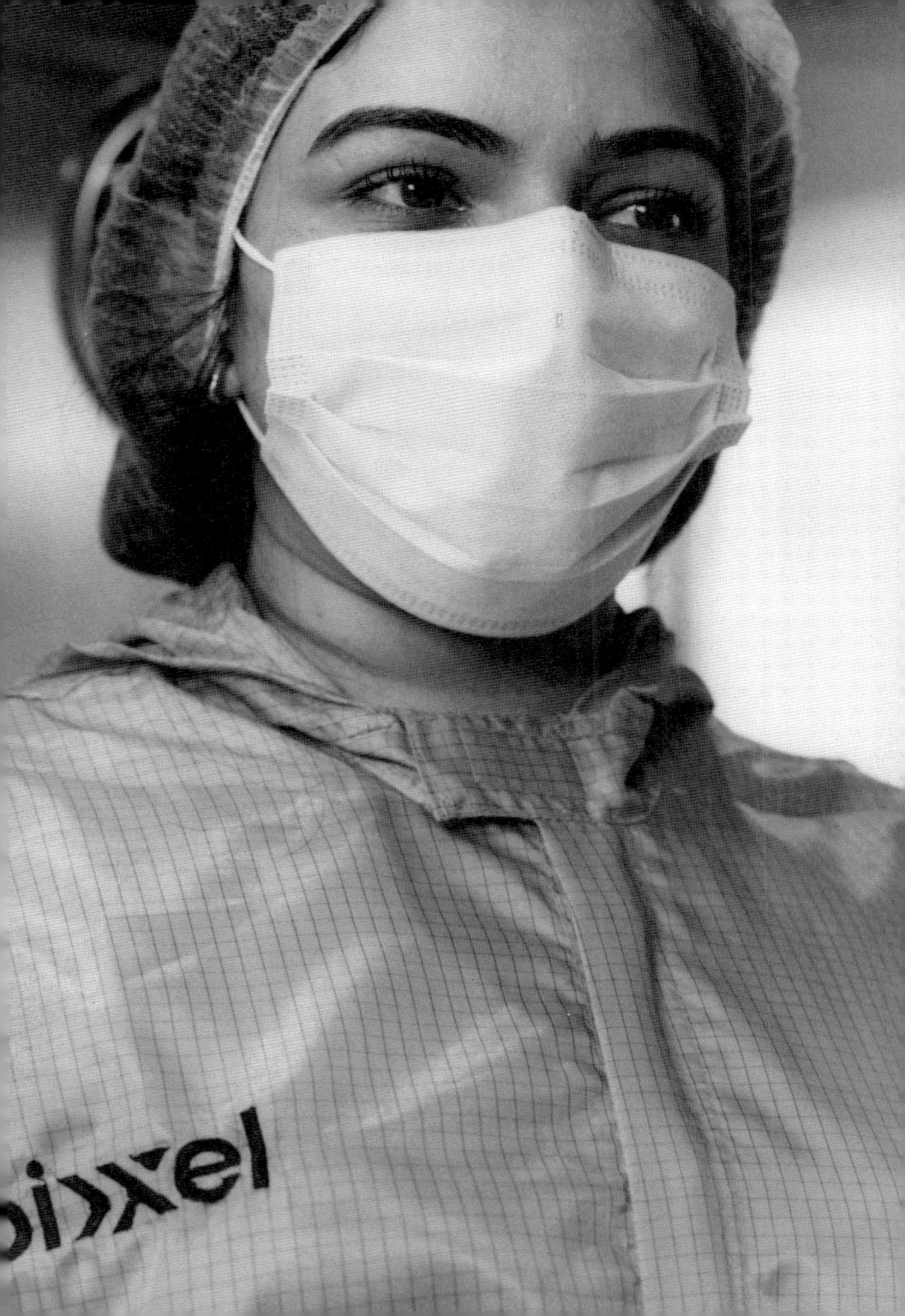

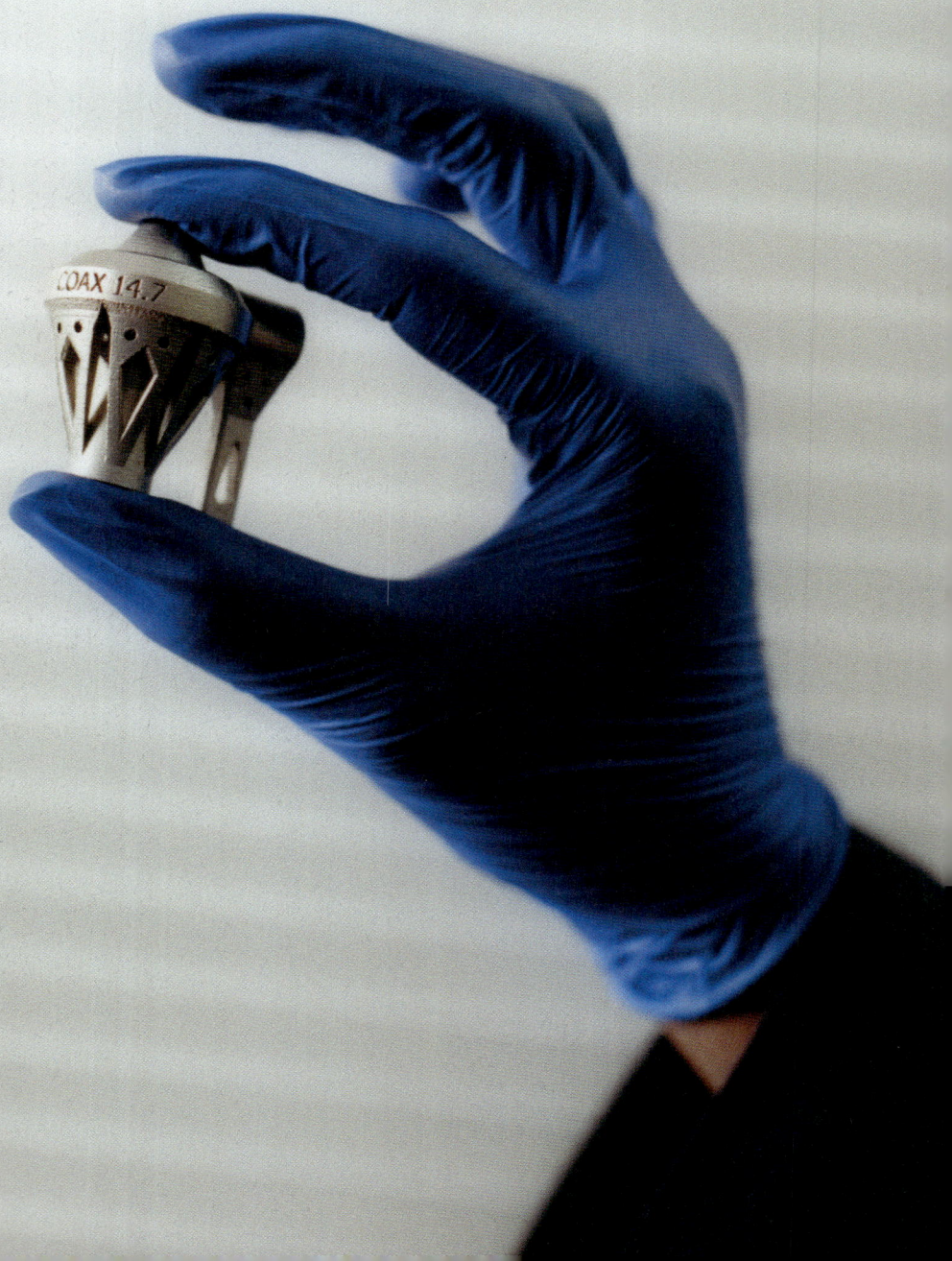

The 2025 Hawthornden Prize for Literature

has been awarded to

Manya Wilkinson

for

LUBLIN

Published by And Other Stories

Hawthornden
Foundation

& And
Other
Stories

WHERE THE NORTH ENDS

A novel by Hugo Moreno

After a fatal crash, Uriel wakes in colonial New Mexico,
accused of heresy. His only way out is fleeing with an Apache shaman
who's hunting him down. Will he be killed? Condemned? Saved?

"Imaginative and unpredictable."
—Kirkus Reviews

Published by UNM Press / Distributed by Simon & Schuster

www.hugos.site

اردو

'*Saalgira,*' the voice of a junior official growled from the immigration office on the Pakistani side, his face and salwar kameez-clad figure hardly distinguishable in the daytime darkness of the room.

It was 2002. I had just crossed by foot from India into Pakistan, over one of the most militarised borders in the world. That August there were tensions between the two countries, threats of nuclear war, and the crossing was deserted. Paddy fields stretched out on all sides, oblivious to the wall of barbed wire that ran like a cicatrice between them. Now and then, through the rain-filled heat of the day, I made out the morose cry of a koel.

I am half Indian, half Pakistani. I grew up in Delhi (the love child of an Indian journalist and a Pakistani politician), and a few weeks before this crossing I had made a journey to Lahore to seek out my estranged father. I'd succeeded in meeting him and, in putting a face to the phantom, rid myself of the gravitational power absences can exert. I had also met a brood of half-siblings, and was returning now for my sister's twenty-fifth birthday. Because of my name, the immigration officer assumed I was of Pakistani origin and travelling on a British passport, a man returning home from a visit to the dark side. He asked me, in a perfunctory sort of way, why I was coming to Pakistan. I said, 'for my sister's birthday', but the word I used – *janamdin,* not *saalgira* – gave me away as someone who could only have grown up in India. The man's 'saalgira' in response was not so much a correction as it was a warning to someone outwardly familiar that their attempt to pass for something they were not had failed. The sympathy for me in the room had evaporated, and was replaced by suspicion.

Hindi and Urdu are like two, fluid, shape-shifting sisters, yin and yang, each containing a measure of the other. Their syntax and structure are identical, but whereas Urdu draws its vocabulary from Persian and Arabic, Hindi in post-Partition India has become Sanskritised. The former is written in Nastaliq, an Arabic script; the latter in the Devanagari script, in letters that Gabriel García Márquez once memorably described as 'clothes hung out on a line'. Both emerged from the same catchment area, namely the natural language of undivided North India, and neither had any distinct identity until colonial times. Even the word Urdu, derived from the Turkish for 'army' and cognate with the English 'horde', came very late into use as a name for the language. Mirza Ghalib (1797–1869), Urdu's greatest poet, would, in a wonderful irony, have thought himself a poet of Hindvi, or Rekhta. He would have landed on several other descriptors, such as Dehalvi, Gujri and Dakhini, for the language he wrote in, before arriving at Urdu. To him, Urdu was less a language than a shorthand for the city of Delhi – an abbreviation of '*zabaan-e-urdu-e mu'alla-e Shahjahanabad*', or 'the language of the exalted camp of Mughal Delhi'. 'No discussion can now afford to ignore the fact,' writes the Urdu scholar Shamsur Rahman Faruqi, 'that there *are* two claimants to a single linguistic and literary tradition, and that the whole issue is more political than academic.'

The story of how one became two is in miniature the story of how a syncretic Hindu, Muslim and Sikh culture in North India was unravelled. The schism can be dated to the establishment of Fort William College in Calcutta in 1800. There, under the auspices of British administrators like John Gilchrist, who were training civil servants and devising textbooks, the shared language of the North was subjected to the violence of a classification along religious lines – Hindi for Hindus and Urdu for Muslims. The absurdity of the division was to be felt even a century later by men like Munshi Premchand (1880–1936), a writer claimed by both languages. I once asked his grandson how Premchand had navigated these treacherous waters. 'He wrote in Urdu,' he told me, 'then he handed his typescript to a stenographer, and said, "*Hindi banado*" – make it Hindi.' The stenographer then went through the text and replaced all the big Perso-Arabic words with Sanskrit equivalents.

India and Pakistan have been separate countries now for almost eighty years, yet the people of these two societies still speak to each

اردو

other with such ease that it can seem as if they've grown up under the same roof. The survival of this shared demotic, running like an underground semantic stream between the two countries, is, for want of a better word, referred to as 'Hindustani'. In India, with its 170 million Muslims, the plurality of which are spread out across the Urdu heartland in the northern states of Uttar Pradesh and Bihar, daily usage is replete with Urdu words. This is without mentioning Bollywood, which plays a large role in preserving a colloquial, shared language. The same was not true of Pakistan. Here, the ear of usage had been infected with religio-national feeling, and in saying 'janamdin' I had given myself away, like a German spy in wartime Britain, unable to recall the verses of a famous nursery rhyme.

Five years later I sat down with an Urdu poet from the old city of Delhi, the 'camp-market' that lent its name to its language, to learn the Nastaliq script. My paternal grandfather was an Urdu poet. I had been named after his main poetic work – *Aatish-kada*, or Fire Temple. My great uncle, Faiz Ahmed Faiz, was among the most important Urdu poets of the modern era. It was a source of embarrassment to me that I could not read their work in the script in which it was written, even though – such are the ironic symmetries created by Partition! – my Sikh grandfather, who came across to India as a refugee in 1947, naturally could.

Zafar Moradabadi, my poet-teacher, was a delicate man, in a safari suit, sunglasses and a white peaked cap. He was full of grief at the division of language into religious camps. But for all his melancholy, he balked at the idea of Urdu written in the Devanagari script – which has been done now for decades in India. 'A script,' he said, bristling at my impertinence, 'contains the very spirit of a language.' Though he would not countenance Urdu being written in Hindi, he was adamant that the soul of Urdu lay not in its purity, but its colloquialism. He loved to tell the story of the English administrator who, claiming to have mastered all of Urdu, approached a poet and boasted of his achievement. 'Then surely you must know what a divot is?' the poet asked. The Englishman was mystified. The poet wanted him to see that this commonplace English word had as much right to be part of Urdu's lexicon as grander words in Persian and Arabic. I remember once asking the Urdu lyricist Javed Akhtar if, in referring to 'death', I should use the Hindi *dehant* or the Urdu *inteqal*. Javed looked at me aghast. 'You must only ever say *death*,' he said, using the English word, '*unki* death *ho gayi* – their death has occurred.'

Urdu was an answer to the riddle of India's three-tiered history – British, Muslim, Hindu. It derived its vitality from its talent for adjusting to the natural register of every new time. It was the queen of demotics, a joyfully low language, the *vox populi* cocking a snook at the Academy. This is also what makes translation out of Urdu so difficult. When I sat down to translate into English the work of one of Urdu's best short story writers, Saadat Hassan Manto, I was struck by the genius of how, in this land of three natures, the spoken language deployed different words for the same thing to convey different meanings. Consider the case of the word 'traveller'. The Sanskrit, *yatri*, evoked pilgrimage. The Urdu, *musaffir*, conjured up a caravanserai, a moonlit night, a hint of romance and danger, whereas the English 'traveller' immediately brought to mind the sterility of modern tourism. Manto loved it all, revelling in the language's many registers.

The tragedy of North India and Pakistan – of Hindi and Urdu – is that this delicate scheme of sound and meaning by which words come over time to be imbued with subtle distinctions has been wrenched from the hands of its most able practitioners – the novelists, poets, filmmakers and lyricists who write a language into being. It is now the province of politicians determined to make language the locus of historical erasure. Taken to its natural conclusion, India's home minister Amit Shah would lose his own surname, for 'shah' is an old Persian word for king. But autocrats are never deterred by absurdity. They thrive on it. ∎

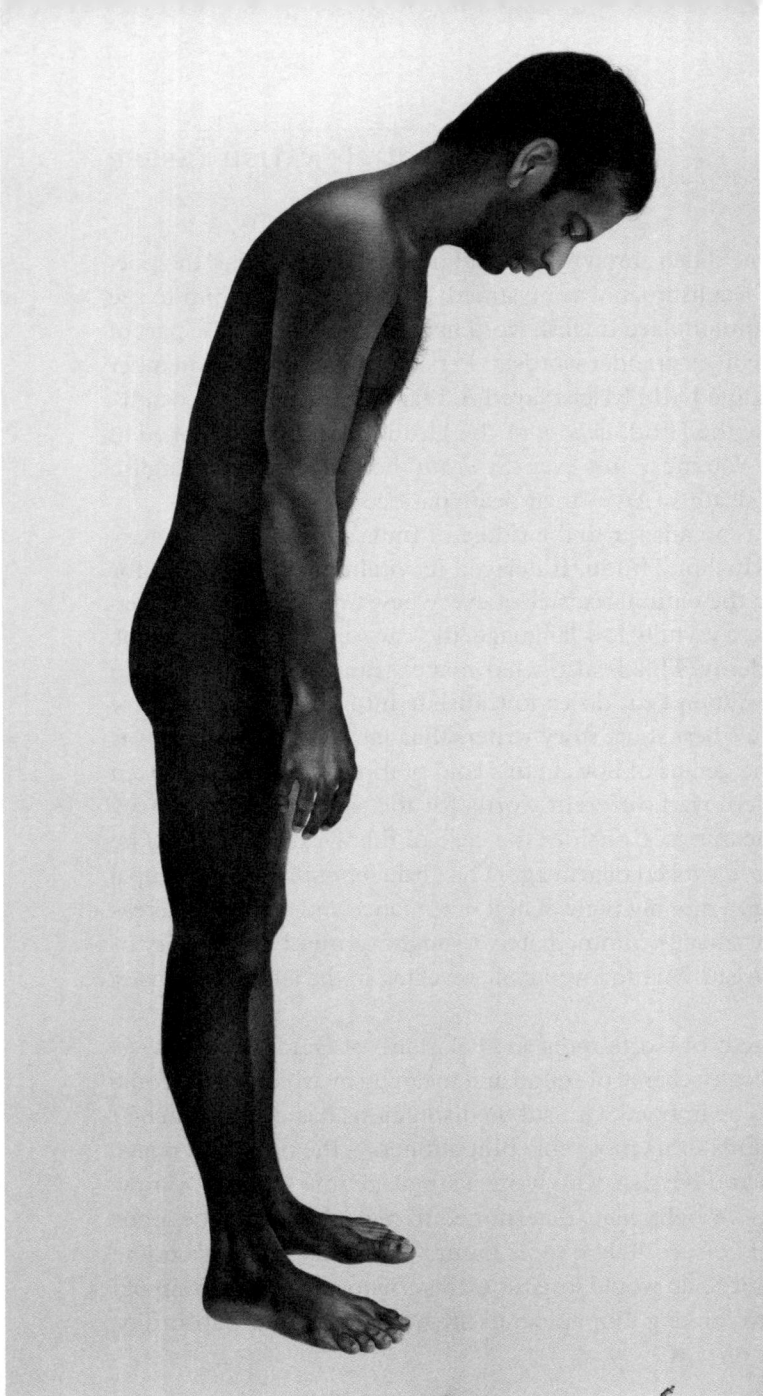

ALI KAZIM
Untitled (Self Portrait), 2012
Courtesy of Cristea Roberts Gallery

A PUBLIC CIRCUMCISION

Saharu Nusaiba Kannanari

Sulfee parked his car in the shed and got out. Ayishumma, his mother, squatted in the yard and husked coconuts using a billhook with a bare tang. Zeenath, his sister, sat on a chair picking her ear with a feather. Her twelve-year-old daughter Paathu greeted her uncle with her latest grin – the grin with a missing bicuspid. Sulfee returned the grin and hurried straight to his room and bolted the door. He took off his mundu and shirt and robed his waist in a bath towel. He pulled the curtains shut. Thinking, not wanting to think. He turned towards the mirror on the almirah. Looking, not wanting to look. A moustachioed oblong face with thick arching brows and black eyes and coarse curly hair and long whiskers and stubbly cheeks and smoker's lips and a bulbous nose and a protuberant chin. He loosened the towel and let it drop to his feet. In the mirror was a bare anatomy that no one other than him had seen. He looked at the upper part of his body, the thick boxer's neck and strong swimmer's shoulders. His chest was hairless except in the midriff and around the nipples and the belly. He did not look beneath his belly. He did not want to, lacked the daring to. This was the most Muslim of embarrassments. To host an uncircumcised dick. To go around carrying a forty-year-old uncircumcised dick in a district full of circumcised dicks. His dick in its Adamic state was directly responsible for this late crisis in his political life and he looked at the culprit without wanting to. This heretic without a cause. This hermit without a choice in his crotch. It looked awful.

As a child the future communist revolutionary was afflicted with aichmophobia, an irrational fear of sharp metal objects. Knives, needles, scissors, broken glass and the like. While in children a mite of aichmophobia is universal, its degree and severity in him was exceptional, a fear which grew more intense and stubborn as he grew older, hitting hysterical peaks by the age of six, already too late for circumcision according to local standards.

Even as a toddler, Sulfee had established a reputation in the neighbourhood for his extraordinary fear of needles and shaving blades. He almost bit off the polio vaccinator's earring. He pulled off a grey chunk of hair from the chest of a barber trying to tonsure his head. He spat on a nurse who tried to give him a tetanus shot. His bowels gave way when they stitched a minor gash on his elbow after a fall. But the fear of shaving blades occupied a higher place in the hierarchy of his fears because they were a weekly terror, an assured nightmare. Kerala, in the early eighties, still saw villagers cutting their nails using either a knife or shaving blade, and Ayishumma was no different. It was a bloody affair, wounds forever on her fingers, and, tired of wrestling with her son, in 1988, when he was four, she brought home a nail-cutter, becoming the first in the neighbourhood to own one. For a long time the nail-cutter was the only sharp metal object he would allow to touch his body.

Yet nothing scared him as much as his impending circumcision. They did it with special super-sharp knives, the other kids said. The barber did it, a specialised barber, not a doctor, whose employability towards the holy task was yet to gain traction in the town of Areekode and its surrounding villages. The barber did it raw, without numbing your dick, they said. One mistake and you are dickless for life, they laughed and worried. Those who had already been circumcised bragged of their temerity and those who awaited their turn confessed to their timidity in anticipation, and both those who had already undergone the circumcision by the barber or witnessed the event gave graphic descriptions of how it's done – with men holding you down spreadeagled to the bed by your limbs – and recounted anecdotal horrors which steadily solidified in him a terrifying mythology, with the image of a goateed barber wielding his special knives and scissors at its centre. At four and five in the morning Sulfee started waking up from nightmares with his hands in his crotch, sweating like a steam-bather.

Ayishumma was puzzled. The boy was so traumatised that, by the time he was five, she couldn't take him on a casual tour of the town because in her every move he suspected a conspiracy afoot to deliver him to a barber, to circumcise him. Five was already late for circumcision but six was certainly unusual and pressure from kith and kin was mounting on her. That's when Mr Abdullaaji – the president of the local mosque – dropped by to enrol new kids at the madrasa, where Sulfee was supposed to have joined the previous year to start learning Arabic grammar, Islamic law and history and the Qur'an. Why the delay?

Ayishumma gave away the reason: her son wasn't circumcised.

She explained the story in detail. She said the prospect of earning his consent looked next to impossible. The president listened. He told her of a Byzantine emperor who called Prophet Muhammad the King of the Circumcised and laughed. Then his face turned halfway serious. He said in madrasa the kids were going to handle the Qur'an daily and it was auspicious to touch it as a proper Muslim, a complete Muslim, not a partial one, and a Muslim was not fully a Muslim until the prepuce was gone. Then he told her something that was even more dumbly persuasive. The president advised her to use force. 'If the kid grows up uncircumcised,' he said, 'one day he's going to find out that he's the only grown-up man with a foreskin in the community and he'll blame the shame and embarrassment on you because it is incumbent on the parents to do the things they need to do to the child with or without their consent, so that when the child grows up he doesn't feel exceptional in his own community. Circumcision is at the top of the ladder.'

This wasn't a possibility Ayishumma had reckoned with in her career as a single mother – her grown-up son accusing her of depriving him his inalienable right as a Muslim to a timely circumcised penis – and the president's hilarious but bleak forecast struck a chord. She had to raise her voice now to stop the boy from raising his later. She had deprived the kid the right to a normal father already. To deny him his right to a circumcised penis would be too much to bear. The boy had to be circumcised. So far she had only cajoled and scolded and badgered, had resisted dragooning him by deceptive or coercive means despite the burgeoning frustration. But now she decided to use force.

She telegrammed her estranged husband – a stevedore in Lakshadweep, where he had a family of his own – about her decision, asking him to board the next ship home. He did. She summoned her only sister home and requested her husband's hands in the deed. She talked to two immediate neighbours and requested their help in the matter, too. So, on the morning of the appointed day, on the appointed hour, four men lay in wait in the house as the barber walked in with his kit of legendary tools.

It was seven thirty in the morning and the boy was conveniently asleep. Ayishumma went out and left Zeenath – who was just three then – with a neighbour and came back. The plan was to wake and overpower him, stretch him flat on the bed, arms and legs splayed wide.

Ayishumma stood guard at Sulfee's doors to stop him from fleeing in case he happened to rouse before his routine time, which usually came past eight thirty, her ears alert and eyes unsure, giving her face a dramatic calm. They were old heavy doors made of mango timber, which did not turn on metal hinges, but in round grooves dug into the upper and lower frame and opened with unpredictable creaks. Ayishumma had to be cautious here not to wake the boy. She lifted one half of the door just a little from the bottom groove and spun it open without even a faint groan. The men moved in one after the other. She closed the door with equal care and stood outside just as before, alert, in case he managed to wrest himself free from their clutches and made a dash for the door by dint of some manoeuvre she knew he was perfectly capable of pulling off even if the men in the room didn't. Worse, she counted on him for it. She waited anxiously for the screaming to begin. It did, followed by swear words she had never heard before. She covered her ears with her hands.

They tamed him quickly, this brittle-boned kid, thin and rather too tall for his age. They woke him up gently and let him realise what it was all about before pinning him down in unison, each man with a limb under his control. '*Bismillahirahmanuraheem*,' the barber threatened with an elfish grin, brandishing a shiny knife in one hand and a pair of stainless-steel scissors in the other, setting off a frantic scream in the kid's throat, which was unlike anything he had ever heard in his five-decade-long career in dick-cropping. He worried the scream could rupture the kid's gullet. That worry was soon replaced by disbelief at the obscenities that followed. He was astounded that this child's mouth was the source of these words. Screaming he was used to, but not this relentless hail of profanities. The barber ordered the boy's mouth shut and the father, who was in charge of his son's left hand, covered his mouth with one hand, allowing his grip around the wrist to loosen a little. The barber climbed onto the bed and kneeled and leaned down on his elbows, bringing his head super-close to the boy's penis, which he lifted with his left index finger and studied with a circumciser's eye.

First Sulfee spritzed those eyes with a forceful jet of hot morning piss, then he squeezed his father's balls hard under his mundu with his left hand.

The barber let go of the penis with a couple of remarkable portmanteau obscenities of his own while the father, an amply bearded Tablighi, with his balls crushing in the palm of the child of their own laborious making, screamed, provoking a confused Ayishumma to open the door and peer in. Urine continued to flow in full force, wetting the bed and making the uncle in charge of Sulfee's left leg let go, laughing at the barber, not knowing that the leg he had just released was going to launch a kick at the barber. The barber, confused in the quickly ensuing mayhem, tried to dodge the kick, but the hand with the scissors was in the foot's way and the scissors hit the man's piss-filled eyes, thankfully handle-wise and when his eyes were closed, but knocking him off balance nonetheless and toppling him down to the floor. Everyone rushed for the septuagenarian, even Ayishumma, even the father who had just managed to wrest his balls free from his son's patricidal grasp, leaving Sulfee's limbs free for a moment, allowing him to escape.

The event plunged mother and son into a month-long cold war. He refused to acknowledge her presence in the house. She sent his father back to Lakshadweep. Entreaties and feelers failed to attenuate his anger or thaw his resolve not to talk to her. What could have placated him was exactly what she was not willing to offer in exchange for his acknowledgement of her in this house of three – the olive branch called the Promise of No Circumcision.

Yet her determination weakened and a month later she offered him her own version of what he wanted with a caveat. Let's fake a circumcision, she said. She proposed a pact: he would circumcise as soon as he was a little older and less afraid of blades and scissors and needles. He promised. And that's what the mother and the son had done. They faked a circumcision. One morning she told her sister that they were going to Kozhikode town to check into a private hospital for a painless procedure. They set out in the morning and returned in the evening, walking past shops and houses, in full view of the villagers, hand in hand, with Sulfee holding his gold-bordered polyester mundu a little away from his belly as if to protect the fresh wound of the circumcision from rough contact with the cloth, rather too believably like a really circumcised boy. She threw a feast of buff to the extended family the next day to lend their story greater credibility and opened the doors of Sulfee's room to exhibit him as he lay on his back in his staged convalescence, with the centre of the sheet over him tied with a rope to a rafter in the roof, again to protect the non-existent wound from accidental friction. Nobody removed and peered inside the sheet to verify the veracity of the account; they were instructed not to. Ayishumma had alerted them that the boy was too shy and embarrassed and angry and they obliged. It was a believable story because these well-wishers were too relieved to see Ayishumma so relieved to allow suspicious thoughts to occur. And so the fiction stuck. Sulfee was officially circumcised without having been circumcised, a normal Muslim boy among normal Muslim boys, offering prayers in the mosque and reading the Qur'an in the madrasa – normal except in pissing. He did not piss with other boys any more, he made sure to wear underwear beneath the towel even when he went swimming, he shunned public urinals and company elsewhere as well. He prolonged his urge. He chose his moment. He waited for privacy. For once in life he was obedient to his mother's advice, advice he had abided by all his life. And nobody doubted the claim that he was circumcised. It was unheard of to have suspected a family of faking a circumcision. It was unheard of to have faked a circumcision at all.

Three years passed and his mother reminded him of his promise. She knew his aichmophobia was gone, she knew the boy couldn't go on forever with an uncircumcised penis and she was acutely aware of and concerned about its sure ramifications for a Muslim man. She repeated the reminder when he was ten, twelve, fifteen, as late as eighteen. Thereafter she never did, and here he was twenty-two years later, looking at his penis in the mirror with new eyes, regretting not heeding his wise mother's request, wondering if his mother was also troubled about his predicament, set to be unravelled by the impending marriage. He wondered if she was also expecting Sulfee to finagle a miracle against all odds, just like his Communist Party in the elections? He believed she was. He knew she was. ∎

SANJIT DAS
Chhattisgarh, 2010
Panos Pictures

THE THIN RED CORRIDOR

Snigdha Poonam

There is no comfort in driving down a road once lined with landmines, even if your companion is the one who put them there. 'We planted them on both sides, so a vehicle would blow up right upon entering – and many did,' Bada Vikas told me. I looked in the rear-view mirror. The driver's face had contracted in terror. Vikas was enjoying himself.

We were on our way to the base of Burha Pahad, the mountain range in the eastern state of Jharkhand. The range stretches across the Latehar district, 110 km west of Ranchi, the state capital, where I grew up. With its steep ravines and thick clusters of sal and teak trees, it is an ideal host for guerrilla warfare. Just a few years ago, the area was still a stronghold of Maoist fighters. The Indian state has devoted enormous resources to eradicating them. But in the forests of Jharkhand, amid the fledgling eco-resorts built to attract tourists, some of the Maoists still hold their ground.

Vikas did not seem concerned by the dozens of armed police we saw scanning the roadside. From his neat clothes and demeanor, he looks more like a man used to working behind a desk than a former insurgent. Forty-seven years old and nearly six feet tall, he has a voice that seems accustomed to issuing commands. For many years, since he was eighteen, Vikas was a Maoist guerrilla leader. Despite his departure from that world, he still feels at ease in the forest and has no regrets about his years of fighting. The landmines he'd once planted here were small contributions to the cause. 'Had we not laid them, the police would have entered the forest,' he told me. That would have meant the end – for him, his comrades, and the parallel government they ran with the ultimate aim of replacing the Indian state.

What did they want to replace the state with? He called it 'sarvahara satta' – the old phrase from Marx, 'the dictatorship of the proletariat'. It may sound antique to some ears, even quaint, but for the run-down people of Jharkhand, one of the poorest regions in India, it acquired a currency that none of the other twentieth century's ideologies ever matched.

For decades, parts of central and eastern India have been home to two intertwined movements: the Adivasis and the Maoists. The Adivasis are the Indigenous peoples of the land. They speak their own languages, and many live off what they reap from the forest. Their customs, from marriage to inheritance, differ sharply from the largely agrarian, caste-bound Hindu traditions of the surrounding cities. In the nineteenth century, the Adivasis made up one of the most determined revolts against the British Empire, with a 7,000-strong army rallied by the leader Birsa Munda. After Independence, Jaipal Singh Munda, a Christianised Adivasi who was educated at Oxford and captained India's hockey team at the 1928 Olympics, became their champion in India's first parliament. The Adivasis have never ceased to campaign for their own state within India, but their fortunes only seemed to change in the late 1990s, when the Bharatiya Janata Party (BJP), looking to undermine the Congress Party's vote share in the region, promised the Adivasis more regional autonomy. The gambit worked spectacularly, and in 2000, the Indian parliament approved the carve-out of a new Indian state out of Bihar called Jharkhand, which means 'land of forests'.

The Maoist insurgency developed alongside the struggles of Adivasis, and often incorporated them into its ranks. 'Naxalism', as the movement is known, started in the late 1960s with a peasant revolt against feudal conditions in Naxalbari, in rural West Bengal. Inspired by the original Maoists of China, radical-left cadres, many of them disenchanted Brahmins, mobilised villagers, many of them Adivasis, in armed attacks against the land-owning zamindars. From there, 'Naxalism' as an ideology, and a method, quickly spread across the eastern and central states of India, drawing in tribal peoples and peasants. Gradually, internal divisions splintered the movement into dozens of 'Naxal' groups, each staking out its own base and defining particular class enemies.

'Maoism' – or what goes under that heading – made deep inroads among the Adivasi and tribal populations, partly because they were a group with which the other Indian social movements of the twentieth century failed to engage. Gandhi rejected class warfare and believed landlords could be persuaded to end exploitation, while the national project of Nehru never identified a place for the Adivasis. The only movements that made a real impact on the local populations were Christianity and Maoism, both of which took caste directly into their sights and made a point of elevating people through schools. Even after Jharkhand became its own state in 2000, a significant portion of the oppressed population was still not satisfied. They found that Hindu upper castes continued to wield power over them, from politics to job opportunities to land rights. It was left to the Maoists to continue radicalising succeeding generations in the area and beyond.

When the state of Jharkhand was created, my father became an administrator with the government. He was posted to Koderma, 170 km north-west of Ranchi, on the border with Bihar. Koderma is an old railway town with a mixed population of tribals and non-tribals, with rich reserves of mica. Formal mining had declined since the 1980s – the forests had been nearly stripped bare – but local contractors carried on the trade openly. In the illegal mines, whole tribal families, including children, were employed. Like other districts sharing a border with Bihar, Koderma was rife with Maoist activity. My father remembers, 'It was difficult in those days to draw clear lines between ordinary villagers, Naxal sympathisers and cadres themselves.' 'The police units used to recite prayers before driving into the rural areas; the threat of landmines was constant,' my mother added. 'One day, a unit of Maoists charged into a police camp. Some said young women were leading the charge. They blew up the camp with explosives and ran away.' When I combed through the news reports of the period, I found one account after another about Maoists attacking police stations. Since its creation, Jharkhand has never allowed the Indian state to rest comfortably.

Earlier this year, the home minister of India, Amit Shah, declared March 2026 the deadline for wiping out India's seven-decade-old Maoist insurgency. The insurgency has long occupied what Indian newspapers call the Red Corridor, which runs as an overlapping chain through eastern, central and southern states. At its peak, in the late 2000s, Naxalism encompassed more than 200 districts across the rural heartlands, boasting anywhere between 20,000 to 25,000 armed cadres. By 2024, government offensives had reduced the insurgency to fewer than fifty districts with significant activity. But in the India of Narendra Modi, the fear of small numbers runs high.

Over the past year, security forces have mounted an aggressive push into some of their strongest bases. In Chhattisgarh, their central bastion, police and paramilitary units, sometimes numbering more than 5,000 personnel, moved in coordinated sweeps to take out entire guerrilla units. In January, a joint operation by multiple police and security forces killed Ramachandra Reddy, alias Chalapathi, a prominent leader. In February, a forest raid in Bijapur gunned down thirty-one insurgents. Then in May came the most successful strike. A brutal attack on a unit in Abujhmarh forest near Narayanpur brought down India's highest-ranking Maoist: general-secretary Nambala Keshava Rao, aka Comrade Basavaraju. Twenty-six of his close associates were shot down in the same attack. All of these actions were celebrated in the Indian press like the extermination of pests.

Since 2000, more than 10,000 Maoists are estimated to have surrendered nationwide, though many of them were merely fellow travellers or low-level figures. I knew the story of the insurgency from my parents, from the media, and through my contacts in the state police. But what I wanted was to meet someone from the other side. 'There is someone you could meet,' an officer with the state police force, whose phone number I got from an old school friend, told me. It was a big fish, he explained. At the time of his surrender in 2015, the man was among Jharkhand's most wanted Maoists – one who inspired as much terror among the police as he commanded respect among the people. Yet he gave it all up to pursue the ordinary life of a villager.

B ada Vikas was waiting for me in the office of the state police, where he had agreed to meet me. My contact in the police introduced us, then left us alone to talk. He began to unfurl the story of his life to me. He came from a family of Oraons, one of Jharkhand's thirty-two Adivasi tribes. Unlike the majority of Oraons in Donki – his village – who were sharecroppers and sold forest produce for a living, his family owned a sizeable acreage of ancestral land: 'A full sixty acres.' But despite their holdings, they still lived at the mercy of upper-caste landowners of the larger estates, who made demands on them and the other local tribespeople, continuing the feudal practice of zamindari. 'At planting season, we had to leave our farms, tilled and ready for sowing, to go and work on their fields.'

Even though most Indian states officially abolished the zamindari system by 1956, the landlords have continued to hold sway in interior regions. 'Many of us worked as bonded labour,' Vikas told me. 'If you refused to go to the fields of the zamindar, their musclemen, loaded with guns, would come to pick you up. Our oxen too were pressed into their service.'

Vikas used the Hindi word 'daman' to describe the landlords' tyranny. No single English word captures the meaning of this – it is equal parts oppression and impunity, intended not only to degrade an individual but to crush entire generations. Vikas remembers resentment simmering among the Adivasis while he was a youth, but few dared to speak out.

One day towards the end of 1995, when Vikas was eighteen, word spread of a rally in the neighbouring town of Daltonganj. Thousands of villagers from Latehar were heading in that direction to attend, and Vikas joined the crowd leaving from Donki. As they neared the rally site, he saw a group of people in olive-green uniforms standing beneath a tree. A large red flag fluttered beside them. The crowd sat in a semicircle around the squad. The leader stepped forward. A rifle slung across his back, his stance was like a soldier's. Others in the group also carried weapons, including bows and arrows.

The squad members were Adivasi, but something about their body language was different. Vikas realised that it was because they carried themselves upright, like they feared nothing. Their leader radiated authority, yet not of the kind the villagers associated with politicians. This was Madal Pal, an influential Maoist leader from Bihar. Unlike his cadres, he wasn't an Adivasi, but belonged to a lower-caste group. College-educated, like others in the party leadership, he spoke softly, pausing often to ask if someone wanted to add something or challenge his way of seeing.

'It was like he had captured the full gamut of our suffering,' Vikas said. The land grabs. The low wages. The abject poverty. The endless march of disease. The daily humiliations. The villains too were methodically identified: feudal landlords, greedy gentry, corrupt politicians, crooked bureaucrats, tyrannical police. The speaker declared that these problems wouldn't go away until the Adivasis seized power from those who tormented them. He called on the public to join the fight.

That evening, about sixty boys hiked to a nearby hillock where the squad had camped for the night. All of them wanted to join up with the Naxalites. The alternative was continuing to work with their families in the fields, or taking exams in the hope of landing a job in the government or the army. By now, Vikas had already sat one army entrance exam and worked in the grocery shop his family had recently acquired. 'But none of that had any attraction once we had been exposed to the movement,' he said.

The insurgents asked Vikas and the other boys a few questions, testing them for their commitment to social revolution as well as their readiness for armed rebellion. Only half were selected. Vikas made the cut. That was the day he became Vikas for the first time – this was a new name, by which he would be known in the movement. In Hindi it means progress. Since a younger boy named Vikas had already joined the party, he was given the prefix 'Bada' – older. Every new recruit was assigned a unit and a role. From then on, they followed wherever their unit went.

Vikas expected to begin his journey as a comrade with political education, starting with lessons in Marxism, Leninism and Maoism. But that would come later. On his first day he was handed a stick and sent with his unit to confront a zamindar. It was planting day on the 500-acre estate. 'Thousands of villagers had reached there already, bringing four hundred or five hundred cattle between them. Men, women, children, entire families,' he said. Everyone was aware of the police camp that had been set up on the estate a few months earlier, after a failed Naxal attack. Since then the police had been watching for suspicious movements.

But that day, the party planned a surprise attack. 'The estate bordered the forest, and an armed unit was staked out along its edges.' At an hour appointed by the local priests, the zamindar emerged from his house to attend a ritual in his personal temple to kick off the planting season. Just as he was approaching the temple, cadres burst out from behind the trees, guns raised. 'They grabbed him from all sides, opening fire. He was killed on the spot.'

I met Vikas again a few days later, this time in Latehar, his home district. He took me to an interior village close to Donki, and showed me a school that he and his comrades had built while they governed this pocket of Latehar as a 'liberated area'. He wanted me to see the kind of social transformation the Maoists had once managed to bring about.

Nothing about the school hinted at its revolutionary origin. There were hostels where girls from remote villages stayed, a kitchen that served healthy meals, and a classroom where an English lesson was in progress. Still, the land it stood on had been gained during the People's War. 'We forced a local zamindar to give us an acre to build the school,' Vikas told me.

Within just a few years of joining the party, he and his comrades had attacked dozens of zamindars and seized large swathes of their estates. 'We distributed thousands of acres among landless peasants so they could grow their own crops,' he told me. 'On every piece of land we freed from control, we planted a red flag to mark its liberation.'

At first, lathis were enough, but then the landlords began to unleash their hired guns. The comrades needed guns to fight back, and the surest way to get them was to rob the landlords themselves. 'In those days, each zamindar owned five or six firearms,' Vikas estimated. The zamindars' goons were built like wrestlers, hardened by years of training, but for them the fight wasn't existential. With each new consignment of seized weapons, the insurgents grew more formidable.

By the early 2000s, some zamindars had come to terms with the new reality: they ended generational bondage, and raised daily wages for farm labour and mahua-blossom picking. A few fled their estates altogether. In Donki and the other villages I passed along the way, the estates, several in ruin, stood out in ghostly splendour. Some resembled Rajput-Mughal fortresses, with grand arches and delicate jharokhas; others evoked European mansions with colonnaded porticos. Vikas told me about some of the gun battles that had unfolded in those now-abandoned fields. About the zamindars who had died in the crossfire.

With the state police's growing determination to uproot them, the insurgents began to spend more time underground, moving through the dense forests that blanketed the mountain. They formed reading groups around classical texts. 'Marx-vad. Lenin-vad. Engels-vad. Stalin-vad. Mao-vad,' Vikas recalled. The Chinese example of the

1940s, when Mao's peasant army had defeated the nationalists, stood out in particular.

The insurgents were growing more organised. By 2004, after a series of mergers, Party Unity – the revolutionary group from Bihar that Vikas joined in 1995 – became part of the Communist Party of India (Maoist), which unified the armed struggles for peasants and workers across the country under a single banner. CPI (M) brought together tens of thousands of guerrillas under a centralised structure governed by a clear chain of command and a common party constitution. Their declared goal was the overthrow of the Indian state through a protracted people's war.

In their time underground, Vikas and the higher-ups around him developed a plan for action. They would build bases in forests and hill tracts and expand their political influence through public meetings. Meanwhile, their armed cadres would keep striking at the state's military apparatus. The idea was not to confront the security forces head on, but to drain their strength and demoralise them. As more areas became 'liberated zones', the state's grip would weaken. In its place, the people's governments, known as Janatana Sarkar, would be ready and waiting.

Vikas was inducted into the Special Area Committee, the second-highest tier of leadership, just below the Central Committee. Commanding a unit of his own, he was responsible now for both strategy and execution: he might set the policy on levies (from local administration, mining corporations, and forest authorities) and also go out to collect them. Another of his tasks was to expand the Maoists' armoury. While they manufactured some of their own weapons – country-made rifles and pressure-cooker bombs – most guns and revolvers were stolen from the police.

'Seven or eight of us, all in plain clothes, would accost the police in broad daylight. Say we were travelling on a local bus. Seven or eight of us are sitting on one side of the aisle, and an equal number of constables on the other. We spot the pistols in their holsters. I pass the signal to the group with just a glance. Then, extending our hands, we'd circle the pistols – calmly. We didn't need to say more than this: 'We are Maoists. Let it go.' They'd freeze. At the next stop, we'd get off and walk straight into the forest.' Vikas reached out and took the water bottle from my hand in one clean, fluid motion. 'This is how smoothly we did it,' he said.

M ao identified three distinct phases of guerrilla war. The first involved creating a protective belt of sympathisers willing to provide food, recruits, and intelligence. The second phase was marked by 'direct action': attacks on the police and the elimination of collaborators, often accompanied by the seizure of weapons. In the final phase, guerrilla forces were to liberate entire territories, replacing existing power structures with the rule of the people.

In Latehar, the Maoists were entering the third phase by the end of 2000s. In this remote region, untouched by governance – with no doctors, no electricity, no running water, no paved roads, no functioning school, and no sewage system – the insurgents were not so much co-opting a society as building one. They established schools and organised medical camps, set rules for the harvest of forest produce, and regulated prices of agricultural goods in the weekly markets. 'Ten to twenty thousand people used to be treated in the medical camps we organised every monsoon, with doctors coming from the cities at our invitation,' Vikas recalled.

Their justice department held public courts to resolve local disputes. 'Property feuds, small fights, thefts, robberies, rapes . . . everything,' Vikas said. 'Whatever the issue, we couldn't allow villagers to go to the police. We feared the police would extract information about our plans and movements.' Still, leaks happened. And so, the public courts also served another function: trying informers and so-called anti-revolutionaries. 'If someone was found guilty, we gave them two or three warnings,' he said. 'If they didn't change their behaviour, we killed them.'

Across their bases, the Maoists cannily erected statues of Adivasi revolutionaries who, since the nineteenth century, had led uprisings against landlords, moneylenders, and the colonial state. In Latehar, Vikas and his comrades commissioned statues of Nilamber and Pitamber, the two brothers from the region who rallied the Indigenous communities during the 1857 revolt against the British.

The boundaries of the guerrilla zones were so clearly drawn that no representative of the government – police, bureaucrat, or politician – could enter without permission. Journalists knew the protocol: honk once before entering the liberated zone on a motorbike. If they failed to, or forgot, a guerrilla stationed behind a rock would press a button and detonate a landmine.

To make these landmines, the Maoists first stole raw materials from mining sites, which were everywhere in Jharkhand. They mixed gelatin sticks, dynamite and powdered ammonium nitrate with fuel substances to increase volatility, then packed the blend tightly into containers, like a pressure cooker or a PVC pipe. Into this explosive mix, they also threw nails, ball bearings and pieces of iron, to ensure sufficient shrapnel. Last they inserted detonators, wired or fitted with blasting caps, and sealed the casing with molten tar.

'Our men were standing guard all over this landscape,' Vikas said, sweeping his arm across the low forested ridge that rose gradually towards the mountain. 'We were the people, we were the government, we were the police.'

The most chilling episode of Vikas's career as a Naxal happened in the forests of Latehar in January 2013. A police officer then posted in the district told me it all started with Jharkhand's security forces receiving a sensational tip. 'Arvind-ji, the top Naxal commander of the region, was going to cross the border at Latehar, with two hundred to three hundred cadres.' The high-profile leader was on his way to preside over a big Maoist convention in Saranda.

Severely ill by this time, the sixty-two-year-old legendary Naxal commander travelled on horseback, flanked front and rear by cadres. 'They were going to halt for weeks at a time in villages along the route. At each stop, he was expected to hold public meetings,' the officer recalled.

The security forces devised a straightforward plan: ambush the unit as soon as it crossed into Latehar. But the Maoists had intelligence on them too, and when a 200-person Central Reserve Police Force (CRPF) contingent crossed the 18-km ridge into the forest, Arvind-ji's unit was waiting for them. The firefight raged from 10 a.m. to 3 p.m. It was a devastating blow to counter-insurgency.

Four bodies were abandoned during the company's retreat. Usually the police would send villagers to retrieve the bodies, but this time, strangely, the Maoists would not let anyone collect them for a couple of days.

A government helicopter finally picked up one of the corpses, and delivered it to a public hospital in Ranchi for a post-mortem. Midway through the autopsy, the doctor discovered a 2.75 kg improvised explosive device had been planted in the body's stomach. It sat in a plastic container, with detonator batteries and a small solar panel. In Ranchi, the officials claimed the Maoists had sought to blow up the hospital. 'This is equivalent to terrorism,' a BJP spokesperson said. 'The Naxalite movement should realise that.'

The Maoists issued a statement to the press: the target had been the police helicopter. 'Those accusing us of dishonouring the dead must answer what the government forces do with the dead Maoists in their custody.'

Now, more than a decade later, Vikas explained the technical flaw in the 'belly-bomb' operation: 'We had timed the explosion carefully. Everything was in place. But too much water had collected in his abdomen. It caused the batteries to swell up. The plug never ignited.' The second booby-trapped corpse was collected by four villagers. It exploded as they were walking back from the forest, killing them all.

One day in July 2016, Vikas told his superiors he was going to visit his family. His wife, five children, two brothers and their wives all lived together in their ancestral house in Donki. 'Usually, when I went home, members of my unit came along, all of us on motorbikes, but this time I rode alone.'

The next morning, he boarded a bus bound for Ranchi. Around noon, he arrived at the state's police headquarters, where Jharkhand's most senior officers were waiting for him. He was giving himself up.

'I had come in civilian clothing, plain shirt and trousers, completely unarmed. They were surprised to see me that way. A constable was ordered to fetch fatigues and a matching cap. They asked me to change into it. Another constable brought a well-used rifle and put it in my hands.'

A high-ranking officer then briefed him: 'He said an official programme had been organised, with journalists invited. In a short while, I would go up on stage in this uniform, holding the gun. The director general of police would be onstage already. I would hand over the gun to him. He would give me a bouquet of flowers. He would then hug me.'

Vikas's surrender was a major achievement for the Jharkhand Police. They wanted the news spread far and wide. The pageantry was fine with Vikas, but he feared the hug would be going too far. The officer insisted. He said that the hug was the centrepiece of the event. It was meant to send a message: lay down your arms, and the police will welcome you with open arms.

Dressed in the fatigues he was given, Vikas looked as if he had walked straight into police headquarters from a bunker in Burha Pahad. The gun he handed over featured prominently in the coverage, as did the ceremonial cheques he was awarded.

The state's surrender policy deferred to the CPI (M)'s internal hierarchy almost as much as the party's own squads did. Compensation was tied to a cadre's last-known rank and how badly the police wanted them. Vikas, a commander in the Special Area Committee spanning parts of Bihar, Jharkhand, and Chhattisgarh, had a bounty of ₹25 lakh on his head. He had spent twenty years in the Maoist movement and faced charges ranging from looting and arson to kidnapping and murder: twenty-seven cases in Latehar, seventeen in Garhwa, and twenty-two across the border, in Chhattisgarh. Only two of his comrades, both Central Committee members, carried higher rewards.

That day, he received three cheques: ₹25 lakh for surrendering, ₹50,000 as the first instalment of a rehabilitation fund, with four more payments to follow, along with ₹15,000 for handing over the gun that they had given him to hold. Two years after his surrender, he was set to receive an additional ₹4 lakh, a gesture of appreciation for staying on the right path. Beyond the cash, he had been promised a plot of land to build a house, a small loan to start an enterprise, and a grant to support his children's education.

None of this compensation, Vikas stressed, was what had motivated him to lay down arms. The money had never been a lure. 'What did I need it for? My family still possessed acres of land,' he said.

But Vikas had become disillusioned with the infighting over the levies that the Naxalites were imposing. Even as the amounts they demanded swelled into lakhs, even crores, of rupees, different party units squabbled over who got to collect them. The problem was that at all levels, Maoist units were filling up with recruits who were in it only to make money: 'Some of them would extort at will, neither informing us nor noting the collection in party records.' After a decade in power, the insurgents were beginning to display the same weakness for corruption that had marked the government and its representatives as their class enemy.

As the infighting grew, Maoist groups left the party to launch their own factions. That further divided the turf available for extortion. Vikas recounted one bloody episode when two party units and a rival faction all converged on a forest site where a contractor was supervising the collection of tendu leaves. A three-way gunfight erupted. Two men were killed, several injured. Vikas claimed that one of his own party members in the other unit took a shot at him. He only narrowly escaped.

'To treat comrades like enemies is to go over to the stand of the enemy,' Mao once warned. But other fault lines were also dividing the Naxalites. As with money, the party's policy on violence had always been contentious. To Vikas, it seemed like the rules meant to distinguish between just and unjust violence had become dangerously blurred. 'People in our guerrilla bases were branded informers without sufficient evidence. They were being executed without even a warning.' He had to step in repeatedly to save individuals from being killed on the basis of hearsay. Unjustified acts of violence, he feared, were costing the movement the support of the people.

Local police officers, following the political fragmentation of the local Naxalites closely, had started calling Vikas on his personal mobile phone. Some of them had known him for years. On more than one occasion, they had let him walk free after arresting him.

'They were now persuading me to leave the party for good,' he told me. 'They were saying, "It's no longer a place for someone like you."'

His surrender was a sign that he agreed. And that the police now had the upper hand.

'Bada Vikas's surrender was a turning point for us,' a senior officer of the Jharkhand Jaguars, the state's specialised anti-insurgency force, told me in his office in Ranchi. The headquarters is a different world: a vast brown field lined with labyrinthine roads leading from one heavily secured office building to another.

The central government launched the Jaguars in 2008 in a bid to tighten its grip on the Red Corridor. In 2009, the home ministry, under P. Chidambaram, declared the Maoists the country's gravest internal security threat, and commissioned a series of specialised CoBRA (Commando Battalion for Resolute Action) units, trained in guerrilla warfare, from the CRPF. In 'affected' states – a bureaucratic label that had become shorthand for regions defined by the CPI (M)-led insurgency – CoBRA units now joined forces with local anti-Maoist task forces. 'Twenty teams of Jaguars were commissioned in 2008, then another twenty in 2009. Fighting the menace of left-wing insurgency became the ministry's topmost agenda,' the officer said. 'The thrust of their plan was to modernise the security forces, from training to weaponry.'

The Jaguars received training in what the coaches termed jungle warfare, from scaling trees for reconnaissance to firing guns from behind rocky outcrops. Their armoury expanded to include drones for aerial surveillance, mine-protected vehicles for safe movement, and bulletproof jackets designed to withstand high-intensity rounds. Advanced technologies, like night-vision devices, raised their surveillance capabilities and the precision of their strikes. 'What also favoured us,' the Jaguar officer told me, 'was that we were recruiting our forces from the tribal heartlands. Our men shared their background, and their familiarity with the terrain.'

The police and the security forces also upgraded their tactics. Informers became the linchpin of their strategy. In 'affected' districts, villagers were paid ₹6,000 a month to pass on tips about Maoist movements and plans, the same amount the rural employment guarantee scheme paid for a month's hard labour. Some police stations also awarded civilians for pointing out landmines. 'We were throwing money at people to pass on information,' another officer who had served in Latehar told me.

Local police began assembling region-specific mercenary forces to unleash them on the rebels. These informal militias were armed by the state, granted licence to collect levies, and often tipped off with intelligence about the Maoists' locations, routes, and timings. Each region became its own war zone, with local power struggles waged through ambushes, informants, and rapid, often deadly, retaliation. By 2012, these new moves were shifting the balance in the long, drawn-out battle.

After surrender, many Maoists were relocated to an open jail in Hazaribagh, where they were given their own rooms and permitted to cook, farm a plot of land, and live with their families while their cases proceeded through the courts. For high-ranking leaders, some accused in a hundred or more cases, the police offered further assurances: they would petition the high court to drop charges. 'After Bada Vikas came out, we tried to have all cases against him taken back. However, the court rejected our appeal on the grounds that it would be unfair to the victims,' said the senior officer.

The senior officer also credited the efficacy of their new techniques to the rise of cheap smartphones. 'The villagers now could see what was happening in the wider world – and the rest of the country. How communism had failed in other places and how powerful the Indian state was. How it crushed militancy in Punjab and in the north-east states. It just can't be brought down.'

Over the past fifteen years, armed cadres in Jharkhand shrank from nearly 3,000 to just over one hundred, according to the senior officer. The dense forest in West Singhbhum in southern Jharkhand is now the main site of the state's ongoing battle with the insurgents. Security forces say the last three members of the CPI (M)'s central committee – all relentlessly hunted since the state's assassination of Basavaraju – are stationed here. 'But our raids are shrinking the hiding radius. We are inching ever closer.'

B y 2025, all but four of the cases against Vikas had been dismissed, as documented in the legal register he meticulously updated. Several of those dismissed cases involved stunning acts of violence. It wasn't easy to figure out which ones he felt comfortable revisiting. On some occasions, he owned up to the killing. On others, he trailed off into silence. With a pained expression, he would admit he shouldn't be 'talking about all this stuff'.

He explained he was concerned about offending certain people. For instance, the police. He was grateful to them for various favours, and he did not want to appear as though he relished talking about having attacked them for two decades. Zamindars too figured in his hesitation. 'I have to live with them in the same villages,' he said.

Yet the sense remained that he took as much pride in his combat victories as he did from the land redistribution and education reforms he'd achieved.

Could Maoism ever regain its foothold in Jharkhand? Vikas did not think so. Not because poverty and oppression were things of the past – he wasn't impressed by the state's narrative about this – but because the fundamentals had shifted.

I knew what he meant. While reporting this story, I heard many arguments for why Maoism had run its course in India. The youth were too busy watching videos on their phones instead of studying Lenin; no corner of Jharkhand was any longer beyond the reach of the police. But the deeper reason was that the state the Maoists once sought to overthrow had itself changed, and the country even more so.

People in Latehar were no less poor than their ancestors, but today the chief minister, a tribal leader, directly acknowledges their needs, promising to 'make their every wish come true'. The government was engaging with the people even if only grudgingly, and the Naxals could rightfully claim credit for this. The insurgency had taught the state a key lesson: deliver just enough (roads, ration, basic welfare) and you can blunt the effect of revolutionary speeches.

The forest path, once scattered with landmines, now lay before us as a smooth ribbon of concrete. It led us to the village of Sarju, where the Naxals ran a Janatana Sarkar – one of several people's governments established in the region during the height of the Maoist movement. We were here for a public meeting. Vikas had contacted an old ally, asking him to gather villagers who might be willing to talk about those years, and about life now.

The gathering spot was an old sal tree, its broad canopy casting a generous circle of shade. Someone had laid out a bed sheet under it. Vikas sat in a plastic chair. Beside him were a few local journalists, men who had known him from his days as a Maoist commander. He announced why we were there. Sarju held a special place in the history of the revolution in Jharkhand. The region had seen the terror of feudal landlords, a brief spell of the Janatana Sarkar, and now, the all-encompassing rule of the state. It had been a battleground and, at times, a laboratory for social change.

Since 2012, the central government had been pouring special funds into so-called 'liberated areas', hoping to bring them back into the fold of the state. That year, the Sarju Area Development Action Plan was launched, promising to build roads and schools, extend welfare schemes, and improve healthcare and education. It was also the year the district commissioner, Rahul Kumar Purwar, defied warnings and visited Sarju himself, to 'show love and build trust with the masses'. Twelve years on, the local administration saw its mission as more or less accomplished. But were people satisfied? Was life better now than it had been under the people's government?

A woman was the first to speak. 'I didn't grow up in this village,' she said, adding that she'd come to Sarju only after her wedding ten years ago. One of her earliest memories was of Maoists disrupting road construction. 'They poured petrol over the vehicle carrying the material.' Vikas nodded, recalling the incident; it must have happened just after he'd left the party. Eventually, the road was built, and it changed things. 'Earlier, it took the villagers four hours on foot to reach the nearest market. Now, it's a thirty-minute ride in a shared autorickshaw.' She turned to the others, looking for agreement. A few nodded, but with caution.

A man wearing an ironed shirt stood up to speak. The truth, he said, is complicated. 'The lands, even though redistributed among us, still belonged to the landlords on paper.' While the landlords who returned have maintained a frozen civility, they wasted no time asserting their legal right to their property. 'They reclaimed what we thought was ours.'

With the special area fund, more roads were built, electricity lines laid out. Still, the man added, that didn't mean the area can be called developed. 'Sure, there's a main road that connects us to the district headquarters. But the smaller hamlets still don't have proper roads. Only some parts of the village have electricity. There are mobile towers now, but most people can't afford to recharge their phones.' Work is scarce, he said. Hunger is still everywhere.

Manoj Dutta, one of the journalists, picked up where the older man left off: the Maoists had retreated too soon. 'They needed to stay dominant for another twenty years. I'm not the only one who feels that way.' Once a district is officially declared 'cleared', the central government pulls back its special development funds. If rebels were still strong in places like Sarju, he argued, the state would be forced to keep functioning the way it was supposed to.

In 2022, Burha Pahad was 'freed' from Maoist control. Amit Shah congratulated the security forces on their 'unprecedented success'. But Latehar, an area that overlaps with Burha Pahad, is still an 'affected' district – with encounters, arrests and surrenders all continuing.

Many of the rebels who once moved through Burha Pahad gave up in the years after Vikas left. Some of them are still in the open jail, waiting for their court cases to be dismissed. Those who have been released were struggling to, as one put it to me, 'integrate with mainstream life'. I met two others while I was in Jharkhand. One was trying to secure a bank loan that had been promised him under the surrender policy – he wanted to open a small shop in his village. The other had returned to working as a labourer on someone else's land.

Vikas started working soon after coming out of jail. He was an established public-works contractor, handling village-level projects such as roads, ponds, and culverts. In his guerrilla days, he would have spent his time destroying the projects he now planned – or at least demanding a heavy levy from them.

Local officers had helped him secure the tenders, even as upper-caste contractors complained loudly. The money wasn't bad either. When we met, he was overseeing a project worth ₹25 lakh to build boundary walls around a tree worshipped by local Adivasis. A few lakhs from that would come directly to him.

He told himself that being a contractor was another way of responding to people's needs. Still, he missed being part of a revolution. 'People know me here for the work I did while being part of the movement,' he said. 'Everyone still calls me Bada Vikas.' Leaving the party has not shaken his faith in what they were fighting for. 'Liberation from poverty. Equality for all humans.' ∎

TLC The Literary Consultancy

MEETING WRITERS ON THE PAGE SINCE 1996

Transformative and personalised editorial services for writers.

EDITING
- Industry-recommended feedback services
- Links with publishers and agents
- Support every step of the way

MENTORING
- Finish your book in 12 months
- Includes full manuscript assessment
- In house day with agent and publisher

EVENTS
- Masterclasses and workshops
- Writing and wellbeing courses
- 1:1 and group coaching

literaryconsultancy.co.uk   info@literaryconsultancy.co.uk   0203 751 0757 (Ext 800)

Literary Review

FOR PEOPLE WHO DEVOUR BOOKS

SPECIAL CHRISTMAS OFFER

Subscribe or give a gift for only £44.50 and save one third on newsstand prices*

To redeem this special offer for *Granta* readers, please visit us online at **www.literaryreview.co.uk/subscribe** and use code 'GRANTAGIFT'

£44.50*
£66.00

*UK only. Please visit us online for international rates.
Eleven issues of Literary Review would cost £66 on newsstands

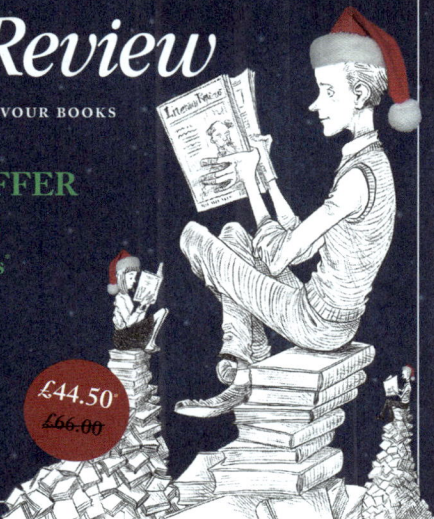

Arvind Krishna Mehrotra

House Painting

At night, after
the workmen had left,
when I looked
at the discoloured
stone floor
where the dresser stood,
there was a house lizard's
tail twitching to join
the reptile it was
part of, its curve
now preserved
in the fossil record
of a brittle page.

Dead Poets Directory

Clearing out a cupboard,
I find letters from the 1960s
when the poets of the 1910s
were neighbours.
I got to know them well.
One became a friend.
He'd stick his neck in the door
and offer free advice. 'Go in fear
of abstractions,' he said.
I heard he was dangerous.
When I started a magazine
I named it after him.
It was mimeographed.
Most of its contributors
are dead. Some I lost touch with.
Phoebe Coan of Fort Lauderdale
wrote me long letters.
If you see her please tell her
that she's alive and well.

Lineman

I know the ritual
  only too well:
He touches,
  as if in prayer,
the lower rungs
  of the bamboo
ladder, kisses the back
  of his hand, puts
his right foot
  on the bottom-most
rung and taking one
  final look at the knot
of power cables
  on the electricity pole,
climbs without harness
  or gloves to the top
where the fault is,
  a pair of lineman pliers
stuck in his hip pocket
  like a fountain pen.

संस्कृत

S anskrit has always been a language of superiority, in contrast to more widely spoken languages, which historically were designated 'Prakrit', meaning 'natural', 'provincial', and, among other things, 'low'. In the twenty-first century, how does one deal with a language that no one routinely speaks any more, a language that is historically implicated in social hierarchy and discrimination – the word itself means 'cultured' or 'refined' – and supported by the Hindutva ideology that seeks to create a theocratic nation and a monolithic culture – and yet, a language that also holds within it exquisite literature, profound philosophical thinking, and the primary texts of more than one great world religion?

For the past forty years, I have worked mostly with one Sanskrit text – the *Ramayana* of Valmiki. I have had ample time to wonder whether, when I translate and teach and write about it, I am complicit in the inequities it implies. The *Ramayana* tells the story of a noble prince, Rama, who is sent into exile by his stepmother the night before his coronation. In those long, dark years in the forest, his wife is abducted by a demon king, a monster with ten heads and twenty arms. The prince makes an alliance with magical monkeys who become the army that he needs to slay his enemy and win back his wife. The story of Rama has an additional dimension that complicates how we talk about it: over the centuries of its composition, the focus of Hinduism moved away from the performance of ritual towards devotion to a personal god. As a consequence of this theological shift, Rama was transformed from a mortal man into an avatar of the great god Vishnu, and the story of the righteous prince was elevated to become a story about a god living among humans. The epic tale became a prescriptive and religious text, with Rama as the paradigm of virtue, the ideal man and king.

The *Ramayana* finds and generates meaning through the operation of *karma* and *dharma*, Hindu principles which were being debated and explored at the same time that the epics were first composed. Dharma (the principle that underpins duty, obligation and responsibility) and karma (the theory of retributive action) come together in moments of crisis for the characters. The old king must send his beloved son Rama into exile for two reasons – one, because he must uphold a promise that he made to his younger wife when she saved his life in battle (*dharma*), and two, because he has been cursed by the bereaved parents of a young man he accidentally killed such that he too would be separated from his child in old age (*karma*).

When free will and determinism collide, the question the *Ramayana* asks of the characters in its story and of all of us is this: in a universe where most possible actions are already determined, what must I do to make the world better, what does it mean to be good? A simple question but surely, one with a hundred different answers that depend on time, place, and ethos.

The *Ramayana* is ultimately about the power struggle between the priestly and warrior classes during a distinct historical moment. In South Asia, around the fourth and third centuries BCE, these groups frequently competed for social dominance. They vied not only for status but for control over resources, authority, and the ability to define the moral and political order. Within a Hindu universe, this struggle for supremacy was inevitably a conflict about hierarchies of caste.

Our discomforts with Sanskrit and its culture do not arise solely from our modernity. Although the oldest version of the *Ramayana* comes to us in Sanskrit, Rama's story has been told over and over again through the centuries in almost every Indian language and by various castes, creeds and religions. In that sense, the *Ramayana* has frequently been and continues to be rewritten: it has been challenged by women and Dalit castes, it has been questioned by people who believe that they are the indigenous inhabitants of the subcontinent, it has been subverted by many contemporary retellings. Women have retold the story in Sita's voice, centring her in the narrative rather than her husband, letting her speak of her years in captivity and her second banishment. Dalit retellings highlight the Sanskrit poet's lowly origins – many stories tell us that he was a brigand before he composed the epic, and they criticise the upper-caste ethics that allow Rama to kill Shambuka for practising austerities above his station. Indigenous people emphasise the roles of forest-dwellers that Rama meets, such as Guha and Shabari, reading their words and deeds as resistance and opposition. All of these retellings are corrections, in some way, of the systemic exclusions of Sanskrit language and culture.

But the *Ramayana* has also been claimed and remade by the increasingly mainstream Hindu right. From the perspective of this political group, the *Ramayana* can be read as a religious battle between good and evil, where good triumphs over those who oppose Hindu values and behaviours. Rama is a conquering hero waging a righteous war against Hinduism's enemies. The army of monkeys symbolises Rama's passionately devoted human followers who are committed to ensuring the establishment of a majoritarian state. As the Hindu right seeks to create a single, unitary *Ramayana* story and belief system around Rama, it erases and silences the many heterogenous voices that have spoken from within the *Ramayana* tradition.

For those of us exiled by birth from a universe of knowledge and power – of meaning and, often, beauty – responses to this exclusion can lie in creating or excavating retellings that include us. We must also create counter-narratives that resist the flattening of history, especially when that flattening is used to consolidate power. The past must be parsed by as many voices as possible – it belongs to us all. ∎

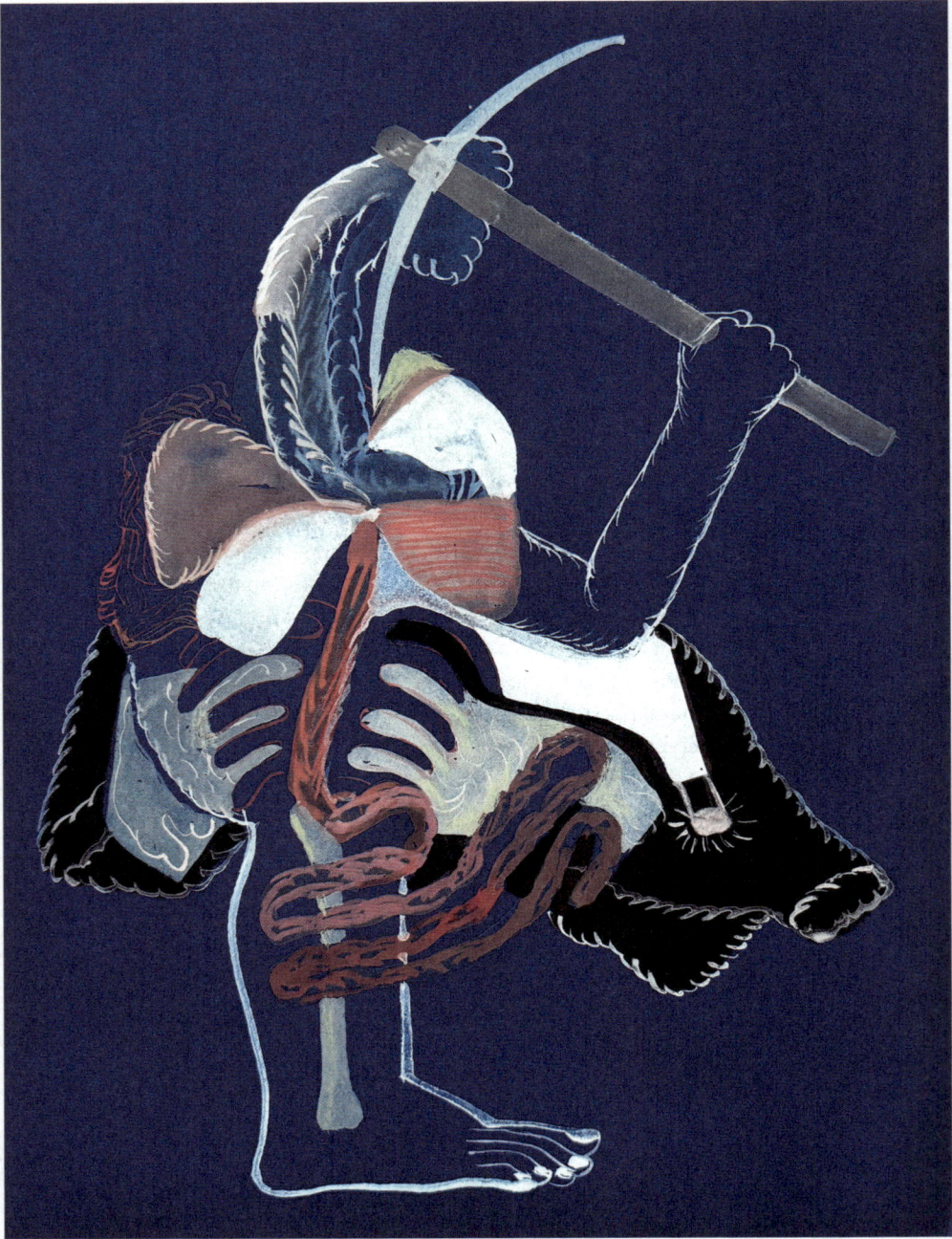

VIKRANT BHISE
Existence: Conflicts, Poverty 09, 2022

KAZHUMAADAN

Jeyamohan

TRANSLATED FROM THE TAMIL BY PRIYAMVADA RAMKUMAR

We did not have the right to go in through the fort's front entrance or its rear. But a narrow cart track forked away from the mud road that headed north towards Kumarapuram, cut across the cremation grounds and wound up at the side of the fort. I had used this separate path a couple of times before. There, where the darbha grass grew tall enough to camouflage an elephant and burst into surfs of white blossoms that rose and fell with the wind, you wouldn't find a single soul from the upper castes, except for when a bier of their dead passed through.

I perched up on a rock; after I had made sure that there was no one in sight, I climbed down and proceeded slowly. Every now and then I cupped my palms around my mouth and called out: 'Theendadhonaakume aayithamunde.' *An untouchable is on his way, take heed.* My voice crashed into the boulders and ricocheted back to me. An untouchable man was entreating me to keep distance.

The path led to the small fort entrance near Perumalkulam, abutting a massive rock on which the Kani-Pillaiyaar temple stood like a canopied carriage on the back of an elephant. Beyond the rock, the blue waters of the Perumalkulam Lake would be full and rippling. The path wrapped around the lake's shoreline, and diverged: one branch leading to the Nayinar Neelakandasamy temple, and the other to the temple-car street. Neither I nor anyone else from my Pulayar clan could enter them.

But there were a number of narrow, person-wide pathways starting at the lakebed – shortcuts that led to the back of every palace in town. They wove across one another, knitting the city together like a web. We could rely on them to reach any corner of the city. We could turn up in the backyards, stand right next to the outlets that discharged urine and faeces and call for the masters. Everyone in my clan carried a small pipe with them. When we blew on our pipe, servants poked their heads out and took note of us.

Both the lake and the rock were old enough to be called ancient. They were here long before the city came up. Three hundred years ago – before Maharaja Ravivarma Kulasekara Perumal built a palace and a mud fort in the area, named it Padmanabhapuram and took up residence – there was only a wooden monastery on that rock. Unclothed, sky-clad monks lived there. As for the land at the base of that rock, it was my clanspeople who had set down roots, building several clusters of hutments over it.

Many generations later, Maharaja Marthandavarma Kulasekara Perumal erected embankments around the lake and built a taller fort out of stone. A treasury, a performance hall, an entrance hall with a pillared veranda, and a public dining hall were added to the palace. Armies swelled, servants multiplied. My people were chased out of the fort. Pushed farther and farther back, they were forced to settle at the foot of the Veli hills. The sky-clad monks left, migrating north-east to the Pandya land.

I spotted a throng of people near the outer fort. Before cupping my hands around my mouth and making a sound, I decided to check what was happening. I fell to my knees and crept through the thick grass, so as to not betray my presence.

On a slant of rock ahead of the fort, a team of men were layering a mortar of lime and sand over the life-sized idol of Pulaimaadan. They were my people.

'Victory to Karuthaal and Kaatuneeli!' I greeted, stepping out of the bushes.

'Victory be!' echoed one of the men as he turned around and

looked at me. He squinted. 'Who is it?' he asked.

'A slave from Ponmana Ammaveedu, the Queen's house.' I answered. 'I bring a message.'

'Oh,' he said. He knew not to enquire any further, even though the queen I referred to was not the queen in power.

'What's going on?' I asked.

'Can't you see? We are decorating Pulaimaadan and getting him ready,' he said. 'He is about to exact a sacrifice, isn't he? A kazhubali. Sacrifice by impalement. His stars have aligned. After this, he can rest for a whole year.'

'Indeed,' I said.

'The impalement platform is being readied above . . . go have a look, if you like,' he offered.

'Above?'

'Yes, that's the best place for it. Impale a man in there and close the door, and our masters in the fort won't hear him, not even if he tears his throat out with never-ending cries. After all, the women and children mustn't be frightened.'

I made my way up the gradient of the rock, to the top. The whole slope was covered with the dried scat of jackals and leopards. Deer droppings were scattered around like seeds. It was a bald and barren rock face, the odd thorny outgrowth notwithstanding.

Sounds emerged from the fortifications above. 'Victory to Karuthaal and Kaatuneeli,' I called out as loudly as I could.

'Victory be,' responded a voice from within. A man peeped out. 'Who is it?' he asked.

'One tasked with slave-duty at the Ponmana Queen's House. My name is Kuligan,' I said. 'I bring a message.'

'Is it about the impalement?' he asked.

'Yes,' I said. The others, too, turned to look.

'They call me Sindan. I'm the seniormost Pulayan,' the older man said. 'What did that boy lack in his life that he had to resort to this? He is the only son to his mother, they say. The lone sapling left to a woman who bore seventeen . . .'

'All that is gods' play, isn't it?' I replied. 'What are you doing?'

'Don't you see? Constructing the kazhupeedam – the platform for impalement,' he said.

'Out of clay?'

They had shaped a waist-high slurry of clay into a kind of raised platform.

'The clay will dry into rock,' Sindan explained. He turned to a young lad who was standing nearby. 'Won't you be quiet?' he chided.

The boy was shivering. A skinny eighteen-year-old, with a soft moustache and a soft beard. Pimples on his cheeks and nose.

'What is he for?' I asked

'We need a mould for the arse-cheeks, don't we? The size has to be perfect, and this kid is the same size as the chap being sacrificed. Sit down, boy.'

The boy shook his head and fell back.

'It's not as if *you're* being impaled! It's just for measurement . . . Hey, Guruma, grab him and pin him down.'

'No, no!' the boy shrieked, as Guruman caught him by the hand.

'Sit down. Now!' Sindan roared. The boy trembled and brought his palms together. Two men set about undressing him. They led the naked boy by the hand, sat him down on the clay platform, spread their palms across his shoulders, and pressed him down.

When he got back to his feet, the shape of his backside was imprinted on the clay. I looked at him. His palms were still pressed together and he was shaking all over. Tears streamed down his cheeks.

Right between where his two buttocks had sunk into the clay, Sindan pointed out the location of the anal orifice. One of the men removed a red cane from its cloth wrapping and drove it into the identified spot. The cane sank three feet in and stood up to a height of two and a half feet.

'He'll be impaled on this?' I let slip. It was a smooth cane, the colour of an ant and gleaming with oil. I wondered if it was a copper rod.

'Yes, this,' said Sindan. 'Bends nicely, and it's soft as a newborn's finger, too. They season it with butter to make it smooth. The to-be-impaled kazhuvan will be brought in with his hands tightly bound behind his back and seated on this platform. After that, they will insert the cane through the anal pore. It'll slip in like an earthworm. Won't hurt. Won't bleed. So, the kazhuvan won't know a thing . . . it might even feel cool and soothing to him.'

It was evident that he enjoyed talking about it. Meanwhile, the others watched with pinched faces.

'There are craftsmen who specialise in inserting the stake. Mekkarai Aasaan is one. He'll pass the stake all the way through the intestines, as if gliding a stick through a tube. Once it reaches the hollow of the chest, they will sit him down, close the door and leave . . . The platform is shaped in such a way that the kazhuvan's legs have to be stretched out a bit. He can't get up. Just the one guard will be left behind to wet his lips with some palm nectar, once every half hour.'

I could not take my eyes off Sindan. He continued: 'The guts will eventually ease back into their original position, yes? That's when the pain will start. But there'll be no bleeding – so the impaled won't pass out. He can revel in the pain with every ounce of his awareness. The pain will dig its heels in and run riot, you know? But we don't want him to lose consciousness to thirst or hunger, hence the palm nectar. He'll scream his guts out for one whole day. Then, his throat will crack. His body alone will keep on shuddering. The pain will last right until life leaves his body.'

I sighed.

'Death won't come right away. Some have suffered as long as eight days before dying,' said Sindan.

Wanting to leave, I cast a glance at the path downhill.

'But there's one thing – when a man dies after knowing such pain, the debts of several lifetimes are deemed to be discharged. He becomes Kazhumaadasamy, one deified by impalement. He is entitled to a hero stone. And annual sacrifices and offerings of blood, too. Thereby, he becomes deathless,' Sindan went on. 'Here, in this land of Thiruvithamkoor, there are four hundred and seventeen Kazhumaadans, no less.'

'And it is you who has to do this?'

'Of course. Isn't that why the Maharaja has bestowed the title of Chief Pulayan on me, along with a house to live in, and the right to bear a staff?' said Sindan. 'It is a right and an authority we've enjoyed since the days of my grandfather.'

I took one last look at the clay platform. As I made my way down, I thought about that boy.

I entered the fort from the side, walked around Perumalkulam, and took a narrow pathway. Given the time of the day, there was no one to be seen in those burrow-like trails. The faecal collectors must have visited in the morning and gone back. They would return for a serving of gruel in the evening, which would be doled out at the same place where they collected the faeces. Rats scurried about. The sound of steaming, bubbling sewage.

I counted the houses as I walked past them. After redoing my calculations to confirm if it was indeed the right house, I blew on my instrument. When I sounded it thrice, a door swung open and a padai-nair looked out.

'What is it?' he demanded, with the quintessential air of a military commander.

I showed him the signet ring that I was carrying. His face tautened.

'I need to speak to Kariyaathan. I am the messenger of the royal consort Valiyammachi Bhagavathi Pillai. I have been sent all the way from Ponmana for that very purpose,' I declared.

'Give that here,' he said, and took the ring from me. 'Is there a palm leaf?'

'No. Only a verbal message.'

He disappeared inside. I was left waiting. It felt as if he was gone a long time.

The door opened again. 'Follow me,' he said. I stepped inside. Eight Nair men were seated in there with spears by their sides.

'There he is, near the manure trough. You can go talk to him,' said the padai-nair who led the way. 'But, no more than ten minutes, all right?'

I walked past the stable and reached the dung pit. Next to it, with his arms and legs chained to iron manacles that were ordinarily used to tether buffaloes, lay Kariyaathan. A swarm of flies had settled on his body, like black film.

When I drew close, the flies took off with a metallic drone. Kariyaathan opened his eyes and looked at me.

I sank to my haunches. 'I am Kuligan, the chief slave of Ponmana House,' I said. 'I have a message for you from the royal consort.'

He stared vacantly. The wounds all over his body were ridden with pus. Wounds where the canes and whips had cut his skin. Wounds where the skin had been branded, now half peeled and blistered. Not a single one of the twenty digits on his hands and feet had a nail on them, nor were there any teeth left in his mouth. I sensed that torture had numbed his mind and left him incapable of thinking.

'Kariyaatha, what has happened has happened. You are the only son to your mother. The son that our gods Malaikuligan and Maadan spared for she who bore seventeen, so that she may have her twilight-gruel. You shoulder that responsibility. To stay alive is your only duty now, understand?'

Only the movement of his eyes indicated that he was listening.

'The Queen Consort has turned her divine gaze on you. She has shown mercy and proposed a way to save your life. All you need to do is follow her instruction. She will take care of the rest,' I said. 'Tomorrow morning, they will take you to Kaatuneeli Isakkiamman's shrine in the outer temple. There, the Diwan Peshkar will pose a final question to you. He will read out the royal missive issued by the Maharaja. Once the scroll is read out with the gods as witness, the Maharaja himself can do nothing to change your sentence. You must do what I'm about to tell you before that.'

Yes, he responded with the look in his eyes.

'As soon as I leave from here, tell the Nair on watch that you want to see the region's administrator. If the Nair asks why, say that you have a royal secret to share. Say this loudly, so that the others hear you too. They will take you to Isakkiamman's shrine. The local peshkar and other officials will be there. You must place a hand on Isakkiamman's sacrificial stone, take an oath, and declare aloud for everyone to hear that you never laid a finger on Devaki Pillai Ilayammai, the princess of Ponmana House. Repeat it three times.'

Before Kariyaathan could open his mouth, I pressed on. 'The man in charge there is Valiyammachi Bhagavathi Pillai's man. He will inscribe your oath on a palm leaf, certify it with his conch seal, and deliver it to the Diwan Peshkar himself. Once that is done, no one can intervene in the matter.

'Don't be scared. It will not be easy for him to execute a Pulayan who has sworn in the presence of the clan-goddess,' I said. 'That will require a whole new set of procedures. First, the Pulayar's grand council will have to be convened. The priest must put you on trial there. Then, the council will lay down three tests for you. You will have to shape a pot from virgin sand, lift a newly fired brick with your bare hands, and swallow boiling hot oil. If all three are done as they should be, even the Maharaja will not be able to kill you. You will escape.'

Seeing that he was about to speak, I raised a hand. 'I see your question. The council will be under the control of my master, Valiyammachi Bhagavathi Pillai, all right? I will be a part of that council too. At that point, we can make sure things happen as we want them to. All you need to do is swear your oath.'

'The one who accused me was Valiyammachi Bhagavathi Pillai herself,' Kariyaathan said quietly. 'Why is she saving my life now?' His lips were swollen, and it had been so long since he had spoken that his speech appeared slurred.

'These games are beyond me,' I said. 'If her daughter, the daughter of a respected family, is seen with a Pulayan, blood is bound to rush to her head a little, right? She must have assumed that you brought disrepute to her family and cried out instinctively, alerting her people. One of the people who heard her was sister Ammini, the wife of the man in real control of the Ponmana family, and what's worse, Valiyammachi's adversary. Once she had come to know of it, they could no longer hush it all up, could they? The news reached the local chieftain and the Maharaja, which triggered everything that followed: the investigation, the punishment . . .'

'The woman croaked happily then, didn't she? She had a good laugh while they tied me up and beat me, didn't she?'

'Yes, my boy. But Valiyammachi Bhagavathi Pillai only realised later what a great stain your execution would bring to her house. No good family will ever come forth to marry a girl from that house. And should the royal family shun all alliance with them, the house will wilt, you see,' I said.

'Think about it,' I continued, lowering my voice. 'If they impale you and make you a god, their family will have to make offerings and sacrifices every year, yes? That shame will pass down for generations . . . the entire family will fester and rot.'

'Yes,' he acknowledged, but I couldn't make out the emotion on his face.

'If you swear that oath in the name of the goddess, it will remove the shame. If they let you go, the shame will go too.'

'Has Devaki Pillai Illayammai sworn so?' Kariyaathan asked.

'You have to swear first. We have to overturn your sentence. After that, they will try her as women are tried – through an ammaivicharam. She will swear on fire in front of a council of matriarchs who will gather at the Goddess Bhagavathy temple. By then, if you too have passed the Pulayar trial unscathed, the Maharaja will let you off. That will be the end of all blame and shame.'

The padai-nair came by briefly and stamped his spear on the ground.

'What does Devaki Pillai Ilayammai say happened now?' Kariyaathan asked.

'She claims that you never touched her.'

'Really?'

'Yes, boy. Devaki Pillai Ilayammai turned up at the village council and declared that you never laid a finger on her. She cried so much that everyone believed her. She swore on Naagathaan's trident, and on a lamp lit in Goddess Bhagavathy's presence,' I said. 'That is in the nature of women. They will not relent, not even at the very end. They will shed every last tear they have in them.'

He was listening to me with downcast eyes.

I lowered my voice further. 'Let's say you take the stake. Once that happens, she will be driven out of her home, too, won't she, with all the fanfare due to a corpse? They won't auction her in the open like they would have before. But she will have no place among her caste. Her children will have no status, no wealth. She will be married off to some pathetic, lowly Nair. Her life will be ruined . . . that anxiety has gripped her now,' I said.

Kariyaathan had fallen to thinking; his gaze was still lowered. He had big eyes. Their lashes long, like those of a calf. In that moment, I felt as if I were looking at a child.

'Don't think twice about taking the oath. You are your mother's only son. Goddess Isakkiammai will understand. Once you are free, your mother can make a vow in her name and atone for your lie. All she has to do is go on a ritual fast and fulfil a votive offering. That will take care of it. After all, the goddess too is a mother, isn't she?'

'Uncle, I want you to know – it was Devaki Pillai Ilayammai who wanted me,' Kariyaathan said.

'I know, my boy. Poothedathu Valiya Namboothiri, the man who presented a sari to Devaki Pillai Ilayammai and announced his wish for an alliance, is sixty. Devaki Pillai Ilayammai is twenty. How would it work? She saw you and felt the heat of desire.'

'She threatened me. She said she would kill my mother if I didn't come . . .' said Kariyaathan. 'I hid from her sight for six whole months.'

'That's typical. Lust blinds the eyes, doesn't it?' I said. 'But let's not get into that now.'

'That day, the maid summoned me and told me to come around to the rice-pounding shed at the back of the house. I went without knowing why . . . When I arrived, Devaki Pillai was already there. But, as soon as her mother saw us, she burst into tears and said that I had tried to grab her . . . she shifted the blame onto me.'

'I understand . . . it's fine, but you have to let it go. Just swear that you did not do it. I'll take care of the rest.'

'No, uncle. I won't swear it,' Kariyaathan said in a firm voice.

'What are you saying, boy?' I exclaimed, in spite of myself.

'I won't swear it. I will take the stake. They'll ask me for my last wish when I'm impaled, won't they? I'll tell them, then, that they must bury me at the market corner along the road that leads to Ponmana, erect a stone there in my memory and make me a god – a Kazhumaadan. Only after I say that will I rest on the stake,' he said forcefully. 'I will remain there, on that road. Let the people see me for a thousand years. Let them worship me . . . a time will come when that family will shed endless tears, when they will say: "Kariyaatha, you have won." But I will not be subdued by sacrifice, nor quelled by magic. Only when the land their house stands on is reduced to a fishpond will I be sated.'

His words reached my ears so quietly I almost believed they were my own thoughts. 'Son . . .' I said, extending my hand in his direction.

'Let the village know. Let the world know. Let the whole kingdom know,' he declared.

'Please listen to me . . . don't do this, son. I have just seen the impalement platform.'

'And I have ascended it a thousand times in my mind.'

'Hand on heart, I came as an emissary just for you, because I want you to live. I swear.'

'To hell with my death, uncle. What did you say . . . they're afraid of the shame that will cling to them, yes? But we have only this shame to give back to them, don't we?' he asked, a faint smile curling on his lips.

'Don't do it, son. Please.' When I said that, I couldn't hold back my tears.

The padai-nair came around again, spear in hand.

Kariyaathan turned and looked at him. Then, he said, 'The Peshkar's interrogation isn't scheduled for tomorrow, uncle. It is now. The Peshkar is heading to the Krishnan temple in Vadassery tomorrow . . . the trial is being held now. They'll take me shortly.'

'Son, don't do it. Please listen to me.'

He was smiling.

'You don't know what you're doing . . . you're so young.'

'To stand at the head of battle as first offering, one ought to be young, uncle.'

'That will do,' the padai-nair said, striding in. 'We have to take him now. The men have arrived.'

I got to my feet, my palms pressed together, tears streaming down my face. 'Don't, son . . . don't . . .' I begged under my breath.

Two other padai-nairs came in, unlocked the chain and freed Kariyaathan. The metal jangle made my heart drop.

They bound his hands together with the same chain. Kariyaathan turned to me with a smile on his face, and in a tongue that belonged only to us Pulaiyars, said, 'But the truth is, I never touched Devaki Pillai Ilayammai . . .'

'Son!' My restraint broke as I cried out and reached my hand in his direction.

They took him away. Chains clanging against the floor, he placed one swollen foot in front of the other and walked forward, calmly. ∎

नेपाली

The Nepali Bazaar in London, Ontario, stocks food so authentic that each item resists elegant translation: *lapsi achaar*, a sweet, sour and spicy hog plum chutney; *timmoor*, a lemony hill pepper that is kin to the high-mountain Sichuan pepper; *kwaati*, a nine-bean mix that is sprouted and cooked as a soup on the final full moon of the monsoon. To wander the aisles is to be transported far away – to Bhutan. The shop is Bhutanese-owned. Its owners would be called Lhotsampa in Dzongkha, the official language of Bhutan. In their mother tongue, Nepali, they are called Nepali.

'It's Nepali, not Nepalese,' many of us in Nepal insisted in the 1990s, as the English language came into wider circulation after a democracy movement ended the absolute monarchy. We had been taught to use 'Nepalese' as a descriptor and 'Nepali' for the language, but since we called ourselves 'Nepali' in our own language, we felt that we should do so in English as well. 'Nepalese' sounded distinctly colonial. It was time to reclaim English.

Some still use 'Nepalese', but for the most part, 'Nepali' took hold. Soon, the people, the language, and all descriptors became Nepali, rendering the word so all-encompassing, so vast and amorphous, that it gradually lost any fixed meaning.

Outside of Nepal, Nepalis live mainly in India and Bhutan, sometimes in embattled conditions. The Gorkhaland movement, simmering in Darjeeling since the 1980s, still bubbles over with the grievances of India's three million-odd Nepalis. While in Bhutan, the country's tiny Nepali population must abide by citizenship laws designed to favour the Druk majority, to avoid the misfortune of the 100,000 compatriots expelled in the 1990s.

For those refugees now resettled in third countries, and for Nepalis in Bhutan and India, the word 'Nepali' invokes the heated pride of the minority, the survivor. The pride is softer in the newer diasporic outposts of Hong Kong, Aldershot, Queens, and Auburn, Australia.

In Nepal, many feel a rush of patriotism at declaring themselves Nepali. But there, at the centre of the Nepali world, feelings are also more complicated.

The Nepali language is the mother tongue of less than half of the citizens of Nepal, who speak one or more of 123 Indo-European, Tibeto-Burmese, Austro-Asiatic and Dravidian languages at home. Because Nepali – or its root language, Khas-bhasa – happened to be the mother tongue of the conquering Shah kings of Gorkha, it became the country's official language.

After democracy, Indigenous rights activists were quick to reframe Nepali as the language of internal colonisation. The word 'Nepal' itself derives not from the Nepali language, as they point out, but from Nepal-bhasa, the language of the Newa community who are indigenous to the Kathmandu valley. Kathmandu is, in fact, not the valley's name at all. Its proper name is Nepa. After the conquest of Nepa, the Shah kings of Gorkha appropriated its name for their entire kingdom. As 'Nepa' transformed into 'Nepal', Khas-bhasa transformed into Nepali. The original, which is still spoken in the country's western region, is not intelligible to today's Nepali speaker.

The Indigenous rights movement is steadily dismantling Nepali hegemony in Nepal. In recent years the Newa have reasserted their own names for the neighbourhoods, cultural sites, architectural structures, and natural formations of the Nepa valley. Settlers like me scramble to learn them. Years after I should have known better, I disappointed a Newa friend by carelessly saying that a temple in Patan (or Yala) was in the Kathmandu valley. 'Nepa,' she snapped when I made excuses; and I stood corrected.

नेपाली

This nuance is easily lost in the diaspora, where a hunger for the lost homeland can make Nepalis of all variety gather around unambiguous symbols of belonging such as Nepal's double-pennant national flag.

I see Nepalis waving this flag a lot in Toronto, where I now live after spending half my life in Nepal. It always confuses me. And it makes me wonder whether, as Nepalis leave South Asia in unprecedented numbers, the word 'Nepali' is transforming into a false friend, a word that is similar in different languages, but which carries divergent meanings.

In this case the divergence comes not from language, but from context.

'This is Nepali food,' someone might say of *momo*, or dumplings, and immediately quibble over whether the recipe is from Nepa in Nepal or Darjeeling in India – or, for that matter, Tibet. In the last case, the dumplings could be not Nepali at all – and yet also, given the history of Tibetan refugee resettlement in Nepal, entirely Nepali. ∎

MUSEUM OF PANDALS

Dayanita Singh

Introduction by Amit Chaudhuri

I never saw the Pujas as a child. That's an exaggeration: I mean I never went to a Durga Puja – the Bengali's annual harvest festival – in Calcutta until I was probably seventeen. This is because I grew up in Bombay, though I was born in Calcutta. I went to Calcutta every summer with my mother to spend the school vacations in my maternal uncle's house. We'd often go during Christmas too. Christmases in Calcutta in the late 1960s, with their fake snow and sparkling Christmas trees procured from New Market, the temperature outside dipping to sixteen degrees, quilts emerging from cupboards and protective winter wear swaddling bodies, seem to me the most dramatic and convincing – the most lifelike – Christmases I have experienced. But during the Pujas, which occurred in a month I had little idea of until much later, Ashvin (September–October), we were invariably in Bombay. There were no Puja vacations. School may have closed for Dussehra, the tenth and closing day of the Pujas, but otherwise we had to comply with the usual life-denying repetition: going to school, attending classes, doing homework. Bombay is in Maharashtra, not Bengal, and the Durga Puja is a Bengali festival, not a national one.

Still, school would end at half past three, and by evening, dressed appropriately in new, uncomfortable clothes, we *would* set out for one of the Pujas in Bombay. Hosted by Bengali families and associations, they were mainly in the then far-flung outposts of the north. The principal Puja was in Shivaji Park. Our car would go past the mosque at Haji Ali, and the dark expanse of ocean, towards the intersections leading to Mahim, eventually slowing in front of what was part commons and part sports ground, where a massive temporary structure had arisen. The mother goddess Durga stood on a dais at one end with her four children on either side, abstractedly piercing the asura or demon with a spear. Their faces were serene; only the asura, discomfited, displayed what the European Renaissance might have recognised as 'emotion'. Without realising it, I found the cartoonish faces of the goddess and her family members deeply congenial. The fact they weren't 'realistic' was part of an education. At some point, the bare bones of the myth were passed on to me: the goddess had been designated by Brahma, Vishnu and her husband Shiva to slay the demon. And there was a filial dimension to the story: she was also here on a visit from the icy peak of Mount Kailash (where she lived with her husband), to her father's home (an excursion, then, that combined work – ridding the world of the demon – and pleasure). We were her progeny on one level of the myth, genuflecting to her in her capacity as Ma Durga when we went up to the dais; but we also, by the end of the Pujas – when she was taken away to be immersed in the Ganga (how this happened in Bombay, which is a seafront city, I don't know) – had become her father or at least part of her father's family as we bid farewell. Durga, at the close of the Pujas, was daughter rather than mother, as she – so the story went – returned to her husband's home. (Bengali fathers often call their daughters 'Ma', and the double register of the word came into play during the Pujas.) This shift in emotion and perspective was undertaken in the course of the ten days without self-consciousness. We were able to make these transitions without being aware of making them, just as we made the transition from being middle-class people generally averse to religion to voluntary participants in a kind of make-believe without any of the sardonic self-doubt Philip Larkin imparts to the narrative voice of 'Church Going': 'A shape less recognisable each week, / A purpose more obscure . . .'

We travelled to Shivaji Park only partly to glimpse Durga. We also went there to meet the Bengalis. These were a set of middle-class people who weren't sure where they belonged. On festive occasions, they indulged their apparent capacity to savour the cultural, even the religious, in a way that was freed from denomination or persuasion. This could happen for them at Christmas, or Midnight Mass, or Eid, but it happened on a greater scale, with a tenderness that emerged from a forgotten rural past, during the Pujas. The priestly rituals on the dais always occurred (as the priest knew) in the midst of something else, and in this 'something else' was the suggestion of a magic that lay in the social and not just the religious – a sacred modernity. Religion was baulked at; contradictions abounded, deliberately uninvestigated.

It was in 1980 – school having become a thing of the past, junior college increasingly something I felt no obligation to – that we may have gone to Calcutta during September or October, and I would have seen my first Pujas there.

Common wisdom had it that the Pujas were to be explored after midnight, since the press of the crowds was intolerable in the evening. We – my cousins, uncle, aunt, mother and I – took up whatever space was available in a couple of Ambassador cars, and then, wide awake, drifted through roads that were hung with lines of light. I knew at once something extraordinary was happening, but couldn't put my finger on what. We moved further into illuminated vistas that, peopled but not crowded, were glittering. It felt not so much like a festival as entering a singular historical period. People who live through exceptional epochs aren't aware of living through them. They're busy with their lives. The present, for them, consists of frustrating oddities that have to be puzzled over. Maybe we can only understand what it means to live inside an epoch while marvelling at its extraordinariness through the window that something like the Pujas create. The transience of the Pujas feels like the transience of a great age.

I saw the Pujas in Calcutta again in 1994. By then I had been married for almost three years and lived in Oxford; my parents had moved to Calcutta from Bombay in 1989. The Berlin Wall had fallen, the Soviet bloc disintegrated, and free market capitalism was everywhere including India, but Bengal, like a renunciate, held out, and was among the few places in the world that had a socialist government. The descendants of the middle class that had characterised Bengali modernity from the late nineteenth century onwards were by now mostly living in other parts of the world, and the industrial decline that had gripped the city in the late 1960s had become a seemingly permanent condition as a result of its disconnection with globalisation.

That year, there was a plague that moved across western India without fully infiltrating Calcutta. Flights in and out were cancelled for a short while from some cities. If I remember correctly, the Pujas occurred around or just after this. It was a chance for us to explore the marquees or pandals in which the Pujas took place – pandals (in which the goddess, her family and the asura were on display) that had been made to look like well-known buildings or even monuments. In contrast with the covered space in Shivaji Park, pandals in Calcutta never resembled themselves. I was struck, occasionally, by their exactitude, but equally by the lights on either side of the street leading up to the pandal, less illuminated patterns than frescoes. As with frescoes or murals, these were meant not only to adorn but to record. Each scene was the equivalent of a page in a pamphlet or a headline. Among them was a rat (the mascot of Durga's older son, Ganesh) being refused entry at a gate – a reference to the plague. The lighting artists, who were from Chandannagar, took as their subject anything that was at hand, along with the this-worldly and other-worldly possibilities it suggested. In fact, this was how modern art in Calcutta – a city only around three hundred and fifty years old – had begun in the late eighteenth and early nineteenth centuries: in the congested pathways outside the temple of Kalighat, with anonymous, often Muslim, painters offering the passer-by Hindu devotional scenes in homemade pigments and watercolour that accommodated some incongruous contemporary detail, like a slatted Italian-style window, or a Prince Albert-style haircut and buckled shoes for Durga's son Kartik. Between the 1860s and 1970s, art moved to the avant-garde enclaves of a new, imaginative, unruly subset of the Bengali middle class; but in 1994, with the bourgeoisie destroyed and delegitimised, with Calcutta out of step with the global order, a predominantly working-class city of the street, of hawkers and vendors, and the Pujas largely a working-class event, it seemed art and its response, both to the immediate and to the world, had also moved streetwards, in these feverish, mutating lights. You couldn't help but laugh. We might have been back in the early 1800s. In 1994, it felt like Calcutta was starting over.

The Pujas have three main characteristics, not counting Durga and her antagonist. They engender what photographer Dayanita Singh recently described to me as their 'fictional' quality. The first has to do with the lights. The Pujas – although we don't think of them as such, because activity, precipitated by the beating of the *dhak*, starts at dawn – are substantially a nocturnal production, using, and improvising on, the surface of darkness for their effects. The lights aren't just pandal-specific: they cast a glow even on parts of the street where nothing's happening. They illuminate – by chance; but without this accident a dimension would be lost – people's houses.

The pandals – depending on the ambition and playfulness of the neighbourhood's commission – can be made to look like a temple, cathedral, the General Post Office, an old cinema house that once stood in that area, or simply some kind of celebratory canopy. Old buildings are recreated with a verisimilitude that includes discoloured walls and surfaces, introducing, to the teeming visitors, a residue of the great Bengali poets' and artists' fascination with atrophy. Inside, Durga and her family comprise a pause for adoration amid the business of exploring the inside of the pandal.

Leading up to the pandals, and on either side of them, are houses. If you're in north Calcutta, the older part of the city, these will be large, with a mix of neoclassical, north Indian, and Bengali elements. North Calcutta is where the great neighbourhood Pujas, hosted by families, started in the late eighteenth century; now (since so much of Bengali civic life shifted to the south in the twentieth century) people resolve to go to the largely unvisited north during the last days of the Pujas.

In the south, the houses are smaller, and have both angular lines and, often, art deco features (semicircular balconies; porthole windows; a vertical frontispiece of glass behind which is the staircase), and fewer neoclassical ones. No two houses are identical. From afar, but even close up, there might be some confusion during the Pujas about which is house and which is pandal. This is because the cultural provenances of these houses are more eccentric, and their appearance more beautiful and unexpected, than even the most remarkably designed pandal-illusion. With their red stone floor and green slatted windows, they remind you – despite Calcutta having once been the capital of British India – how un-English Bengali modernity was: that these houses' location is not to be fixed in prefabricated historical trajectories determined by colonialism or nationalism.

The fact that Bengali history (as we largely know it) and modernity are to an extent coterminous means that the city has little 'history' in the conventional sense. Its monuments – the Victoria Memorial, say – are largely uninteresting; only when they're fictionalised, as they are during the Pujas, or, in those ten days, confused with the non-monumental, with the mystery of the sacred-secular middle-class domain from the 1920s, 30s and 40s, do they spring for a while to life. To 'see' the Pujas is not only to see the goddess or the lights or the pandal – it's to see the neighbourhood. This is the 'fiction' that, I think, moves Dayanita Singh. We're being invited into a space – a larger zone than the pandal, at once historical and lived in – and asked to reconsider it. This is why seeing a Puja in isolation, as was the case in Shivaji Park, as is the case with Pujas in America, is to miss out on its larger, estranging fabric.

After Durga's immersion, the structures are pulled down. The fragile, workaday skeleton made of bamboo is exposed. The neighbourhoods are being demolished, too, by developers. South Calcutta, with its desirable addresses, has especially been under duress as buildings promising 'luxury flats' and gyms come up where that unique agglomeration of features that comprised a Calcutta home once was. The delicate fiction of the Pujas, already threatened by the increasing commercialisation of the pandals, must give way at some point – as the houses around the pandals cease to exist – to stand-alone spectacle. ■

London Review
OF BOOKS

'It is one of those unaccountable facts of modernity: Nasa launched a chimpanzee into space before women had access to reliable, frog-free home pregnancy testing.'

CAN'T YOU TAKE A JOKE?
JONATHAN COE

The magazine for curious minds

An *LRB* subscription is perfect for anyone with an interest in history, politics, literature, current affairs and the arts.

Subscribe today at lrb.me/granta25

Get 12 issues for £12

हिन्दी

In Hindi, the same word names the passing of time and the certainty of death. *Kaal*: literary, religious – unsurprising since so much literature once sprung from, was inseparable from, religion – and portentous. This is death with a capital D: death in the abstract, death personified, death deified. Shiva the destroyer, Kali the devourer. A death that will pursue you, toy with you, play games. On rare occasions, it may even be kind. But it is what awaits everything; it is the end. Or if one prefers, The End.

A word so freighted is bound, over time, to hold or gather other meanings. And so kaal is also time: a stretch, an era, a season. Not as casual as *samay*, the word you'd use for what a clock tells you, but a word one could use to say *greeshmakaal*, summertime, or *pratahkaal*, morning time. It works in more ominous contexts too: *yuddhakaal*, wartime; *aapaatkaal*, a time of emergency; *coronakaal*, the time of Covid. These are words now familiar to us from 24/7 news and 72-point headlines – words that bring the two meanings of kaal into uncomfortable proximity.

What does it mean for a language – for a people, for a culture – to have the same word for time and death? What does it do to them? Does it make life feel more transitory? Does it bring a certain lightness, a freedom, or a lack of responsibility? And what is the value of life if the shadow of death clings so close to time? Lately, I have been returning to the Hindi poet Shrikant Verma and to *Magadh*, his death-obsessed final book, written in the shadow of the aapaatkaal, the Emergency in the 1970s – an episode we seem doomed to repeat in this time of dying democracies.

What does it tell you about languages, people, cultures, if their words for time and death are different? If they have no single word to hold the weight of both ideas? The Greeks differentiated between Kronos and Thanatos; the Romans did the same. Did this make the weight of a life there heavier or lighter? I think of Goya, shut away in the Quinta del Sordo – the Deaf Man's House – painting those indelible, terrifying visions. Saturn devouring his son: the crunch of bone between teeth, the sound of tearing flesh. The old man's eyes, unforgettable. *The Black Paintings*, they call them.

It should not be surprising that kaal is also the word for black. The dictionary is oddly specific: a dark blue-black. The black of the eye. The complexion of God – think of depictions of Rama, Krishna, Shiva – 'compressed sky', in a memorable phrase coined by the art historian B.N. Goswamy. It brings to mind black holes, compressed so dense that nothing can escape their gravity, not even light. ∎

DAYANITA SINGH
File Museum

INDIAN TEMPTATIONS

Interview with Sanjay Subrahmanyam

S anjay Subrahmanyam is a leading historian of the subcontinent and Europe. Born in 1961 in Delhi into a Tamil Brahmin family, he studied economics at St Stephen's College and did his PhD in economic history at the Delhi School of Economics.

Subrahmanyam moves fluidly among the intellectual and academic cultures of India, Europe, Britain and the United States, where he is a professor of history and social sciences at the University of California, Los Angeles. His scholarship explores the interactions and exchanges between the European empires and India in the early modern period, from the fifteenth to the eighteenth century. His best-known books include *The Portuguese Empire in Asia, 1500–1700* (1993); *The Career and Legend of Vasco da Gama* (1998); and *Europe's India: Words, People, Empires, 1500–1800* (2017). Alongside his scholarly work, Subrahmanyam is one of the finest essayists of his generation. *Connected History* (2022) collects some of his articles on Indian literature and history, many of which originally appeared in the *London Review of Books*.

The editor of *Granta* conducted this interview with Subrahmanyam this September while he was visiting Paris. A longer version of the conversation is available on the *Granta* website.

EDITOR: The writer Vivek Shanbhag has argued that 'English is not merely a language in India, it's a kind of power.' Would you agree?

SUBRAHMANYAM: The relationship between English and the Indian languages is a tortured one. Part of this can be attributed to the 'cultural success' of the British Empire's education agenda, if you compare it with the Dutch in Indonesia, for example. You may not like the status and cultural cachet that English enjoys today, but you can't do without it for certain purposes, and acquiring English is often seen both as a means and a sign of social ascension, not only in India but in many other former British colonies. You see this with India's cricketers, who often come these days from small towns and modest backgrounds.

At the same time, over the last sixty years, the struggle with the hegemony of English has not destroyed the sphere of the Indian languages, or their resonance in many spheres, including politics. And these are languages that are often spoken by tens of millions of people: Bengali by more than 200 million (also in Bangladesh), and Tamil by 80 million or more, including in Sri Lanka and Southeast Asia. Together with the struggle, there has been a more creative side, some linguistic adaptation in both directions, which one can even see in popular music and its lyrics. The fear that haunts many people is of a genuine linguistic impoverishment, when groups in search of social and economic mobility will let go of their grasp of their mother tongues, fail to properly enter the Anglosphere, and remain in a kind of linguistic limbo or no man's land. I hope this proves an exaggerated fear, though it is a legitimate one. These were issues that the post-independence modernizers failed to grapple with adequately.

EDITOR: Were they too concerned about further cracks and break-aways from the nation under construction or was it more the weight of the English-speaking bureaucracy that they were inheriting? Did they have other options?

SUBRAHMANYAM: There were certainly no easy options, and still are none, but the matter required sustained political and intellectual engagement. Certainly not the iron fist used in the Soviet Union to impose Russification and Cyrillization. In the first two decades after Independence, the southern states were probably not given enough of a voice in these discussions, as many of the dominant politicians on the national stage came from the 'Hindi belt'. After Nehru's death, there were the violent anti-Hindi agitations and the invention in 1968 of what came to be called the 'three-language formula' – a national educational policy that mandated students learn English, Hindi, and one regional language – which was in turn perceived as asymmetric in the burdens it placed. In sum, the question remains a sort of open sore, albeit not the only one.

EDITOR: Twenty years ago, William Dalrymple predicted that the future of the Indian novel was in the diaspora. Your review of Aravind Adiga's 2008 Booker Prize-winning *The White Tiger* was effectively an obituary of that tradition. What exhausted that literary form? Did the diaspora simply run out of actual experience in the country to make their writing credible?

SUBRAHMANYAM: I think the diaspora can most credibly write about itself, but that is a subject of limited interest as such, since it can so easily descend into self-pity about cultural alienation. Dalrymple's idea that diaspora writers are 'natural bridges between cultures' also suggests he has not spent that much time talking to Indian diaspora communities. Of course, there can and should be writers in the Indian diaspora who don't want to write about India at all, and who we want nevertheless to read not because of their identities but because of the quality of their writing and imaginative powers.

The problem, as Dalrymple acknowledged only in passing, is that in the 1980s and 1990s, we entered the era of huge advances, even running into millions of dollars. Writing the next great Indian novel from a perch abroad became an industry of sorts, something like flying in to Los Angeles to meet an agent for a movie audition. But as I know from living in LA, most of those would-be movie stars wind up waiting tables in restaurants. Similarly, there was a vast over-production of repetitive novels from the diaspora using similar literary devices, often with blurbs written by the same self-promoting arbiters of good taste, that caused a market crash. To analyze this, we may not need literary critics as much as marketing specialists, who will also possibly tell us how these more 'highbrow' works fit in with popular bestsellers written by the likes of Chetan Bhagat or Vikas Swarup, which lend themselves easily to popular film adaptations.

EDITOR: The International Booker Prize has recently gone to two writers in vernacular languages, Banu Mushtaq and Geetanjali Shree. How do you think about this development?

SUBRAHMANYAM: From an Indian perspective, this is excellent to provide some balance to the excessive prominence of the Indian English novel and short-story tradition. The two books are of course very different, in their form as well as in what they set out to achieve. Mushtaq's short stories translated from the Kannada seem more like gritty social realism, with an unmistakeable feminist political undertone. In the case of Shree, with whom I had friendly relations in the late 1990s when she was frequently in France, I have read some of her earlier works in their Hindi versions, and I know that she is in fact almost perfectly bilingual, but prefers to write in Hindi. One realizes though that in the case of such international competitions like the Booker, much depends too on the quality of the translator.

Perhaps the publishing industry will be willing to spend more on translations, and not just on multi-million-dollar advances. This does evoke a version of the problem set out in the late Pascale Casanova's *The World Republic of Letters* (1999) of how one compares literary works produced in vastly different cultural milieus.

EDITOR: When we think of the development of modern Indian

literature, it can be hard to avoid seeing it as a companion of the national movement itself. How do you think about the relationship between literature and the Indian nation-state?

SUBRAHMANYAM: I understand that there is a temptation to bring everything in India, whether it's literature, music or art, around to its relationship to nationalism. But as my friends in the art world have always taught me, that is surely impoverished as an analysis, because there were also many writers and artists whose central concern was not the nation-state, and even writers like Tagore or later Manto had far more to them than their views on nationalism. Though I am far from being a specialist, my understanding was that even the canonized Hindi poets we were taught in school and who belonged to the movement called 'Chhayavad' were also grappling with their relationship to language and sound, as well as philosophical and metaphysical questions, which had far more resonance to them than merely their engagement with nationalism.

Reading Velcheru Narayana Rao's histories of modern Telugu literature, I come away with the same feeling that reading these writings through the lens of political attitudes has not always been particularly fruitful, because they also had to do with formal experimentation, registers of the language, and so on.

Besides, for many writers, loyalty was above all to a region and a linguistic community, rather than to India writ large. We see this is the case of both Punjab and Bengal, two regions which had to grapple centrally with Partition, and where the reading public was not willing to abandon writers just because they now belonged to the 'other side', as a career like that of Kazi Nazrul Islam exemplifies.

EDITOR: One of the major political episodes in your own formation would have been the Emergency – the 21-month period from 1975–1977 when prime minister Indira Gandhi suspended civil liberties and ruled by decree. How did the Emergency affect you? How do you think it affected elite Indian culture?

SUBRAHMANYAM: I was in high school during the Emergency years, from 1975 to 1977, but many of us were well aware of what was going on. In those years, my parents were in Madras (Chennai), so I lived away from home and my informal foster-parents were a couple from Maharashtra who were close to the socialists from that part of India, some of whom like Mrinal Gore and Madhu Dandavate had been thrown in prison.

Since I and my friends at that time were very interested in music, a case that caught everybody's attention was of the south Indian actress Snehalata Reddy who died of mistreatment in prison, and whose son was a popular musician. Besides this, my brother gave me regular news and gossip from Nehru University where he was studying at the time, and which was a major site of repression.

I would consider this period my political coming-of-age, and rumors were rife in school about the forced sterilization campaigns of the megalomaniac Sanjay Gandhi, and the ruthless demolitions of buildings in Old Delhi. As a consequence, I developed a visceral aversion to the Nehru-Gandhi dynasty and all the feckless privilege that they represent. This was only exacerbated by having to live through the anti-Sikh pogrom of late 1984, which the Congress organized.

EDITOR: You were too young for the first major dosage of Maoism injected into Indian intellectuals, peasants, and tribals in the 1960s. Nevertheless, at an intellectual level, especially in your field of history, the prominent presence of Marxists is unmistakable. What was the source of the appeal of Marxism to Indian intellectual elites in the 1950s and 1960s and later?

SUBRAHMANYAM: India was not that different in this respect from many other parts of the non-Western world, where Marxism was very appealing in the middle decades of the twentieth century, whether in Turkey, Japan, or Latin America. Further, after 1947, there was no real repression against Marxist intellectuals, as happened elsewhere.

They were able to even assert themselves and become a kind of lobby, supporting and promoting each other, until a major factional struggle broke out, which it did in the 1960s. The appeal of Marxism was of course its claim to unsentimental rigor, its concern for real social change, where the Congress by the 1950s had begun to lose credibility, even among its erstwhile supporters.

Eventually, the establishment Marxists allied to the Soviet Union's line were outflanked on the left by the Maoists with their more radical agenda, but they still remained important. There were also disparate groups of intellectuals who claimed to be 'liberals', but as the analyses by Ram Guha and Chris Bayly have shown, this is a term that is very difficult to make sense of in the Indian context. Some liberals were in favor of a free market and for less state intervention, while others were just ecumenical in their intellectual tastes, so that 'liberal' came to mean someone who was in her/his own view not doctrinaire.

The difficulty that the Marxists faced was that along with some remarkably creative minds like the great ancient historian D.D. Kosambi, or Ranajit Guha, or Susobhan and Sumit Sarkar, they also attracted many people who were extremely rigid, repetitive, and doctrinaire, and this became even more evident when they were the ones to call the shots in the institutional landscape.

EDITOR: But there must be something more exceptional about the Indian situation. Marxism made more headway in India than it did in many other former British colonies. The conditions seem to have been more propitious for its reception than, say, Pakistan with its larger, more formidable land-owning class. Is part of the reason that the Congress, with its acquiescence toward landlords, left itself vulnerable to criticism about persistent caste inequalities and the like?

SUBRAHMANYAM: From a certain point of view, the resentments created by Pakistan's class structure should have helped the Marxists, except that already in the late 1950s, there was US-backed Army rule. In India, while there was periodic repression, it was more limited, and the communist parties found a place in the system but at the price of a great deal of compromise. They may have had a social and economic agenda, but their leadership was very much drawn from the upper castes. And in the case of West Bengal, over several decades of rule, the Communist Party of India (Marxist) became a machine for the distribution of patronage and thoroughly entrenched in a corrupt rural politics. Leaving aside the Maoists, who are not concerned with governing, the two other main parties have gradually been 'normalized'. Concerns about caste-based inequality are now carried mainly by other parties.

EDITOR: The BJP has now been in power for more than a decade. Do you think there is anything like a right-wing intellectual milieu in the country?

SUBRAHMANYAM: There are relatively few historians, sociologists or anthropologists of quality in India today who both have genuine scholarly stature, and openly sympathize with the BJP. To be sure, there are now such people like Sanjeev Sanyal who have penetrated the market for popular history and biography with some degree of success. But this is easy enough with the backing of trade presses and their marketing machinery, even if one writes slapdash and derivative books.

In literary circles, there are certainly a fair number of pro-Hindutva figures, including some trained in cultural studies in the US, who are adept in channelling post-colonial vocabulary, including Saidian terminology. The other major exception is possibly among the economists, who are the group among social scientists who have always been the most attuned to power, and amongst whom there were pro-BJP figures even before 2014. This was sometimes based on the fond hope that Hindutva and free-market liberalism would go hand in hand. It remains to be seen whether in another ten years, things will change further if the BJP retains power. For that to happen, the intellectuals in question will possibly have to persuade the spokesmen of the BJP to abandon some of their more ludicrous positions, which even fly in the face of common sense. Certainly, I can see a number of younger popular historians already with their fingers in the wind, looking for openings.

EDITOR: When one listens to the BJP home minister Amit Shah talk about the greatest threats facing India, it can sometimes be difficult to tell whether he and the rest of the BJP think it's Naxalites, Khalistan supporters, farmers, human rights activists and western NGOs, or Pakistan. Then there is the matter of trying to manoeuvre between the US and China. What do you think the greatest strategic dangers to India actually are?

SUBRAHMANYAM: As Tzvetan Todorov wrote in his book *The Fear of Barbarians* (2008), many forms of nationalism generate paranoia, and see enemies everywhere, both within and without. To me, one can translate this into a different language. There is obviously concern on the part of the Indian state that with a form of accelerated economic growth that is accompanied by widening inequalities, various sizeable groups of disenfranchised people – whether the urban poor, or marginal peasants and footloose rural labor, or tribals whose lands have been expropriated – will want better political representation and living conditions. These struggles could turn violent in India, as elsewhere. That is undoubtedly a long-term threat to the viability of the political system as it stands, and it needs more than band-aids as a response. On the external front, the focus has been on threats from Pakistan and China for decades now. But it has turned out that in the short to medium term, the real 'rogue' polity is the US, which cannot be counted on as an ally either by India, or even by Europe, or Japan. The emergent new world order of which my father – the defense strategist K. Subrahmanyam – wrote, in the years before his passing in 2011, seems hopelessly optimistic now. India will have to brace itself for a rough ride, but so will the rest of the world. ∎

KALPESH LATHIGRA
Memoire Temporelle

ALL AT ONCE

Geetanjali Shree

TRANSLATED FROM THE HINDI BY DAISY ROCKWELL

He had known at that moment something would happen, but what or when, he had no idea. Something stirred inside him, and didn't return to its original state of repose, whatever it was. As though it had lost its former equilibrium and pace.

Or as if he were all at once pregnant and there was something inside him now and his stomach was no longer flat.

A permanent swelling swaying. Not large, but here to stay.

In the coming days whenever that something gently shifted inside him, he felt as though his blood were colliding with it, with that sway-swing-swelling, and his heart would miss a beat.

It's called atrial fibrillation, it has to do with the heart, that's what the doctor said, you should have paid attention.

On the surface, everything had continued as it always had, so why would it occur to anyone to pay any special attention?

And who would have thought that a motichur laddu would be the trigger, and that he would suddenly stop dead in his tracks when he saw his daughter eating said laddu?

That's all it was. He had been in his bower, evening was falling, he was coiling the hose after watering the plants to drag it inside and stow it under the kitchen sink. Just then he heard the rattling of a latch. Of the cabinet. It must be Shambhu or Shambhu's sister, his

ugngrbqtqtGEETANJALI SHREE

jijji; Premila had installed a tinkling bell on the latch to keep an eye on the servants, so the moment they touched it, there'd be a jingle. How delighted she'd be if he suddenly pounced and caught them red-handed among the sweets. He would have smiled, but he wasn't in the habit of smiling about such things. Usually he said, let them take it, when Premila complained about the large quantities of the fruit, vegetables, rations he brought back from the Saturday market. Are you trying to make it easy for the servants to take whatever they wish? she accused.

Let them take it, he said. They don't touch your jewelry, money, or valuables, do they?

What's it to you! Sometimes she was beside herself. You run this house for the benefit of the servants. If you left it up to me, I'd bring everything, and everyone, back on track in two days.

Which never came to fruition because she never had the time to run the house, and when she returned home from work, she needed to relax, and when she could not, because his voice was too loud, as was that stuck-up Shambhu's, and because of the rattlerattle clackclack of Amma's wooden cart, which she used to scoot around the house by pushing her hands along the floor, Premila would stamp her foot and go out alone, or with Chiya, slamming the door behind her every time, to announce that no one cares I've come home exhausted, I can't sit for two minutes of peace in my own home. Out of habit. Everything had become a habit. Yelling, complaining, noise, hollering, carrying on. But all more or less meaningless, because everything was peaceful and orderly in the house.

Which he liked.

This was something he understood when he saw an aberration in the order of things, which made him feel jumpy inside, which threw his blood off course and made it run into things and hop and skip a beat.

All because of a motichoor laddu, which he had bought, and which Chiya was eating.

He had been walking crabwise across the veranda, coiling the hose. He pressed his hand against the end of the hose to try to stop it from

248

dripping. It was patched with fabric in several places from which the droplets were oozing. He was walking along, holding the hose high, away from his body, and he was looking behind and below to keep from making a trail of water on the veranda on his way to the kitchen.

What was happening was exactly like in that tale, the one with the pebbles and breadcrumbs, which he used to tell Chiya when she was small, when Hansel dropped reminders along the way so he and his sister Gretel could escape the jungle and their stepmother's evil plans and find their way back home and fall into the arms of their beloved father. Little Chiya always breathed a sigh of relief when the children returned to the embrace of their beloved father and she would fall asleep leaning against her own father.

He would have to retell the story with exactly the same words the same feeling the same vibes every day and sleepy Chiya would sob in the same places, giggle in the same spots, and if a single word feeling vibe was rearranged, she'd perk up and scold him, no not like that like this. He said, Hansel said, don't be afraid, in the morning we'll follow this trail of pebbles and return to our father, hooray, and Chiya would interrupt, No, Hansel said, don't worry, my darling sister, in the morning we'll follow this trail of pebbles and reach our beloved father, hurrah.

A child's heart finds pleasure in rote and formula.

One day, Chiya herself ruined the rote and the formula of a story. In those days he'd started going to other cities for work, which Chiya objected to. So Premila was telling her a story, and Chiya kept interrupting to tell her the right tone, expression, words. It was a different story. This too a favorite of Chiya's. Chiya's tiny heart would beat pitapat for this one too, anxious until the father and daughter were reunited at last.

It was the tale of King Midas, greedy for riches, who asked for the boon of turning everything he touched to gold, and was filled with monstrous glee as he created more and more gold, but when he touched his daughter's hand and she turned into a golden statue, the king began to weep, and Chiya also wept, and she tearfully repeated the king's lines, I don't want gold, oh lord, take back the boon, give me back my daughter, when the golden statue transformed into a living breathing princess once again and father and daughter embraced, she fell asleep peacefully.

Premila had been telling her this story because he had gone to another city. The king had just turned his daughter into a statue and his greed had turned to regret and he had just begun to weep, when Chiya placed a hand on her mother's lips, not to correct her, but to tell the story herself, which she expanded upon like this: oh lord, take back your boon, give me back my daughter, I don't want any of your stinking gold, I want my daughter, and she began to sob, oh lord, I don't want any stinky gold, I want my papa, give me my papa, papa, papa, give me back my papa, papa, papa, come back!

How easy it was to come back and give the daughter a father and the father a daughter, when she was small and he was big. Loving was lovely, no trouble at all, between small and large. Laughing and crying were simple. Sulking and admonishing were two sides of the same coin. He'd pick her up and dance her in the air, laugh and scold when she pounded him with her sulky fists, and bring her motichoor laddu which she'd loved since she was small, but didn't eat now, not if it was brought by him anyway, so he pretended it had been brought by someone else.

He was staring at the ground, trying to avoid making it wet, and himself as well, so the hose was askew, held high, away from himself, and he was thinking, I'll wipe it all up right away, who knows if Shambhu is free right now or not and what if Amma comes barreling along in her cart, she'll smack her palms against the wetness. He was just about to enter the kitchen when he saw that it was neither Shambhu nor Shambhu's jijji but Chiya who was standing there, eating laddu, the motichoor laddu which he himself had bought, and she knew he had bought it, and he had thought now she wouldn't eat the laddu so he'd distribute them to everyone else, Shambhu and Shambhu's jijji will live it up.

But it was Chiya.

Standing up.

Eating.

Laddu.

That he had bought.

Cupping her left hand beneath her mouth so the crumbs wouldn't fall, greedily scarfing down every morsel.

He stopped. Outside the kitchen. But right in front of the door. Holding the hose crooked. If he turned around, he'd make a noise. He was silent. As though silence would make him invisible. Standing there staring.

A lizard chirped. The fridge stabilizer began to hum. A leaf rattled on the vine swinging outside the kitchen window. The sunlight wrapped itself around the hose. The droplets from the hose had formed a trail like Hansel's pebbles and continued to drip, making the still unstill.

If he fled, he would become visible. Same thing if he walked forward. Even if he just stayed standing. The whatdoIdo pose.

This time he hadn't brought the laddu from the temple, where Shambhu always said he had got them when he went to take darshan. These laddu were from a new style of sweet shop. They were encased in striped paper baskets, like cupcakes, and now Chiya had freed the rest of the laddu from the paper wrapper into her cupped palm, so she could lean over and lick it up. Now she scoured the basket with her fingernails so as not to miss a single crumb. She scraped at the paper basket with her teeth, the way she'd done as a child, when she'd laugh at being scolded, then ram the paper in your mouth too and afterwards suck on it like a toffee, squeezing it dry. Uff, filthy girl.

Then she threw the paper away, shut the cabinet, and turned.

She walked right by him, digging out the bits stuck between her teeth with her fingernail, her eyes wide open, smacking her lips.

He didn't turn to see if she was gone or not.

The warning bell had jingled. The laddu had been consumed. The trigger was pressed and the bullet fired. Something had collided with the flow of his blood. ■

অসমীয়া

I first encountered the Assamese term *byonjonar otripti* in a description of a short story by the writer Indira Goswami. I was in my early teens, and I was struggling to adapt from fables and fairy tales to the adult short story. My mother was an academic, and she used the phrase to explain that gone were the days of stories that would start with 'Once upon a time . . .'

In Goswami's story, a Brahmin widow called Domoyonti has been forced into sex work by abject poverty. One day, she receives a strange proposal from the wealthiest man in the village – will she rent her womb to him? Pitambor, who is from a lower caste, is a moneylender who made his fortune under British rule in Assam. He has heard from the village elders that unless a male heir sets fire to his pyre after his death, his soul will not get peace. After repeated home-induced abortions, Domoyonti's body is failing; she barely has enough to eat. At first she agrees, but late in her pregnancy she decides to break their agreement. In the story's haunting climax, she wakes in the middle of the night to the sound of Pitambor digging up the grave where she buried the foetus.

Why did Domoyonti do this? She was ready to sleep with a lower-caste man, but she cannot tolerate the idea of her upper-caste womb being polluted by a lower-caste child. The story has numerous unresolved ends: what happened to Pitambor? Did he find someone else as a surrogate mother? Did he go crazy? And Domoyonti? This is pre-independence India: wouldn't she be ostracised by her community and her own caste? The pity and fear lingered, and those questions left me with a sense of unease.

This is byonjonar otripti. In Assam, our storytelling traditions have always celebrated the unfinished, with sudden endings that leave the reader partly frustrated. One of the earliest written reflections on the art of modern storytelling comes from Rabindranath Tagore, India's first Nobel laureate for literature, who highlighted in the poetry collection *Sonar Tori* (1894) the meaning of this dissatisfaction. He describes a good story as something that should embody the feeling of '*sesh hoyu hoilo na sesh*', which roughly translates as 'ends but doesn't really end'.

That feeling – of not knowing what to do with your unease – is byonjonar otripti. The term comes from the world of food, where byonjonar is a dish or meal. Byonjonar otripti describes the opposite of satisfaction. It is a 'dissatisfying meal', a taste that remains or won't resolve, that continues to tease the taste buds. It emphasises the importance in Assamese storytelling of celebrating the absence of neat endings, part of a wider South Asian tradition that pushes against the conventions of the contemporary Anglophone short story. The ending is artificial; it serves as the closure of the text, but the story continues. ■

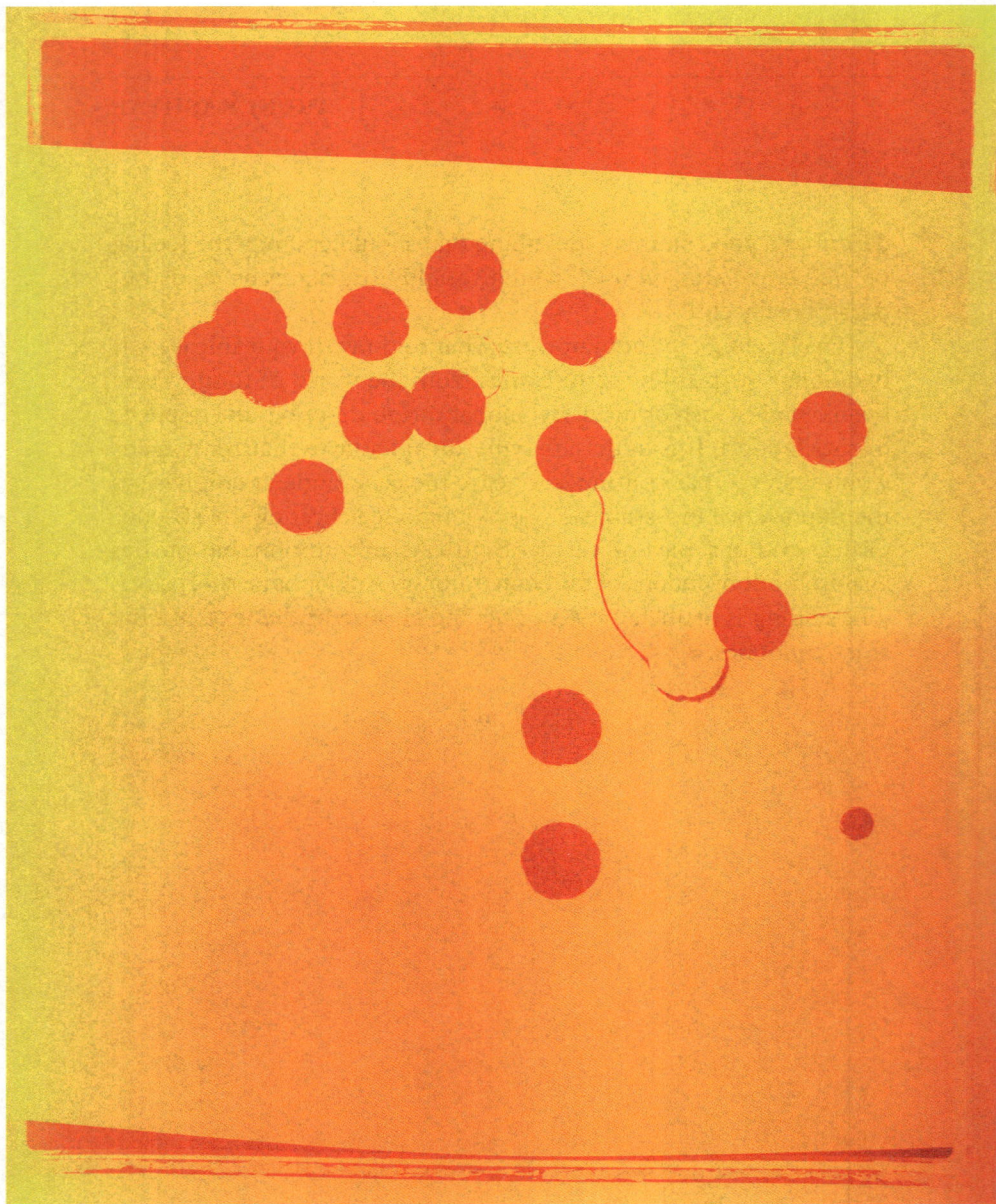

ATHUL PRASAD
Photogram

HOMA

Devika Rege

1

In the park, no one wanted Homa on their team. She owed her only friends to her older sister's popularity and their mother's insistence that she be taken along. She struggled to accept the unfairness of how other children treated her and her sister, especially since Ruhi barely noticed and was even a little embarrassed by their regard. In the family though, Homa had advantages. Her father adored her for inheriting his wide-set eyes, and her mother, who prized tidiness and manners, found her easier to train. At weddings, she was also the child they liked to parade, and yet, when the sisters argued, Ruhi's tears got more sympathy. Homa once asked her uncle why, and he said teasingly, 'Even as a baby Ruhi would cry quietly, as if she was sorry to trouble us. You, Homa, would clench your fists and scream in rage.'

Homa went to the public primary school, where she read faster than her classmates and outran them on the field. At the annual PTM, her teacher had no complaints; his only concern, after a pause, was that she ate her lunch alone. His advice to her mother was to reserve her praise only for those occasions when Homa did something for others. Soon enough, Homa learned that offering help was a reliable means to secure affection. The moment she met someone new, she would study them for what they needed. Ruhi made no such efforts, yet she was elected as the leader of the children in the park, who relied on her for judging disputes. At times Ruhi refused to take even her sister's side, which left Homa appalled. When Homa asked how she knew who was in the right, Ruhi replied, 'A voice inside told me.'

In secondary school, Homa made two friends. They met at the canteen table reserved for those who ate alone. Both shared her sense of allegiance, and they now stood together with a defiant pride. As the group expanded, Homa received her first invitation to a movie. Her parents congratulated her; Ruhi even raised a salute. Then, a day before the outing, the newest entrant informed Homa that she had been cast out. She may have shared her lunch money, taken the blame for group pranks – but it was not enough; they had judged her 'good only on the outside'. Homa rushed home, fell on the bed and refused to cry.

After this incident, Homa gave up on charming her peers. She focused on her teachers instead, eager for the praise: *good girl*. Gradually, she arrived at an understanding of her worth that was free of people's whims altogether. A good girl followed rules – if an adult still punished her, it put *them* in the wrong – and the most important rules were those prescribed by her faith. Where she had once lit the lamps to please her mother, she now did so to please the gods. Around puberty, she had fantasies of tonsuring her scalp and becoming a monk. Brutal privations followed, like meditating in a lake of ice, until one of the comely deities in her grandma's oleographs was moved enough to marry her.

This religious phase ended when Homa became the school captain and discovered the demands and rewards of a public reputation. Leading the assembly, the badge on her chest was never askew and her braids were oiled tight with black ribbons. She was known to go beyond her duties by telling on couples she came across in the hedges. If a boy rested his eyes on her too long, he was met with disdain. When Ruhi teased her that she was acting from fear, Homa said she had no time for local boys. Everyone knew she was headed for a future bigger than their city, where summer evenings still carried a whiff of dung and a night out meant a milkshake at the bakery.

Homa's father owned a textile shop and was from the same mercantile caste as his wife. They were traditional enough to believe that running a business was better suited to men, but modern enough to aspire to daughters employed in 'the services'. They pushed Ruhi to study medicine, but she failed the entrance tests and ended up at a local college for life sciences. Meanwhile, Homa awoke at dawn to prepare for her board examinations. Her father started to question aloud the need for sons, and she responded with promises to look after him in his old age. In praising her to the neighbours, her mother did not mention that they feared her temper and were careful never to upset her routine. When she got admission to the country's finest public university to study law, they had visions of Homa as the country's first female chief justice.

The law school was housed in a Gothic building in the capital. The students were from humble families, which meant that grades were their only currency, and Homa was in demand. She decided these peers were worth her while, and would advance and retract favours to keep them in line. Studying law affirmed her instinct that the world could be made legible through procedure. Better a harsh justice, she believed, than a capricious mercy. And it was good to think that this was what was implied by the school's emblem, with its sapphire scales over the Latin phrase: *Ne Vile Fano.*

2

With one child away, it was a comfort to have the other at home, and Ruhi's parents came to think that it was enough if she led a simple, respectable life. But even this was asking for too much. After college, Ruhi worked in the Forestry Department before drifting into freelance conservation. Then she gave that up too and got a diploma in homoeopathy while her mother convinced the neighbours she wasn't idle. She turned down several marriage proposals, less from pride than indifference to the life they promised. She was often low and spent hours on the terrace. And advising her with little effect only confirmed Homa's intuition that her own childhood suffering had been the price of lucidity in a middling town.

Homa's first job was at a corporate law firm in the capital. The brisk air of their glass offices made her feel a cut above the advocates queuing in the musty courts. She worked hard to cultivate mentors and a social circle marked by the give and take of a series of rising rivals. So it was a surprise, at least initially, that when it came to marriage, she chose a mousy civil servant. They met on a pro bono project her firm had signed on to extend its reach within the government. His boyish politeness reminded her, with tenderness, of her manners around elders as a child. For the rest, he was closer to Ruhi in temperament; only his desire for status, which was not unwelcome, made him more predictable. He often asked what Homa saw in him and looked smudged when she replied, 'A good man.'

Homa's husband had more of a start in life, with a rent-free flat owned by his parents and family connections he was too halting to pursue. Homa brought their union drive and strategic clarity. She refurbished the flat in a modern, minimalist style and hosted dinners for his superiors where she pushed him to demand recognition for his work. Sitting like a guest in his own drawing room, he resented her need for control, but with a less ruthless partner, he feared that they might slip into mediocrity together.

A decade into his success, his doubts about his calibre mellowed. It helped that other women were responding to his rise. He came to agree with his mother that he might have done better than to marry a woman whose unkindness he had mistaken for a crudity of manners rather than of spirit. There was still no child because Homa had worried that motherhood would interrupt her early career. One evening when he missed a fertility appointment, she called him impotent. Both knew that he was not, but the word, full of the sourness of old insinuations, had him slam the door and drive off. Homa went about her day certain that he would return. Then she phoned her mother, who agreed that the name-calling was innocuous yet felt the need to say, 'Be careful. Even a worm turns.'

A week later, Homa's in-laws sent their driver to collect her husband's things. *You coward*, she texted him. He showed up in person the next morning and asked for a divorce. Through the legal proceedings, Homa felt an emotion she could only describe as boredom. She moved into a flat in a noisier suburb and did not bother to change the decor. Then her father died of a heart attack at the age of sixty-nine. Though he had never brought it up, she felt a deep shame in having disappointed him. In the year after, she developed an incurable acid reflux and underwent surgery to cauterise an ulcer. She was determined to start a new life, but her existing one only got narrower. She eliminated foods, friends, and clients. On weekends, she flew home to visit her family. Her sister had weathered their father's loss far better, perhaps because her life had acquired a nurturing solidity.

Ruhi had married a veterinary doctor and lived in a cluttered row house at the edge of the city. They had a daughter whose sweet, gap-tooth smile would have made Homa jealous if she wasn't relieved to recognise that she might make a better aunt than a mother. Some years before, she had helped Ruhi register a 'wellness clinic'. The patients came with aches and fevers; anything serious was referred to the hospital. In the evenings, they often visited Ruhi again at home, where she was generous with tea and advice. The poorer ones asked her and her husband to intervene in family disputes; they carried respect as a 'doctor couple'. Ruhi's husband mused that she could stand for the local election but Homa knew that she never would. There was a gossipy air and pride in the paltriness of it all, as if it were vain to strive for anything better. Yet Ruhi's was the only place where Homa didn't wake at night thinking about the cabinet under the sink. When she mentioned this, Ruhi told her it was time to come home.

3

At the age of forty, Homa returned to her native city, where her firm had a growing clientele. She rented a flat near one of the new business parks though she had no energy for its restaurants and bars. Then one Sunday, she accompanied her mother to a devotional gathering. The host, a family friend, had become a member of a mission called the Society. Homa expected an audience of retirees, but the room was full of office-goers her age. The priest was a young man in a scarlet robe, his scalp shaved around a tuft at the crown. He sat with a laptop on a carved stand and a drum tied in muslin to his side. The tenets were familiar from Homa's childhood, but unlike her mother, who irately justified them as *how god likes it*, the priest delighted in meeting the most sceptical questions with cool, logical replies. Over tea, Homa learned that he was an engineer from one of the country's finest colleges.

Homa returned the next week and the week after. Each time she raised her hand to speak, the priest lit up. And the pleasure she took in her effect on him was heightened by her sense that his sympathy was without reserve. One time he lent her an autobiography by one of the Society's elders. The opening pages described a young man in anguish, a darkness so like her own that she read straight through the night. What had healed him, the elder wrote, was a truth he would rediscover over decades of meeting seekers from malarial villages to the halls of parliament: that man's greatest desire is for unconditional love. Peace lay in cultivating this love within oneself until it overflowed and shaped the world. Alone in bed, Homa felt that all the yearning and confusion she had known since childhood had its source in this desire. She read with mounting reverence for the elder's renunciation of his easy life, his search for a master, and his service since, which had brought solace to thousands.

When Homa told the priest that she wished to join the Society, his smile held no triumph, only enthusiasm for her next step. As a registered member, she donated one per cent of her income to its offices and was eligible for discounts and special talks at the library. She was also assigned a counsellor, in her case the same priest, who was responsible for a close group of protégés. Under his guidance, Homa took her first vows on vegetarianism and chanting beads. She liked that the practice was free of the zeal of converts: the rituals were no more than a stricter version of her mother's; most members continued with their regular lives. The founder himself had been a businessman who suffered from chronic migraines. He did not claim to be a messiah, only to have found relief in connecting with his ancient faith.

Homa once again opened her home to guests. Her drawing room was fitted with a tall marble altar; folk paintings replaced the modern art on her walls. Some members might have found her intimidating if they did not pity her as a woman ripe for redemption. The Society, as a rule, condemned divorce – except when a chaste, deserted wife turned to service. As the priest who was her counsellor put it: her husband's exit was merely Fate marking her for a new role. Two years later, his advocacy saw her name added to a list of members ready for initiation as disciples. Her master would be the same elder whose autobiography had drawn her to the path.

On the day of the ceremony, the Society hall was scented with camphor and strings of jasmine. Sixty aspirants sat in the front rows as the elder discoursed on the nature of evil. His voice was objective and capacious, yet with every turn of thought, Homa felt that all the tendencies he described were still alive within her. Then he announced that he had prayed for his new disciples and invited each to receive a blessed rosary. As Homa knelt before him, her hands began to shake. He asked what was wrong. Surprising herself, she whispered, 'I am not kind. That is why my husband left me. I do not deserve these beads.' The elder said gently, 'Whatever his reasons, your affliction is the sign of one who sees herself without disguise. Purify your nature, and it will become the instrument through which you attain your destiny.'

Homa lowered her head on her master's feet. She returned to her spiritual practice with greater patience, and slowly, she began to notice changes in herself. The most remarkable of these was her vanishing acid reflux. She came to believe that beneath the rational mind she once revered lay a latent, mysterious self, one that could be moved through repetition and supplication towards discernible, even biological results. Though there were still days when her temper returned and regrets flared, it was through the contemplation of this unknown source and its effects that she felt she had come closest to a spiritual revelation.

As her vows intensified, Homa found it hard to reconcile her job as a corporate lawyer with her life as a disciple. Other members balanced the two well enough, but as her counsellor noted, Homa had a 'passionate' nature that disliked half-measures. On his advice, she quit the firm to become a legal advisor to their chapter. Her first assignment was to settle a dispute over a plot of land designated for a temple called the Sanctuary. Though the procedure was routine, its aim felt momentous: built of red sandstone, the Sanctuary was to blend ancient and modern architectural techniques to stand for a thousand years. The donors – among the wealthiest in the city – were pleased to have a qualified and articulate woman on the job. Homa's own pay was nominal but her expenses were covered and she was given a flat in a building owned by the Society.

The Society operated like a franchise: the headquarters were in the capital, and besides a few fixed tenets, much of the stewardship was left to the local management. Women could not become priests or elders but they could rise to the highest administrative offices. This suited Homa since her talent lay less in theology than in enterprise. Over the years she became a crucial voice in her chapter's expansion. The premises, which had comprised a brick temple, a hall and some offices, grew to include a restaurant, a seminary, and housing for the entire staff. The calendar was now so packed that members joked about forgetting the rest of the city.

When Homa was fifty-one, her mother was diagnosed with renal failure. Doctors among the members gave her hospice care, and Homa had the satisfaction of doing her duty by at least one parent.

She regretted the funeral her father had received, with leery priests releasing his ashes into a river thick with sewage. When her mother died, the Society took over: a tent was erected, a senior priest arrived, and a group of women sat in the doorway to sing. Ruhi resented the presence of these strangers. The lunch had dishes her mother never prepared. She complained her sister was going too far and that these were 'not our customs' – a phrase that baffled Homa. Still, when the singing began, it released the mourners' grief, and Ruhi opened her mouth on her palm and cried like a child. Homa's eyes were wet too, but she made no sound.

4

Early one winter, Homa learned that her counsellor, the priest, was having an affair with the wife of one of his protégés. The news got out when the husband failed to take his own life. Since the case had no legal implications, Homa was not consulted. The priest was brought before two trustees and the temple president. An ombudsman looked up the guiding principles, which were put in place after a child abuse scandal in the Society's early days, and nothing pointed to the priest's expulsion. Finally, invoking the scriptures and the dead founder, he was dismissed from his spiritual post for breaking the vow of celibacy, though he was allowed to remain a lay member. He also had to undergo some 'purification' practices, such as never eating food prepared by another man's wife even at a devotional gathering.

Homa kept her response brief: God had tested his servant with temptation and found him wanting. But other women among the members could not contain their indignation, which, she suspected, had as much to do with how chaste the handsome priest had been with them. Any similar feelings within her were absorbed into a tender, almost maternal disappointment. Under pressure from the elders, the priest finally married his lover and moved to a village where they started a religious school. Homa assumed he kept his distance to protect her reputation, and she often prayed that he should find peace.

But the rumours continued. People said he still lived like a priest 'in all respects' and the wife was in despair. When the story reached the tabloids, Homa's master, the elder, visited the chapter to check on his disciples. Homa told him of how the scandal had unsettled her faith: the purification rituals had been petty, the members' vows futile against their malice. The elder listened in silence. He then explained that the Society was becoming insular. The first generation of followers, whose leaders had been initiated by the founder, was fading. The one after had no personal experience of him, so they took his messages out of context and applied them in dangerous ways. It was up to younger members like Homa to keep the institution from eating itself. His parting words were: 'Faith stagnates like water in a trough when it cannot flow outward.'

Before his death, the elder put Homa in touch with the Society's national council to help draft a new legal framework for abuses of authority and disputes with secular courts. Homa pored over the records of thirty-seven chapters across the country to compile the precedents. As her trips to the capital increased, she gained a wider view of the mission, and steadily, her motivation returned. Then, in the middle of this, news arrived that the Sanctuary was in trouble. Its sandstone spires were nearing full height and already a landmark; it was how her chapter was recognised. Now the time had come to widen the only access road, but the district officials would not clear the file. They said the road passed through a 'sensitive' settlement. The residents had moved there after riots pushed them out of a temple town and feared another one would rise around them.

Homa assured the authorities that the Society had no desire to displace or offend other faiths. When they did not relent, the elders advised her to be patient. A nationalist party was rising in the polls; temple projects would see better days. But Homa did not have to wait that long. Word of her advocacy spread and a local minister from the same party called her office. With a little public support, he said, he would have an excuse to push for her file. When Homa made it clear that she would not fund a political rally, he sounded hurt, as if he had been misunderstood. He was only proposing a pilgrimage. He would arrange for the permissions and security. All he wanted was the honour of attending the Sanctuary's inauguration.

Homa knew what the minister stood to gain: a hold in a wealthy sect and a chance to rouse villagers before the national election. The Society had more at risk, its reputation could not afford another flare. She went in a group to survey the site. For miles along the marsh the road was rutted; the van's engine sent up clouds of starlings. Then, just as the Sanctuary's spires appeared on the distant rim of the water, the track narrowed. Rickety houses piled on each other like in a city slum. Young men sat idle on the steps, their gaze more curious than cold. To one side rose a brick wall topped with coils of wire. A girl darted up with sharp black eyes and a tray of hair clips before her mother called her wearily back inside. Homa did not recognise a single politician on the vinyl hoardings. When she looked up, the roofs bristled with flags.

Homa thought it best not to wait for the election. Losing the road meant losing the Sanctuary to all but barefoot pilgrims, and the donors were getting restless. The procession need not pass down the settlement; it could take the winding paths through the villages around. This would avoid a confrontation, while also uniting those who wished them well. When the council of elders got behind Homa, the temple president gave in. For weeks after, the members organised buses and portable toilets, rallied neighbours, and practised songs. Their flyers announced that the pilgrimage was a peaceful event; anyone was welcome to join. But on the day, a news report called it a test of whether the faithful could defend what was theirs.

Homa was surprised by the scale of the procession. At every junction, busloads from the city were joined by villagers holding garlands. Marching past the childlike rapture of the members were groups of men with stony, purposeful faces, some waving national flags. After six hours on foot, the procession reached the gates of the Sanctuary, where women were singing hymns in welcome. Local leaders took the mic to speak on the public's right to worship. Priests invoked the glory of the faith. In the haze of the electric lights, the foundations might have been an ancient ruin. And for a moment, Homa was seized by a fear of the eyes on the marsh and a vision of an explosion that would splinter all that sandstone to red shrapnel.

That night, tired and relieved, Homa lit the lamps at her altar. In her mother's shrine, the gods had been numerous. There was the silver infant who stole butter in pastoral tales. The soft-chested youth whose mischief extended to sex and war. Some deities had animal faces, some were primordial forms with eyes. Homa's altar now held a single idol, the brass figure of God as a grown man, handsome, composed, his gaze upon her unfaltering. If her blood ran warm like a warrior's, his was the cool blood of a sovereign. She could almost hear him say the words: *ne vile fano.*

5

Headlines announced that the new regime would propel the nation into the future by reviving the glory of its ancient past. When a reporter pressed Homa for comment, she affirmed that the Society was a spiritual mission. Internally, the members saw the election as heralding a golden age for their faith. The trustees were elated at the thought of the donations such a climate would bring. The chapter's online group, where members shared invitations and festive greetings, became clogged with links to the news. Some members objected to the debates: those with an interest in politics were asked to form a separate chat. Homa, the obvious choice, was invited to preside.

Many in the new group had been involved in organising the Sanctuary campaign. Little press had followed but none of it was hostile, and whether or not the minister needed it to pressure the officials, he kept his end of the bargain: the file was finally signed. The settlement on the marsh did not retaliate, though trouble was expected once the work on the road began. Now, as if by osmosis, most members accepted that priests need the protection of kings to survive. In a democracy, this also meant being alert about who should become king. When the regional election came around, the Protectors, as the group now called themselves, took vows to 'awaken' their communities. No one in the chapter protested when they drove their neighbours to rallies and helped their servants get registered to vote. Of course, none of this was done in the name of the Society but from a sense of 'personal obligation'.

When the nationalist party won the regional election as well, the Protectors hailed the victory. But the chaotic run-up had revealed that democracy could not be relied on to protect them, and the Society must build its own cadre for self-defence. Homa offered to draft a memorandum to this effect. The plan was to circulate it among the other chapters for signatures before presenting it to the elders on the council. There was also constant talk of personal safety: what if one's van was stopped on the way to the Sanctuary? A martial arts master was hired to teach a class. Homa joined only the warm up, but her words made it to the bulletin: 'As a woman, I cannot meditate in a forest and be safe. My inner journey would go nowhere without the police station at the end of the street.'

In time the Protectors' rising clout began to strain the chapter. The priests and counsellors, regarded as the insular old guard, drew close around the temple president, while Homa, speaking for the new, held sway with the council, other chapters, donors and politicians. The trustees leaned this way and then the other. In moments of uncertainty, Homa recalled her elder's advice about faith flowing outward. The Society's future did not lie in becoming a cult. Their practices had emerged from within her way of life, and she saw herself among the elect, a custodian of the millions who already practised her religion.

One afternoon, the minister behind the pilgrimage invited Homa to his new residence as the head of Tourism and Heritage for the state. As his wife served them tea, he asked Homa, not entirely in jest, if she would consider joining politics. Homa replied in full seriousness that she would not. The minister praised her purity but hoped she might say a few words at a training camp he had organised. The theme was 'self-making' and she had a gift for explaining their tenets in simple analogies. Homa was uncertain; she only engaged with politicians as a necessity and had no desire to be seen on a stage together. But she changed her mind when she learned that delegates from two rival missions would attend.

The camp was held during the summer in an empty schoolhouse. Teenage girls arrived from districts across the state. Their fathers were clerks, tenant farmers, truckers; their mothers, housewives and maids. The room was full of teeth and the occasional bruised ear. That the other missions sent male priests made Homa smile. Throughout their sermons, the girls sat at the wooden desks as if they were mute. Around Homa, they giggled and raised their hands. They were rapt when she told them that in their civilisation, ferocity was a feminine trait. They were strong in the way of the goddesses that personified God's wrath to balance the cosmos. They did not need to wear jeans or behave like men, who were too cowardly to protect their honour, let alone that of the motherland. It was their duty to rebuke unmanly husbands and to raise their children to be virtuous.

Homa was repeating what the Society preached with the vividness of the visions that stirred her as a child. At the lunch table, the girls crowded her with questions about her life. They gasped when she told them that her husband had deserted her. But she had not despaired; as she saw it, fate had relieved her of her household duties to become a guardian to any young aspirant. By the end of the afternoon, the girls were calling her Mother. It was not only her words that emboldened them; they were taking in the day together, making little groups and speaking in voices louder than they must otherwise dare. She told herself they were her children. ■

தமிழ்

Sometimes the most obstinate problem in translating a text is its title. So it was with the short story 'Kazhumaadan' by the Tamil writer Jeyamohan, which appears in this issue. The title is a conflation of two words: *kazhu*, meaning stake, and *maadan*, a rural deity. Translated literally, the title would read 'Stake-God', which makes little sense in English. In Tamil, though, the word unravels to communicate an entire idea: 'one who, by virtue of being impaled on a stake, becomes a god'.

Centuries of unconscious practice ensures that this unravelling happens instinctively in the Tamil reader's mind, attuned as she is to how the language's grammar accommodates the combination of independent words to make a compound expression. Such a construction is called a *tŏkai-nilai-todar*. *Tŏkai* means 'to hide' or 'to omit'. Since these compound expressions are created through a technique of omission, they came to be known as *tŏkais*. Tamil grammar defines different types of omission; it allows for the secreting away not just of case markers, but of whole ideas – phrases, similes, even time itself through the effacement of tenses.

In my translation practice, it often seems to me that translators are not just purveyors of words, but of silences, too. To translate with felicity is to translate not only the said, but also the unsaid. To hide, therefore, is not to omit or dispense with; rather, it is an act of enlargement, of containing more within less. It is a synthesis, a process of making a whole greater than the sum of its parts. This is illustrated in tŏkai also being used in the sense of a 'collection', such as *Kuruntŏkai*, a collection of intensely evocative classical Tamil love poems that has engendered many translations.

Tŏkai as synthesis – two variant forces producing something more potent than their individual components – could be seen as a metaphor for the evolution of Tamil literature itself. Tamil is characterised by strong diglossia: a formal register for the written word and an informal one for everyday life. While the formal register has its roots in classical Tamil, the colloquial has always existed alongside it. When these two worlds began to fuse in the late nineteenth century, modern Tamil literature took shape. The writer and activist Subramania Bharati, renowned for his poetry, is credited with revolutionising Tamil prose by folding the spoken tongue into the written register. Later, as modern literature became more provincial, many Tamil writers advanced this blending of the written and spoken by incorporating local dialects, which change not only from region to region but also between social groups. Including these vernaculars was more than aesthetic inventiveness – it allowed writers to present their worlds in a literature as rich and varied as the spoken tongue.

Beyond register, synthesis also took place in form and style. The writer Pudhumaipithan – and his contemporaries who wrote in *Manikodi*, a path-breaking little magazine in Tamil – coupled Western forms with Tamil life to produce a scintillating repertoire of short stories. Ki. Rajanarayanan folded oral folklore traditions into the short-story form to make it uniquely his own. Ashokamitran, inspired by the style of writers like Hemingway, ushered in a spare aesthetic in Tamil prose, one that could express the vicissitudes of Tamil urban life.

Such synthesis, of course, is not singular to Tamil. Every language grows by absorbing and layering the absorbed with its own genius. The act of translation has long been a lubricant for this form of exchange, helping create the grand collective of world literature – the tŏkai of tŏkais. Without it, we would struggle to receive inspiration from the 'other', an act that eschews ideas of linguistic and cultural purity.

'Kazhumaadan' opens with an arresting image. The narrator, an untouchable, walks through an overgrowth of halfa grass – known as *darbha* in India, where it is a sacred element in Vedic rituals. The juxtaposition of the untouchable and the divine enacts, within a single image, this same synthesis: two seemingly opposed elements combined to produce something larger in meaning. It strikes at the heart of the story: a questioning of the very idea of purity, which, when defined externally, is invariably destructive. In society, such ideas lead to oppression; in language, they lead to stagnation.

Synthesis is the way of growth. The constant movement in Tamil literature – where writers blended inspirations from several parts of the world, from several realms of life, to create new legacies – is what makes it a vibrant corpus, one that enriches the grand tŏkai of world literature. ■

REUTERS

THE KILLING OF A CANADIAN SIKH

Karan Mahajan

1

The killing occurred at 8:30 p.m. on Father's Day, 2023. Hardeep Singh Nijjar, a forty-five-year-old Sikh leader in Canada and father of two, had finished giving a speech at the temple over which he presided. From his pickup truck in the parking lot, he called his family and told them he'd be home soon. His son said there would be pizza for dinner, and seviyan, a sweet vermicelli dish, for dessert. But as Nijjar drove out of the temple's parking lot, a white sedan swerved in front of his car at the gate. Then two hooded men in black, wearing medical masks, jumped out from under a gazebo-like wooden structure and fired scores of rounds through the window of Nijjar's Dodge Ram.

It was an audacious murder. Sunday evening is a busy time at the Guru Nanak Sikh Gurdwara, which, even more so than most Sikh temples, is both a place of worship and a community center, boasting a free twenty-four-hour canteen, a senior center, a pre-school, and a recreational field. A knot of people were chatting nearby in the parking lot. A few men practiced soccer in the field, and when they heard the shooting they rushed towards the Dodge Ram. One of the players chased the killers until one turned around and trained his gun on him. In the truck, Nijjar was slumped over to the right, as if reaching for something on the passenger side. His blue turban had come off his head and his light purple shirt was darkened with blood.

Surrey, in British Columbia, is a heavily Sikh town. A quarter of its 700,000-strong population is Sikh; and Punjabi is the second-most spoken language. Sikhs started emigrating to Canada from India in the 1900s to work in lumber mills. Despite discrimination, they established themselves as a social and political force, especially in British Columbia. By the 1980s a large segment of Sikhs had moved to Surrey, a flat, cheap exurb with watercolor-blue mountains on the horizon. Surrey is now a collection of two-story housing developments and dun-and-white strip malls that sell everything from turbans and paan to Punjabi books, Indian fabrics, and jewelry. Immigrant law offices, travel agencies, and notaries are, predictably, rampant. The Guru Nanak Sikh Gurdwara is one of the hubs of the community, and Nijjar, a plumber by profession, was a well-known man. News of his death spread on social media, and within hours hundreds of angry congregants showed up at the grounds of the gurdwara. Moninder Singh, a close friend and Sikh leader, was there too. He remembers some of the younger congregants blocking off the four-lane road in front of the gurdwara. Taking control of a mic, Moninder urged calm, then said, 'Make no mistake: this is a political assassination. And it's been carried out by India.'

Moninder had reasons to suspect India. For years, Nijjar had publicly espoused the cause of Khalistan, an independent Sikh state in India, which a fringe of Sikhs in the diaspora wished to carve out of Indian Punjab, as well as Pakistani Punjab and other states that had once been part of larger Punjab under British rule. In 2014, when Nijjar started planning symbolic referendums for Khalistan in the West, the Indian government had termed him a terrorist. But the charges against Nijjar – that he was directing bombings and assassinations in India – did not meet Canada's evidentiary threshold, and Canada declined to extradite him. Nijjar continued his activism, and, in the year before his death, spoke to his followers about an active threat on his life. 'The coming time is very dangerous,' he said in what turned out to be his last speech. It was one reason the congregants were so angry; they felt Canada had not done enough to protect him.

Three months after the murder the community gained a well-placed ally: prime minister Justin Trudeau, who stood up in Parliament that September and stated he had 'credible allegations of a potential link between agents of the government of India and the killing of a Canadian citizen' – Hardeep Singh Nijjar – adding that, 'Any involvement of a foreign government in the killing of a Canadian citizen on Canadian soil is an unacceptable violation of our sovereignty.' It was a major turn in the affair. Canada and India have been intricately connected trading partners for decades. Hundreds of thousands of Indian students flock to Canadian colleges every year, and Canada is home to the largest Sikh diaspora in the world, at 800,000 souls. But Canada would not release its evidence, and so India accused Trudeau of pandering to a fundamentalist Sikh base. Since 1967, when the Liberal Party's immigration reforms opened the gates for the arrival of Sikhs in larger numbers, Sikhs have reliably voted Liberal, so much so that in 2016 Trudeau was able to quip that, 'I have more Sikhs in my Cabinet than Modi does' – four versus two. Now, mutual expulsions of diplomats followed Trudeau's accusation. India suspended visa services to Canada. Indian and Canadian relations became strained.

This stalemate of conflicting narratives might have continued were it not for the fact that two months later, in November 2023, the US Justice Department unsealed an indictment against an Indian intelligence agent for trying to carry out a very similar hit against a Khalistani activist in New York. Indian officials again argued that an indictment was not evidence, but the US presented a cache of recordings and text messages, and India soon arrested the accused Indian intelligence operative, Vikash Yadav, on other charges, perhaps with the intent of making him appear like an officer who had gone rogue.

What appeared to be a single extrajudicial killing now looked like a program to eliminate Khalistani activists across North America.

2

India has changed since the election of prime minister Narendra Modi and his Hindu nationalist Bharatiya Janata Party (BJP) in 2014. Dissent is no longer tolerated. Critics are hounded through the press and social media, by police, the tax department, and the judiciary. So it is not entirely surprising that India would extend its campaign of repression abroad. The Sikhs I met in North America this year were jittery but determined. A woman at Nijjar's gurdwara told me that, after Nijjar's death, she started scanning other congregants for signs they were Indian agents. When my phone call with a Sikh activist in the US briefly dropped, he asked, 'Did you hear something funny on the phone just now?' adding that he'd heard 'what sounded like a broadcast of some kind for ten seconds on the line.'

But, what is a surprise, in this case of transnational repression, are the targets. While it was true that Nijjar and his allies used their megaphones in the West to agitate for Khalistan, they were, at best, irritants. Only a small percentage of Sikhs in Canada, the UK, and the US support Khalistan. In India, meanwhile, the movement – active in the 1980s and early 1990s – is long dead, and there are few signs that it is being resuscitated. If anything, India's campaign against the Khalistanis had given the quixotic movement unexpected oxygen, alerting the world to the cause. Why did India do it?

In the new era of its geopolitical arrival, when India was seen by the US and its allies as a crucial bulwark against China, India was communicating to the West that it would not wait for its dubious 'due process' to eliminate individuals it deemed terrorists. The assassination was also a warning to the prosperous Sikh diaspora not to besmirch India's reputation abroad, a message that revealed a profound misunderstanding of how Sikhs, a proud minority, have traditionally responded to threats from the majority. But, as I learned on my trip this year to Canada, there was also a more immediate political reason for the killing, one which led back, through various curves, to Punjab itself.

3

Sikhism arose in fifteenth century Punjab as a reaction to Brahmanism. Founded by the charismatic mystic Guru Nanak, it is a monotheistic religion with an ethos of service and volunteerism. In Sikh temples, congregants are supposed to cook and eat together, and to offer free meals to the public, all of which runs counter to the caste system. Sikhism, however, was always a non-converting minority religion – even today it is only practiced by less than 2 per cent of India's population – and its reputation rested on its martial strain and its history of resistance. Martyrs are revered. As Guru Arjan, the fifth Guru of Sikhism, supposedly said in the sixteenth century, 'The true test of faith is the hour of misery.' (Tortured to death by the Mughal emperor Jehangir, Arjan was, according to legend, boiled in a cauldron of water with red-hot sand poured onto him from above). In the seventeenth century, the military strain of Sikhism was formalized through the establishment of the Khalsa, a sect of religious warriors identified by the so-called five Ks: kesh (unshorn hair), kara (steel bracelet), kirpan (sword or knife), kaccha (cotton shorts), and kangha (a comb). The men took on the last name 'Singh' (lion) and the women 'Kaur' (princess) – a practice that continues to this day. Then, in the early 1800s, Maharaja Ranjit Singh, a Sikh ruler, united a vast swathe of northern India under his reign. It was only in 1849, a decade after Ranjit Singh's death, that the British annexed Punjab. Sikhs went on to be overrepresented in the British Army, which is why they were mobile in the empire, and came to Canada as early as 1900.

When India gained independence, Punjab was partitioned, and Sikhs sided with India rather than Islamic Pakistan. They didn't gain their own country, but Nehru promised their rights would be safeguarded. By the 1960s, though, many Sikhs felt their fertile state – India's breadbasket – was giving more to India than it was gaining in return. The so-called 'Green Revolution' increased agricultural productivity in Punjab, but it also worsened indebtedness as farmers took out loans for seeds, fertilizers, pesticides, and equipment. Sikh parties – dominated by the land-owning, restive Jat caste – called again for greater autonomy for Punjab, including control over its river waters and the new capital city of Chandigarh, which was shared with a neighboring Hindu-majority state. Autonomy never arrived. Instead, in the late 1970s, a Sikh fundamentalist movement took hold, led by a preacher in his thirties named Jarnail Singh Bhindranwale. Bhindranwale didn't openly call for independence, but his armed followers targeted Sikh apostates and Hindus who fell afoul of them. India's prime minister, Indira Gandhi, and her Congress party initially believed they could control Bhindranwale and use him to divide the Sikh vote. They were proven wrong. By 1982, Bhindranwale and his militants took refuge in the sacred, marbled precincts of the Golden Temple, the central seat of the Sikh religion, in Amritsar. They eventually turned parts of it into a sandbagged headquarters for their attacks.

The movement for Khalistan solidified in 1984. This was the year that Gandhi finally ordered the Indian Army to storm the Golden Temple to flush out Bhindranwale. But the method the army employed – a siege, with pilgrims present, using tanks and armored carriers, near an important religious holiday for Sikhs – made the event seem like an attack on Sikhi itself. 'It would be like shooting at St Paul's Cathedral in London,' the BBC journalist Mark Tully remembered. After the disastrous raid, which lasted days longer than expected, the Akal Takht (the Eternal Throne), which is where the central religious body of Sikhism holds court, lay in ruins. The Central Sikh Museum and Reference Library, housing innumerable ancient documents, was gutted by a fire. The militants were killed, but so were hundreds of soldiers and over a thousand civilians. In the days that followed, Sikh visitors could be seen pressing their faces to the bullet holes on the walls of the complex and their cheeks against the bloodstains on the tiled floors.

4

E ven moderate Sikhs were outraged by the military action, code-named Operation Blue Star. Gurpreet Singh, a well-known journalist in Surrey who grew up in India, was a teenager when the attack occurred. 'I used to dream in Hindi,' he told me on my visit to Surrey this year. 'I used to think in Hindi. Punjabi was still alien to me, because I had been outside Punjab for most of the time. But after Operation Blue Star, I made a conscious decision to learn Punjabi and start thinking in Punjabi.' Another moderate Sikh civic leader remembers telling his wife, 'They're going to kill her.' Meaning: Indira Gandhi. These were common sentiments, and in fact, four months after the siege of the Golden Temple, Gandhi was shot dead by her two Sikh bodyguards as she strolled across her lawn. In response, Gandhi's Congress party unleashed massive 'riots' in Delhi. More than 3,000 Sikhs were murdered (50,000 are said to have fled the city entirely, with another 50,000 seeking shelter in government and volunteer camps).

Buoyed by the vengeful anti-Sikh violence, the Congress won the 1984 election by a landslide. In response, the Sikh militant movement – an insurgency devoted to taking control of Punjab and creating an independent state of Khalistan – began in earnest. Many Sikh youth took up arms against the state and Hindus; Hindu families fled the region; and thousands of Sikhs were killed, tortured, or 'disappeared' by police and paramilitary forces. A segment of Canadian Sikhs supported the movement with money, protests, media coverage, and manpower. In 1985, Canadian-based Khalistani separatists blew up an Air India jet over the coast of Ireland, killing 329, the largest terrorist attack in history before 9/11. (Another bomb, timed to go off around the same time on an Air India plane leaving Tokyo, detonated earlier than planned, killing two baggage handlers at Narita Airport.)

Hardeep Singh Nijjar was seven in 1984. He grew up in a rural Punjabi family that occasionally sheltered militants who were on the run from the paramilitary forces and police (Punjab has no real mountains or forests for guerillas to hide in). These militants included some of the top commandos of Khalistani outfits, such as the Babbar Khalsa, accused of carrying out the Air India bombing. Nijjar was inspired by these individuals, but his actual role in the movement is unclear. What is known is that in 1995, ten years into the militancy, his friends assassinated the chief minister of Punjab, Beant Singh, in a car bombing, killing him and seventeen others. This turned out to be one of the last major actions of an insurgency that was beginning to give way. One of the reasons was that the Indian police and paramilitary repression had been brutally effective. K.P.S. Gill, the Sikh head of police in Punjab credited with crushing the insurgency, told a journalist, 'In a war, human rights just don't factor into it.' By 1995, tens of thousands of Sikhs had been detained, tortured, executed and disappeared by Indian counterinsurgency forces. At the same time, the militant groups themselves began to splinter. They were guilty of their own abuses, and the population was losing patience. It began withdrawing support from the militants. 'Khalistan' was on its way to becoming a verboten term, even though none of the underlying problems of religious or political autonomy had been addressed.

Soon after the assassination of Beant Singh, Nijjar was picked up by police and tortured. He was released after he paid a bribe and reportedly fled to the UK, where his brothers lived. In 1997, two years later, he arrived in Canada, carrying a passport with a Hindu name, Ravi Sharma, his beard and hair shorn. Though his application for asylum was repeatedly rejected – as was an attempt to gain residency through a last-minute marriage to a Punjabi woman – Nijjar was allowed to stay on under Canada's then-lax immigration laws.

At the time, the Khalistan movement was fizzling out in India, but could still be discussed openly in Canada. In 1998, the year after Nijjar arrived, Khalistanis in fact set up their own gurdwara in Surrey, Dasmesh Darbar, with pictures of militants on bold display in the communal dining hall – including a photo of Talwinder Parmar, widely considered the mastermind of the 1985 Air India bombing (to this day, despite ample evidence to the contrary, Khalistanis insist that India conspired to have its own jets blown up). Khalistanis began to fight for control and influence over other gurdwaras in Surrey, seizing on seemingly trivial issues such as the use of tables and chairs in community kitchens when, traditionally, they said, one was supposed to sit on the ground. Bloody hand-to-hand battles were fought in gurdwaras over the topic, though some observers wondered if this ruckus was being raised to distract from the fact that the Canadian police had finally closed in on the suspects in the Air India bombing. In 2000, four Sikh men were charged, all members of the Babbar Khalsa. Only one was convicted.

The long-running Air India trial caused a chill among Khalistanis, but by the mid-2000s, the movement began to revive again. A new generation of Canadian-born Sikhs was coming of age, and they increasingly deployed the language of identity politics and human rights to talk about the pogrom of 1984 and the state-sponsored repression that followed. Issues such as Punjab's opioid crisis, a lack of industrialization, and an influx of poor migrants from other states were viewed as plots engineered by the Indian state to keep Sikhs in check (some of these problems, such as the drug crisis, in fact stem from Punjab's vulnerable position as a border state). Meanwhile, a publicity-seeking lawyer in New York City, Gurpatwant Singh Pannun, lobbied the UN to have the 1984 massacre recognized as a 'genocide'. Pannun also organized educational 'camps' in Canada, and this is where he met Nijjar. It was 2007. Pannun remembers Nijjar being 'very quiet, to the point . . . he talked to me about my thoughts on Khalistan – is it only about justice, what can be done?' Soon enough the two men became close. Pannun represented Nijjar as his lawyer, and Nijjar in turn became one of Pannun's prime activists in Canada.

Nijjar also met other Sikh activists in Surrey, such as Moninder Singh, who was deeply involved with Dasmesh Darbar, the Khalistani-leaning gurdwara. Moninder, who was three years younger than Nijjar and had grown up in Canada in a Khalistani family, remembers that Nijjar 'came straight up to me and hugged me' in the gurdwara after Moninder had given a speech. 'He was very impressed that a person born and raised in the Western world was speaking so openly and powerfully about Khalistan and what happened in 1984. And from there, we just started getting closer and closer.' Moninder was also skilled at using the internet to connect with younger Sikhs all over the world. Over time, this combination of the internet – on which images of massacred and martyred Sikhs could circulate forever – and organized petitions to international bodies gave the movement renewed prominence abroad. Whereas the original movement in the 1980s and 1990s had evolved in India out of an emotional upwelling, pressed at the point of a bayonet, this version was being conducted in the West, through the lobbying of foreign governments.

Interestingly, many of the key players in what one might term Khalistan 2.0 had not been to India in years. Moninder, born in the logging town of Clearwater, with a population of around 2,000, had last visited India when he was four. Pannun had been in self-imposed exile since he had immigrated from Punjab to the US in 1992. Nijjar too had not returned. As a result, these men were increasingly out of touch with the populace of Punjab, which, having suffered a terrible civil war, no longer had any serious interest in independence. This did not deter the Khalistanis in the diaspora. For these Sikhs, Punjab had become a mythical landscape, the land where the ten Gurus of Sikhs had once roamed, and which Maharaja Ranjit Singh had unified in the 1800s. The time for apologies and redressal by the Indian government – which had delayed justice through a parade of slow-moving inquiries – had passed. Khalistan was the only form of salvation possible.

5

And how could Khalistan realistically come about?
I asked Moninder Singh this question on my trip to Canada. It was the evening of Nijjar's second death anniversary at the Guru Nanak Sikh Gurdwara. Hundreds thronged the nine-acre premises, listening to sermons and drinking thandai. We were standing on the sidelines in the rapidly cooling Surrey summer evening. From my spot in the parking lot I could see the gate where Nijjar had been ambushed and beyond that, the frazzled lively greenery into which the shooters had fled.

Moninder is a tall, bearded, bespectacled man with a confidential style and perpetually-surprised-looking eyebrows. He was dressed in the traditional blue garb of the Nihang Sikhs – a warrior order – with two ceremonial knives under his jacket, and mouthed hello to congregants as they passed by. Turning to me, he suggested that 'if one major power like the United States no longer has any need for India, or sees India as a problem,' then it would be easy for the CIA to break up India. He reminded me that, in 'the 1950s, 1960s, 1970s, the Soviet bloc would never have broken in people's minds' but 'it happened.' I asked him what his Khalistan would look like. 'Constitutions are written after countries are made, right?' he said. 'Like, political systems – will it be a theocracy? Will it be a democracy?' He said a panchayat or village council system could work and that his Khalistan would be open to all faiths. And would Khalistan be limited to Indian Punjab, I asked, where the majority of Sikhs are concentrated? (There are only 5,000 Sikhs left in the Pakistani Punjab). 'I don't think any of us have it in our mind that that's where it would end,' he said. 'We would start looking at other areas – maybe towards Lahore and other places. And it's like, well, is that even feasible or possible? Once we have Khalistan, then it's up to us, how we negotiate on further terms. Would it lead to war, would it lead to clashes? Possibly.'

As for why Moninder had not been back to India in forty years, he said that his father's pro-Khalistan activism in the 1980s and 1990s had made it impossible for his family to visit India. Then, in 1997, when his father's name was finally removed from the blacklist as part of a process of granting amnesty to former Khalistanis, Moninder was unable to get a visa to visit. He chalks this up to his growing activism. It was one of the paradoxes of being a Khalistani in Canada: the more you declared yourself one, the less time you could spend in Punjab. But listening to him talk, I wondered if his lack of curiosity about the actual landscape of Punjab went deeper. Moninder had written about how Sikhs could never 'be full-on Canadians in this country', and I now wondered whether an imagined Punjab filled an important space for him and for others who born here – and whether seeing the real Punjab, with its usual Indian chaos and underdevelopment, would tamper with the imagined one.

6

While Khalistan 2.0 was coming into its own in Canada, another force was building in India: Hindu nationalism. Hindu nationalists believe that India is a holy land for Hindus and that other religions and peoples in the region must be neutralized or subsumed for the sake of Hindu self respect. Sikhism, in this regard, is something of an exception. Several of the Gurus of Sikhism bear the names of Hindu Gods, and many Hindus see Sikhism as a warrior-like simplification of their faith – a paternalistic view that religious Sikhs resent. When Modi was elected in 2014, he demonized Muslims but reached out to Sikhs. He reopened certain 1984 riots cases; referred in a speech to the 1984 riots as a 'horrendous genocide'; gave compensation to victims; and inaugurated the Kartarpur Corridor, which allowed Sikh pilgrims from India to visit a shrine in Pakistan without a visa, a concession Sikhs had wanted for decades.

Sikhs, however, had never warmed to the BJP – precisely because it was seen as a party of Hindus. Moreover, the Modi government continued the previous governments' and intelligence officials' fixation with the Khalistan movement, taking an even harder line against individuals who they felt impugned Hindu India's territorial integrity. After his arrest as a youth, Nijjar likely again became a subject of interest to the Indian government in 2013, when he traveled to Pakistan to meet Jagtar Singh Tara. Tara was the prime suspect in the assassination of Beant Singh. He had been apprehended in 1995, but escaped Indian prison in 2004 by hand-digging a tunnel and fleeing to Pakistan, where he was operating freely (India has often accused Pakistan of supporting and inflaming the Khalistan movement). Nijjar and Tara met and were photographed together on the rooftop of a gurdwara. When Tara was arrested the next year in Thailand, Nijjar flew again to meet him, as did Moninder and Pannun, the latter of whom tried to fight Tara's extradition to India, arguing that Tara was not a terrorist because he didn't target civilians and simply wanted to 'put an end' to 'the extrajudicial killings ordered by Beant Singh.' Pannun lost the appeal, but the intervention by North American Sikhs likely enraged the Indian government.

That same year, Pannun and Nijjar announced a plan to hold non-binding referendums on Khalistan among the Punjabi diaspora. India swiftly responded by designating Nijjar a terrorist. Nijjar was accused of being the new mastermind of the banned terrorist organization previously run by Tara – the Khalistan Tiger Force – and of planning a 2007 bombing in a cinema in Punjab that killed six and injured forty-two. India filed a 'red notice' against Nijjar within Interpol. This is not actually an arrest warrant, but a request for extradition, and Canada apparently declined it due to insufficient evidence. (According to *The Globe and Mail*, Nijjar's name didn't even appear in the court transcripts for the case. All the others accused were acquitted, with one dying in jail.)

India did not let up. In 2016, photos began to circulate in the Indian press showing a turbaned Sikh man in a Nike sweatshirt holding an automatic weapon in his right hand against a backdrop of tall Canadian firs – 'proof' that Nijjar was running a terror training camp in the town of Mission in British Columbia, which possesses a shooting range. In fact, the man in the picture wasn't Nijjar at all – though the photo was often accompanied by another (real) photograph of a short, potbellied Nijjar in a red Banana Republic T-shirt standing barefoot before a door and holding an AK-47 in the crook of his right arm. India issued yet another red notice against Nijjar in connection with the 2007 bombing, and reporters swarmed the Nijjar family's home in Surrey for several weeks to cover the training camp story, so much so that Nijjar's son recalls having to change the route he took to and from school to avoid journalists. Nijjar initially denied to the press that he had views on Khalistan, or that he was politically active at all. Soon after, though, he wrote a letter of complaint to Trudeau in which he called himself 'a Sikh nationalist' campaigning for 'Sikh rights.' 'In an earlier attempt to label me as a "terrorist",' he wrote, 'the Indian government accused me of transporting ammunition through "paragliding" which is absolutely preposterous . . . and is more like a bad Bollywood movie plot.' It has since been reported in the Canadian press that Nijjar had in fact given 'weapons and GPS training' to 'five orthodox Sikh men in their 20s and 30s' in 2015, though the training itself 'did not resemble a "camp".' So there was a nugget of truth to India's accusations, but it had marred its own credibility by exaggerating its evidence.

Still, India was on the rise geopolitically, and in April 2018 India and Canada signed an intelligence-sharing agreement. Nijjar was detained for questioning in Canada, only to be released 24 hours later. In 2019, Canada froze Nijjar's accounts and put him on the country's 'no fly' list. Nijjar's debts were called in, his credit cards were canceled, and he would now have to make long drives between Canadian cities for events (Nijjar, who ran a plumbing business, was not exactly poor: he owned three homes in Surrey, now worth nearly $4 million. The source of his increased wealth is not known, though Indian critics have pointed the finger at Pakistani intelligence). The frenetic attention from the Modi government perversely raised Nijjar's profile, and he was unanimously chosen as president of the massive Guru Nanak Sikh Gurdwara in 2019 (Nijjar was re-elected president in 2022). Though the job of president is mostly administrative, the president also delivers a weekly speech. Nijjar included a mention of Khalistan in all of his speeches, telling his congregants on one occasion that, 'we will have to take up arms . . . Those who advocate peaceful methods, we need to leave them behind. What justice will we get this way?'

Then the tide turned against Modi. In late 2020, tens of thousands of farmers converged on the outskirts of Delhi in what has been since called the largest non-violent protest in history. It was a reaction to three farm laws that Modi had tried to slam through Parliament at the peak of the Covid-19 pandemic, without consulting the farmers' unions. The laws might in fact have helped certain farmers by making it easier to sell their produce in the free market, but it scarcely mattered; the farmers believed this was a highhanded attempt to dismantle guaranteed price supports for cash crops like rice and onions, and to pass control to monopolistic industrial houses (a similar move in the state of Bihar some years earlier had resulted in exactly this). The protests also revealed the massive economic discontent roiling under the surface of the Hindu nationalists' success: for years there'd been a lack of investment in agriculture, and levels of indebtedness and suicide among farmers remained high.

Punjabis and Sikhs took the lead in these protests, running encampments with the same ethos of voluntary service and community kitchens seen in gurdwaras. Diasporic Sikhs joined in as well, staging protests abroad and making donations to the farmers' movement. In turn, Modi's party tried to tar the entire protest as being run by Khalistanis. This backfired spectacularly, leading to the term 'Khalistan' being normalized among Sikh youth abroad, while fundamentalist Sikh preachers gained short-lived currency in India.

When I visited Canada this year, Mo Dhaliwal, a brand consultant who used to argue with his friend Moninder Singh that using the term 'Khalistan' was 'a remarkably unstrategic and stupid call,' talked about being branded a Khalistani 'terrorist' himself by the Indian press. His crime? He had shared an activist toolkit that was then retweeted by Greta Thunberg and Rihanna. In his hipster office in downtown Vancouver with its exposed brick walls, Dhaliwal said, 'It wasn't until years later that you start realizing that the term "Khalistan" isn't actually a term for the movement in common usage. In common usage, it was actually a weapon that the Indian media and government would use to scatter any energy that would be gathering for Punjabi or Sikh activism.' He went on, 'If a term can be used against you as a weapon and it's your own term, then your only choice is to actually fully embrace it.'

Trudeau, too, picked up on his Sikh constituents' enthusiasm for the farmers' protests. In November 2020, he became the first international leader to express concern about violent clashes in India, saying, 'Canada will always be there to defend the right of peaceful protest' and that he 'had reached out through multiple means directly to the Indian authorities to highlight our concerns.' Modi's government retorted that this was an 'unacceptable interference in our internal affairs'. (In 2018, Trudeau had accidentally caused a brouhaha in India when, on a state visit, his wife had posed for a photograph with a convicted Khalistani-terrorist-turned-Liberal Party activist who was also invited to an official dinner. In 2019, perhaps to placate Modi, Trudeau's government included the phrase 'Khalistani extremism' in a security report for the first time, only to scrub the phrase when Sikhs protested.)

The farmers' protests lasted over a year, and the farmers would not back down, despite successive Covid waves. In October 2021, capitalizing on the fervor of the protests, Pannun and Nijjar held their first theatrical Khalistan referendum in the UK, with thousands of Sikhs, some still wearing blue Covid medical masks, lining up to cast their ballots on the anniversary of Indira Gandhi's assassination. (Other such referendums followed in the next couple of years in Switzerland, Italy, Canada, and Australia.)

Soon after, in November 2021, in a rare defeat, Modi was forced to roll back the three farm laws, admitting, 'We have failed to convince some farmers despite all our efforts.' But Modi did not forget the role of Trudeau and the Khalistanis abroad in abetting and cheerleading protests that were already tricky to contain. This concatenation of events may have been what led to the green-lighting of the assassination of Nijjar and other activists.

7

Nijjar was warned in July 2022 that a hit was coming. Canadian police officers visited him at his home and served him what is called, in Canada, a duty to warn. The police did not say who might be behind the attempt on his life. The 'duty to warn' policy was designed to deal with warring gangsters, and so does not come with any promise of protection: the police simply tell you to get out of town or lay low. Bulletproof vests and firearm protection are not an option since they are illegal for Canadian civilians.

Moninder Singh received a similar warning, and the two decided that India must be behind the threat. That same month, another prominent Sikh had been shot dead in the driver's seat of his red Tesla in Surrey. The dead man, Ripudaman Malik, had been one of the four accused in the Air India bombing but had since renounced his ideology and had publicly thanked Modi for letting him visit India. For the past year, he had been feuding with Nijjar and Moninder over his attempts to print the Sikh holy book – considered the final Guru of Sikhism – in Canada, when previously it was only allowed to be published in India. Now, Nijjar and Moninder feared that India would kill them both and try to pass it off as a tit-for-tat murder for Malik's death. In fact, mere days after Malik's death, India's National Investigation Agency offered a bounty of a million rupees for 'information' that might lead to the 'arrest or apprehension'

Ripudaman Malik
Getty Images

of Nijjar for directing the killing of a Hindu priest in Jalandhar in January 2021. Helpfully, the NIA published Nijjar's Surrey address online.

Moninder, the more cautious of the two men, rented another flat to be away from his kids and avoided public places like grocery stores. Nijjar, according to Moninder, shrugged off the threat and continued living as he had before. Nijjar's family reported 'vehicles slowing down in front of their house, then speeding off' and a truck circling Nijjar while he was filling up his car at a gas station. In the spring of 2023, Nijjar found a tracker on his vehicle while it was being serviced. Meanwhile, in India, authorities searched the Nijjar family's one-story farmhouse in northwestern Punjab.

Pannun and Nijjar spoke on the phone the night before he was killed. Nijjar told Pannun that Canadian intelligence had come to see him and warned him again about a threat to his life. Nijjar also mentioned that Sikh activists who hung around in clubs with gangsters had heard that individuals were out looking for 'high-powered guns' to shoot Nijjar and Pannun. When Pannun told Nijjar to be careful, Nijjar started laughing. '*You* take care,' he said.

The next day he was gone.

8

At the same time a plot to kill Pannun was unraveling in New York. In May 2023, according to an indictment released by the US Justice Department, an Indian intelligence agent named Vikash Yadav got in touch with Nikhil Gupta, a fifty-one-year-old Indian businessman involved in 'international weapons and narcotic trafficking,' and told him that charges against him in India would be dropped if he helped organize Pannun's murder. Gupta contacted an American criminal who in turn introduced him to a man claiming to be a Colombian cocaine dealer and hitman. Gupta offered the hitman a payment of $100,000, with an advance of $15,000, and told him to track Pannun's movements in New York. On 18 June 2023, mere hours after Nijjar was killed, Yadav sent a video clip to Gupta of Nijjar dead in his vehicle. Gupta texted the hitman to tell him that Nijjar 'was also the target' and 'we have so many targets.' Gupta added that, given Nijjar's murder, there was 'now no need to wait' to kill Pannun.

Unbeknown to him, though, the American criminal he had contacted was a confidential source for the US government. The hitman himself was an undercover DEA agent. Gupta was arrested on 30 June in the Czech Republic.

Still, the US and Canada, who share intelligence, waited several months before announcing the possibility of Indian involvement in the killing of Sikhs abroad. The reason was simple. They were trying first to establish contact with the Indian government through diplomatic channels. According to the Canadian 'Foreign Interference Commission Report', Canada's national security advisor met her Indian counterpart two months after the murder and passed on the information that Canada knew that Nijjar had been extrajudicially executed by India. India didn't respond. Later that month, Canada's minister of foreign affairs talked to her Indian counterpart, but India again did nothing. In September 2023, a Canadian delegation to the G20 Summit in Delhi tasked with improving bilateral relations instead found itself meeting with Indian government officials to 'try to get India to cooperate with the investigation.' Finally, during a quick powwow on the sidelines of the G20, Trudeau told Modi directly that 'Canada knew India was involved, and that this would likely become public.' Modi stalled by saying 'that Canada had people that India wanted to see arrested,' and asked Canada to share the intelligence it had about the killing. (India's Ministry of External Affairs did not respond to a request for comment.)

Trudeau's announcement in Parliament later that month, then, was an act of desperation – a sign of weakness in the face of India's powerful defiance. When the US unsealed its indictment against Gupta in November 2023, Biden said nothing, perhaps to protect his county's relationship with the Modi government.

9

W hat were the consequences for India? Very little. By June 2025, when I went to visit Vancouver and Surrey, relations were thawing. A new prime minister – Mark Carney – was in power, and that month, after much subterranean diplomatic chatter, he invited Modi to the G7 Summit in Alberta, a big win for the Indians, who had done little in response to the various charges apart from arresting the agent who had plotted to kill Pannun. (Nor had more evidence emerged publicly of Indian involvement in the Canadian plot. In May 2024, Canadian police arrested three young Sikh men linked to a Punjabi gang and charged them with murdering Nijjar. Their trial is scheduled for 2026.) By August 2025, India and Canada would reinstate each other's high commissioners. It was hard not to think that India had achieved all they wanted – extinguished an influential activist, and, after a moment of outrage, escaped almost without notice.

The Khalistanis, understandably, were defiant, and they protested Modi's visit in several cities. But when I attended one of the Khalistani demonstrations in Vancouver, I was surprised by how small it was. Outside the impassive stone office building that houses India's consulate in Vancouver, about thirty activists had gathered, and that too an hour late. Most were middle-aged and elderly, with a few younger people and kids sprinkled in. As they chanted 'Kill Modi – Politics!' and 'Khalistan Zindabad!' and 'Raj Karega Khalsa!' and broke an effigy of Modi dressed in prisoner's stripes with sticks, I was reminded of something a moderate Sikh leader told me: 'I bet there'll be more press than there are protestors.' He was almost right. I was beginning to see the symbiotic relationship between a tiny group of Sikhs in Canada and the Canadian press. (The Indian press is just as rabidly attentive: recently, when a sign proclaiming THE REPUBLIC OF KHALISTAN went up on the premises of the Guru Nanak Sikh Gurdwara, dozens of Indian newspapers and sites ran a story on how Khalistanis had set up an 'embassy' in Canada.)

The gathering that same day for the second anniversary of Nijjar's death was bigger. Hundreds of people sat on the astro-turfed lawn in front of the temple building, eating puris, chana, and halwa served on plastic trays. In the back I came across a tented area where two teenage boys hawked T-shirts of slain militants and activists in a rapper-gangster aesthetic ('The Immortal Jathedar Hardeep Singh Nijjar', read one; 'Chopper Dropper', read another.) I went to the bathroom and sure enough, as befitting a plumber president, the fixtures were top-notch: Sloan urinals with frosted dividers and automatic Sloan taps and soap dispensers, though some of these, alas, were not working.

The temple had changed since Nijjar's death. Where there had once been a solitary Khalistani flag on the premises, there were now a dozen festooning the tatty three-story white structure with its crockery-white domes. Posters of martyred turbaned Sikh militants and activists – some holding sheathed swords, others sporting bandoliers or toting automatic weapons – had been added in the front and the back. Nijjar was there among them. The Khalistan movement had gained a new martyr.

10

A month later, in New York, I went to see Pannun.
It felt like going to see an outlaw. Pannun, who had been declared a terrorist by India in 2020, made hectoring Instagram videos, such as the one in 2023 in which he had warned Sikhs, 'Don't fly Air India after 19 November; your life may be in danger.' He had a penchant for filing nuisance lawsuits against visiting Indian politicians. A Khalistani sympathizer in Canada called him 'the Alex Jones' of the movement. On the phone, though, he was more direct than I had expected. He was the only Khalistani who talked openly to me about Nijjar's friendship with Tara and the fact that Nijjar's name *did* in fact appear in the court filings for the murder of a Hindu priest in 2021. And so, on a sweltering day, I went to see him in Elmhurst, Queens.

I expected a tired mildewed grey officer tower, but instead found myself staring at a surprisingly grand Art-Deco granite complex. Inside, Pannun's office was a series of dark interconnected rooms full of filing cabinets, and on arrival a white, thick-necked and tattooed bodyguard patted me down in a conference room.

Like many actors, Pannun – who is fifty-six with a bushy white beard and dramatically twirled whiskers – is much smaller and more fine-boned in person. He was dressed in black with black rectangular spectacles and a patka covering on his head instead of a turban (Pannun is not very religious and believes in Khalistan as a political, rather than religious, cause). He sat on a brown office chair, a yellow Khalistani flag draped behind him over shelves of law volumes. His videos gave the impression of being filmed in a TV studio but this studio turned out to simply be a corner of this room: a computer with a few camera lights and a green cloth covering a wall. Several identical black jackets – the kind he wore in his videos – hung from the handle of a cupboard. A small steamer was close to hand to give them a do-over.

What role had he played in the militancy in the 1990s? I asked. He was cagey: 'I would not like to discuss what happened in Punjab . . . but from my zeal and the passion that I'm ready to die, you should know what would have happened.' Pannun worked in IT in Wall Street for ten years after his arrival in 1992, but his goal, he said, had always been to dedicate himself to full-time activism for Khalistan. After enrolling in law school, he did just that. He was boastful about his achievements, claiming for instance, that there had been no Khalistani flags before he started using them in 2014. I wondered again how he could afford to run a movement from this office complex and hire full-time bodyguards. Had Pakistan ever funded the Khalistan movement? I asked. Pannun said that Pakistan gave refuge to 'worthless' Sikh militants but that he himself does not receive funding from Pakistan's intelligence agency, the ISI. 'ISI can't even pay their bills,' he said in his accented English. 'They can't even pay my cappuccino bills for a month.' (He then offered me a cappuccino.)

We got to a subject we had touched on over the phone. If, as he kept claiming, the new Khalistan movement was non-violent and fully legal, why did he espouse violent rhetoric in his videos and posters? In one video from 2020, he urged Sikhs in India: 'Wherever you are doing vote registrations, keep weapons. Keep weapons in your home . . . because Hindu death squads are going to come and do the genocides of you. Remember 1984.' In another video, he brought up the 1993 bombing of the Bombay Stock Exchange, adding that, 'This year, on 12 March 2024, we are going to destroy Nazi India economically and the first target is going to be India's stock exchanges.' He hedged this later: 'We won't use a bomb but we'll shut it down.'

In his well-practiced way, Pannun denied that he condoned violence. Then he said something striking. 'The audience,' he told me. 'You have to see: this is a modern world, right? How much time do you spend on videos – one minute, thirty seconds, maximum? If you feel it's interesting, you will spend two minutes, right? None of my messages go over two minutes, that is the bottom line, and also my videos are confrontational – that's the only way to put your point across.'

It was the talk of any other salesman in the attention economy. I thought about how India's over-focus on Khalistan had led to this. A murder, after all, is an extreme form of both giving and attracting attention. It creates a void that can be filled with hundreds of theories and narratives.

India, when it killed Nijjar and targeted Pannun, did not want to be caught. But it wanted status – for Modi to be seen as a strongman to whom jurisdictions did not apply, who could fell 'terrorists' abroad, just like Putin, Netanyahu, MBS, and the US Presidents: Trump, Biden, Obama. India had joined the club. Meanwhile, the Khalistanis, too, had their moment in the press. Their campaign is now a small satellite in robust orbit around Hindu fundamentalism.

And what about the people of Punjab? Nobody knew. Worse, nobody cared. ■

JOURNAL ISSUE 12

A free, peer-reviewed journal
on contemporary art

LIVE NOW

contemporary.burlington.org.uk/journal

BURLINGTON
CONT
EMPO
RARY

Die Frauen der Antike
(*Women of Antiquity*), by
Anselm Kiefer. 1999–2002.
Mixed-media sculptures
in a greenhouse, 17 parts,
dimensions variable.
(© Anselm Kiefer; photograph
Charles Duprat).

বাংলা

The great Bengali litterateur and Nobel laureate Rabindranath Tagore (1861–1941) spent many years moving between Calcutta and his family's estate at Shelaidaha in eastern Bengal, now Bangladesh.

During his time there, Tagore came to know Gaganchandra Dash, who worked as a *harkara* at the local post office. He delivered letters to Tagore and collected letters on his behalf. But in rural Bengal in the late nineteenth century, a harkara was more than a messenger or courier – he would also bring news and official notices. Gagan Harkara was a Baul poet and singer as well, and on his visits, he would also perform songs for Tagore. Bauls belong to a syncretic religion as well as a musical tradition practised by common folk in eastern India and in Bangladesh, and can be both Sufi Muslim and Vaishnavite Hindu.

Through Gagan Harkara, Tagore was introduced to the songs and world view of the Baul spiritual leader Lalon Shah, a celebrated philosopher, poet and social reformer. Struck by this music, Tagore subsequently helped to bring the songs of both Lalon and Gagan to a wider audience of the educated, intellectual Bengalis, principally based in Calcutta. One could see this as Tagore's way of *seeding* the public mind with the Baul world view, as a means of cultural reclamation and renewal.

In 1905, at the time of the communal partition of the province of Bengal into a Muslim-majority East Bengal and Assam, and a Hindu-majority West Bengal, Tagore was moved to write a song in protest. 'Amar Sonar Bangla' was his ode to a 'Golden Bengal', an invocation of unity. In the same year, Tagore also called for a reinterpretation of the Hindu festival of Rakshabandhan (where a sister ties a *rakhi*, a band, around her brother's wrist) and asked Hindus and Muslims to tie rakhis on one another as an expression of brotherhood and solidarity. When Tagore set the lyrics of 'Amar Sonar Bangla' to music, he chose the melody of Gagan's 'Ami Kothay Pabo Taare'.

Who is the *taare* or person that Gagan Harkara refers to in his song? The third-person-singular pronoun in Bengali, or Bangla, is gender neutral. The lyrics make clear that it is the singer's *moner manush*, a person after one's own heart, the true self, or inner human, in Baul philosophy. It gets to the heart of Baul philosophy. One could thus see the song 'Amar Sonar Bangla', sung in the melody of Gagan's song, as Tagore's inner vision of a unified 'Golden Bengal' and her land and people, thus reclaiming her expressive and philosophical resources, the shimmer, of Bangla itself. In 1971, during the liberation of Bangladesh, Tagore's song became the new nation's national anthem. ■

Sumana Roy

Elephant

Most of my friends chose Gandhi
when the drawing teacher said –
'Draw someone with the fewest lines possible . . .'
Lines that'd identify them
like those on our palm,
a synecdoche for our destiny.
She was teaching us economy:
an arc for a bald pate,
a lazy line for a stick,
another reclining arc for a stooping back,
a doodle for his glasses.

Only *I* drew an elephant –
with nearly the same lines:
the trunk almost like Mohandas's stick,
the elephant's back the man's aged spine,
the two rounds of his glasses
straightened for the elephant's tusks.

All I needed was just one line.

I still look for Gandhi's tail.

Gadha

What we call character
is only a function of repetition:
goodness a military reiteration of correctness,
evil a habitual borrowing of aberration.
Some become humans from walking on two legs,
some donkeys from carrying the weight of others.
That is how god became a beast of burden.

Evolution's a windy thing,
like the wind a slap of surplus –
turning man to donkey.
Ga-dha: two komal notes in Malkauns.
Repetition comes from stubbornness:
raag, animal, idiot, life.
Repetition comes from constancy –
the seasons change, but not the heart,
speed changes, but not time.

Salt was changed to cotton –
what would dissolve in water
became an absorbent.
But not the donkey's trust in the river
(like that of sadness in tears).
What we call mistake is a function of repetition:
idiocy a military reiteration of constancy,
cleverness a habitual performance of originality.
Some become humans from walking on two legs,
some donkeys from carrying the weight of others.

ಕನ್ನಡ

M y school in Bengaluru insisted that its students speak English to one another, and for a brief while there was a rupee fine for those caught speaking anything else, which was usually the local language Kannada. The fine was too radical an idea to last, but no one had any doubt that our futures lay in English. It was during a Kannada class in this English-medium school that a beleaguered teacher challenged us with a question she said could not be translated into English. The operative word in it was ಎಷ್ಟನೇ or *eṣṭanē*, an interrogative to which the answer must always be an ordinal – first, second, third. An approximation in English might be 'whichth'. The question was: 'whichth son of your father are you?'

Supposedly untranslatable words – *schadenfreude, saudade* – don't so much resist translation as lack a single-word equivalent in English. A cluster of words usually does the job of conveying the meaning. My teacher's question, for instance, could be expressed as 'what is your position of birth among your brothers?' or something equally awkward. I've heard the example many times over the years when someone wanted to score a point for Kannada over English. It is always offered half jokingly, but with a touch of defiance, as if to say: you strut around like your English can do everything, but can it do this?

The two languages have had a complex and evolving relationship. Kannada literature goes back over a thousand years, and it has had the depth – and confidence – to absorb English influences while holding its own. The oldest surviving text in Kannada is a ninth-century treatise on poetics called *Kavirajamarga* that mentions now-lost prose and poetry predating it. Attributed to the king Amoghavarsha Nrupatunga and his court poet Srivijaya, it celebrates the Kannada language, land and people, and serves as a guide to literary composition. In the tenth century, Pampa, Ranna and Ponna wrote in a mixture of prose and verse about Jain religious figures and episodes from the Indian epics. The twelfth-century *vachana* poets like Basavanna and Akka Mahadevi led a powerful religious and social reform movement, and their words continue to be sung and recited widely.

In 1921, the writer B.M. Srikantaiah published *English Geetegalu* (*English Songs*), a collection of poems by Shakespeare, Shelley, Wordsworth, Burns, Byron and many others, translated into Kannada. The collection transformed Kannada poetry, introducing fresh subjects and attitudes, along with a new approach to metre and rhyme. In the last century, many of Kannada's literary figures were teachers of English literature, and some wrote in both languages. Kuvempu, widely considered the pre-eminent Kannada writer of the twentieth century, started by writing English poems; the critic G.S. Amur wrote in both languages; Girish Karnad translated his own plays into English; Shankar Mokashi Punekar wrote novels in Kannada and poems in English.

That relationship has been considerably more fraught beyond the world of literature. From the 1970s, as English increasingly began to be seen as the language of economic opportunity, it began to take precedence in schools. The situation was further complicated by languages like Hindi and Sanskrit that laid claim to a broader Indian identity. By the 1980s, the state of Karnataka, of which Bengaluru is the capital, saw large protests demanding the primacy of Kannada in education. Several people died in the ensuing unrest.

In Bengaluru, nameboards without Kannada began to be vandalised by groups of 'language activists'. Establishments responded by displaying their names in Kannada as well, but in a smaller size than the English. The tokenism only added to the insult. Last year the Bengaluru city corporation introduced a '60:40' rule that made it compulsory for all nameboards to dedicate 60 per cent of the space to Kannada.

In 2014, the city of Bangalore officially became Bengaluru, as it is called in Kannada. The change had been proposed by the Kannada writer U.R. Ananthamurthy, who described the name change as 'the

ಕನ್ನಡ

first step to cope with retaining identity in the times of globalization and an increasingly anglicized world. It is to force [the] English language to accept – within its sound system – a word like Bengaluru, which ends in a vowel rather than consonant.'

Perhaps another way to cope with that anglicised world is to embrace it on one's own terms – through translation. Through the translations of writers like Ananthamurthy, Jayant Kaikini, Vivek Shanbhag and most recently Banu Mushtaq, Kannada has moved outwards into English. Kannada gains when English texts are translated into it; it gains something different when its own texts are translated into English. There's probably an untranslatable word in some language that means: 'the comfort that comes from knowing that one's language has a place in the wider world'. ■

THE MAGAZINE OF CHATHAM HOUSE. BRINGING GLOBAL AFFAIRS TO LIFE SINCE 1945

HOW TRUMP 2.0 WOULD UPEND THE WORLD

What another term of America
First could mean for allies and foes

PUTIN'S SPIES
The European states
thwarting Russia's
espionage network

NEW HORIZONS
Why Britain must
make better friends
in Africa and Asia

CHATHAM
HOUSE

Autumn 2024
Volume 80, Number 2

The World Today

The global affairs magazine from Chatham House

Commentary, analysis, reporting; Four editions
a year; Online archive going back to 2000;
Subscriptions from £32

www.theworldtoday.org

CONTRIBUTORS

Amit Chaudhuri is the author of eight novels, including *Sojourn*. He is also a musician, poet and essayist. His novel, *Château Rouge*, will be published in 2026.

J. Devika is a researcher and translates fiction from Malayalam to English, and social theory from English to Malayalam. Her forthcoming work includes the autobiography of the first-generation Malayali feminist Kochattil Kalyanikkutty Amma.

Sarabjeet Garcha is a poet, writer, editor, translator and publisher. His five books of poems include *All We Have*. He is the founder and director of Copper Coin.

Sujatha Gidla's first book, *Ants Among Elephants: an Untouchable Family and the Making of Modern India*, which tells the story of her mother and uncle up to the 1970s, was published in 2017.

Gopika Jadeja is a poet and translator working in English and Gujarati, and the coordinating editor for *PR&TA*. Her new poetry collection, *What Parvati Does Not Say*, was published in 2025.

Jeyamohan is a Tamil writer and literary critic. He has written novels, short stories, volumes of literary criticism, biographies, introductions to Indian and Western literature, translations and books on philosophy.

Ruchir Joshi is a writer and film-maker. His novels include *The Last Jet-Engine Laugh*, published in 2001, and *Great Eastern Hotel*, published in 2025.

Saharu Nusaiba Kannanari is the author of the novels *Chronicle of an Hour and a Half*, published in 2024, and *The Menon Investigation*, published in 2025. 'A Public Circumcision' is an extract from his forthcoming book.

Raghu Karnad is a writer and journalist and the author of *Farthest Field: A Story of India's Second World War*. His writing has appeared in *National Geographic*, the *New York Times*, *n+1*, the *Caravan* and the *Wire*.

Aruni Kashyap is associate professor of English at the University of Georgia. He is the author of *How to Date a Fanatic*, along with four other books of fiction, and the translator of five novels from Assamese.

Madhu H. Kaza is a writer, translator, artist and educator. She is the author of *Lines of Flight* and the editor of *Kitchen Table Translation*.

Rita Kothari is professor of English at Ashoka University, where she co-directs the Ashoka Centre for Translation. Her recent work includes *Uneasy Translations: Self, Experience and Indian Literature* and *Ittehad: A Life Together*, an English translation of the first novel by a woman writer in Sindhi.

Keerthana Kunnath is a visual artist based between India and London. Her work has been shown internationally, with recent exhibitions at Rencontres d'Arles and the Saatchi Gallery.

Karan Mahajan is the author of *Family Planning* and *The Association of Small Bombs*. His third novel, *The Complex*, is forthcoming in 2026.

Arvind Krishna Mehrotra's recent books include *Collected Poems, Book of Rahim* and *Of Least Concern*. He is also the author of *Selected Poems and Translations* and *Songs of Kabir*.

Srinath Perur writes on travel, science and books, and translates from Kannada. He is the author of *If It's Monday It Must Be Madurai* and the translator of, most recently, *Sakina's Kiss*.

Jerry Pinto translates from Marathi, Hindi and Konkani. He writes in English, most notably the novels *Em and the Big Hoom* and *Murder in Mahim*.

Snigdha Poonam is a journalist based in India and the UK. Her first book, *Dreamers: How Young Indians Are Changing the World*, was published in 2018.

CONTRIBUTORS

V. Ramaswamy has translated Subimal Misra, Manoranjan Byapari, Adhir Biswas and Shahidul Zahir from Bangla. His latest translation, *Tagore Never Ate Here* by Mohammad Nazim Uddin, was published in 2025.

Priyamvada Ramkumar is a literary translator whose work includes the collection *Stories of the True* by Jeyamohan, published in 2025, as well as *White Elephant* by Jeyamohan, forthcoming in 2026.

Devika Rege is the author of the novel *Quarterlife*, published in 2023. 'Homa' is an extract from a work in progress.

Daisy Rockwell is a writer, artist and Hindi-Urdu translator. Her translations include *Tomb of Sand* by Geetanjali Shree and *The Women's Courtyard* by Khadija Mastur. Her memoir, *Our Friend, Art*, is forthcoming in 2027.

Sumana Roy is the author of *How I Became a Tree*, *Provincials, Plant Thinkers of Twentieth-Century Bengal*, *Missing: A Novel, My Mother's Lover and Other Stories, Out of Syllabus* and *VIP: Very Important Plant*.

Salman Rushdie is the author of twenty-three books, including *Midnight's Children*, *Victory City*, and most recently *The Eleventh Hour*.

Arshia Sattar's abridged translation from Sanskrit of Valmiki's *Ramayana* has remained in print since 1996. Her most recent publication is *Vasanta: Stories from Sanskrit Plays*, published in 2024.

Vivek Shanbhag is the author of five story collections, three plays and five novels, including *Sakina's Kiss*. *Ghachar Ghochar*, the first of his novels to be translated into English, was translated into more than twenty languages.

Yash Sheth is a photographer based in Mumbai. His current projects include work on the monsoon, Uttan village in Dharavi Island and Indian weddings.

Geetanjali Shree is a Hindi writer whose translated novels include *Tomb of Sand*, *Our City That Year* and *The Roof Beneath Their Feet*. Her latest novel, *Sah-sa (All at Once)*, was published in Hindi in 2025.

Umesh Solanki is a writer, journalist, photographer and documentary film-maker from Gujarat. He has written three poetry collections, two novels and a collection of essays.

Rahul Soni is a writer, editor and translator. He has edited *Home from a Distance*, and translated a selection of Ashok Vajpeyi's poems *A Name for Every Leaf*, Pankaj Kapur's novella *Dopehri* and Geetanjali Shree's novel *The Roof Beneath Their Feet*.

Dayanita Singh is an artist whose photography has been exhibited internationally. Her books include *Sea of Files*, *Book Building* and *Dancing with my Camera*. 'Museum of Pandals' features photography from the upcoming work of the same name.

Sanjay Subrahmanyam is a historian of the early modern world. He has taught in Delhi, Lisbon, Oxford, Paris and Los Angeles.

Aatish Taseer is the author of several works of fiction and non-fiction. His latest book, *A Return to Self: Excursions in Exile*, was published in 2025.

Manjushree Thapa is the author of eight books of political fiction and non-fiction on Nepal, as well as a translator of Nepali literature. She is currently at work on a new novel.

GRANTA TRUST

Granta would be unable to fulfil its mission
without the generosity of its donors. We
gratefully acknowledge the following
individuals and foundations:

Ford Foundation
British Council
Jerwood Foundation
Pulitzer Center
Amazon Literary Partnership
Sigrid Rausing
The Hans and Marit Rausing Charitable Trust
Anonymous
Bloomsbury Publishing Plc
SALT
Open Society
The Common Humanity Arts Trust
Jonathan and Ronnie Newhouse Fund
Hawthornden Foundation

We also thank the following readers, including
those who wish to remain anonymous, for
their kind support:

Anonymous
Gail Anderson
Christine Bartels
Ria Bhavnani
Robert Cenek
Geoff Cohen
Alex Fardon
David Fobel
Monzurul Huq
Michael Isard
Patrick James
Hongnian Jow
Angie Libman
Helen Meads
Cristine Milton
Andrew Nugée
Luiz Otavio Ortigao
Marynel Ryan Van Zee
Laura Schwartz
Rob Shelton
John E. Simmons
John Sirek
Andrea Sydow
Lynnette Widder
Nancy York

If you would like to contribute, please make
a donation at granta.com/donate.

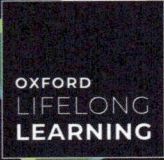

UNIVERSITY OF OXFORD

OXFORD LIFELONG LEARNING

CREATIVE WRITING WITH OXFORD

SHORT AND PART-TIME COURSES

Need an extra push to finish your novel, poem or play? Want to explore new genres?

Whether you're a beginner wondering where to start, or an experienced writer looking to elevate your skills, we have a course for you.

Short courses in Oxford and online
· Workshops and day schools
· Weekend events
· Weekly learning courses
· Summer schools in Oxford

Part-time qualifications
· Certificate of Higher Education
· Diploma in Creative Writing
· Master's in Creative Writing

SCAN TO LEARN MORE

@OxLifelongLearning
www.lifelong-learning.ox.ac.uk